CW00501989

Frank Merriwell's Diamond Foes

Straight Over The Plate

BURT L. STANDISH

Author of the celebrated "Merriwell"
stories, which are the favorite reading of
over half a million up-to-date (194)
American boys.

BOOKS FOR ATHLETICS

LONDON
IBOO PRESS HOUSE
86-9 PAUL STREET

Frank Merriwell's Diamond Foes
Straight Over The Plate

BURT L. STANDISH
Author of the famous Merriwell Stories.

BOOKS FOR ATHLETICS

Layout & Cover © Copyright 22 iBooPress, London

Published by
iBoo Press House

3rd Floor
86-9 Paul Street
London, EC2A4NE UK

t: +44 2 3695 89
info@iboo.com II iBoo.com

ISBNs
978-1-64181-945-9 (h)
978-1-64181-946-6 (p)

Frank Merriwell's Diamond Foes

Straight Over The Plate

BURT L. STANDISH

Author of the celebrated "Merriwell"
stories, which are the favorite reading of
over half a million up-to-date (194)
American boys.

BOOKS FOR ATHLETICS

MERRIWELL SERIES
Stories of Frank and Dick Merriwell
Fascinating Stories of Athletics

A half million enthusiastic followers of the Merriwell brothers will attest the unfailing interest and wholesomeness of these adventures of two lads of high ideals, who play fair with themselves, as well as with the rest of the world.

These stories are rich in fun and thrills in all branches of sports and athletics. They are extremely high in moral tone, and cannot fail to be of immense benefit to every boy who reads them.

They have the splendid quality of firing a boy's ambition to become a good athlete, in order that he may develop into a strong, vigorous, right-thinking man.

Contents

I.	COLONEL CARSON, OF CARSONVILLE.	7
II.	WHY BILLY LEFT SCHOOL.	12
III.	LIKE FATHER, LIKE SON.	17
IV.	COLONEL CARSON'S REVENGE.	22
V.	THE VILLAGE GREEN.	27
VI.	A CHALLENGE.	32
VII.	CHIP GETS A LETTER.	37
VIII.	GETTING DOWN TO WORK.	42
IX.	COLONEL CARSON MAKES A BET.	47
X.	HOW THE GAME OPENED.	52
XI.	THE CLIPPINGS GET WILD.	57
XII.	CLIPPING THE CLIPPERS.	62
XIII.	BEATEN AT HIS OWN GAME.	67
XIV.	"SOUR GRAPES."	69
XV.	THREE CHEERS FOR CHIP!	74
XVI.	A WILY PLOTTER.	79
XVII.	A NIGHT ATTACK.	83
XVIII.	THE INITIALS IN THE HAT.	87
XIX.	FATHER AND SON.	92
XX.	LURED AWAY.	97
XXI.	WHERE IS MERRY?	102
XXII.	INVESTIGATING.	107
XXIII.	THE THIRD DEGREE.	112
XXIV.	QUICK WORK.	117
XXV.	WON IN THE NINTH.	122

XXVI.	CAPTAIN OF THE NINE.	127
XXVII.	A CHALLENGE.	129
XXVIII.	LAYING THE WIRES.	133
XXIX.	A THOUSAND DOLLARS IN CASH.	138
XXX.	CRIMINAL WORK.	143
XXXI.	BEFORE THE GAME.	148
XXXII.	WHO GOT IT?	153
XXXIII.	ACCUSED OF THEFT.	158
XXXIV.	A MYSTERY.	163
XXXV.	THE FIGHT OF HIS LIFE.	168
XXXVI.	THE JUMP BALL.	173
XXXVII.	A DESPERATE FINISH.	178
XXXVIII.	CAUGHT WITH THE GOODS.	183
XXXIX.	CONCLUSION.	188

FRANK MERRIWELL'S DIAMOND FOES.

CHAPTER I.

COLONEL CARSON, OF CARSONVILLE.

hip Merriwell, in running togs, had just taken a rail fence at a flying leap. As he dropped into the road beyond the fence, he halted suddenly and gave vent to a startled exclamation.

Almost at the same instant, a second figure in athletic shirt and track pants came hurtling over the fence, pulled up abruptly, and stood hanging on to Merry's shoulder. This second person was Billy McQuade, with whom Frank Merriwell, junior, was spending a few days of the spring vacation.

The two friends had left home for a cross-country hike together. It was now the middle of the forenoon, they were on their way back, and had still four miles to go before reaching Carsonville.

The crisp spring air of morning gave the two runners new life at every breath. To many a languid youth it spelled laziness and lack of all effort, but Merry and his friend knew from experience that "spring fever" is only a convenient name for doing nothing. Both of them were looking forward to a luxurious relaxation in the long grass by the Carsonville mill pond that afternoon, but they intended to make it all the more enjoyable by an honest physical weariness.

At the point where the two friends struck the highway, it curved in a wide horseshoe bend in order to avoid a tongue of undrained swamp land that struck up from the river. Merriwell had come to the road on one side of the curve, intending to follow the highway back to town.

As he took the hedge bordering the road with a flying hurdle, he had caught sight of a buggy in the white stretch directly ahead of him. That one flashing glimpse had shown him a man in the buggy, and, as he came to earth, he saw the horse give a sudden leap, shying frantically at sight of the flying figure.

Merriwell regretted instantly that he had not looked before he had leaped, but it was now too late. Before Billy McQuade took the leap in turn, the mettlesome steed hitched to the buggy was tearing around the bend of road, while the lone occupant stood up sawing savagely at the reins.

"That's a lesson I should have learned before this," Merriwell murmured regretfully. "The horse shied when I came over the hedge, and he's run away."

"No doubt about that," commented Billy, watching with startled eyes. "He looks as if he didn't intend to stop this side of Fardale."

The course of the runaway was anything but reassuring. The startled horse was racing madly around the horseshoe bend, with the buggy leaping and rocking behind him, threatening at every instant to go over.

The driver still stood erect, however. He was shouting in an angry tone of voice, and trying vainly to curb the frightened animal. Disaster was imminent at any moment.

"My eye!" Billy ejaculated soberly. "We've done it this time, Chip!"

"Then we'd better undo it," snapped Merriwell, rousing himself. He pointed across the marshy land to the opposite bend of the road.

"Come along, Billy! We can cut straight across over there, and beat the horse to it. He's forced to go clear around the bend."

"Practical lesson in geometry," murmured Billy, with a resigned look at the boggy strip. "The shortest distance between two points is a straight line. Go ahead, old man, I'm with you. Hope the buggy will still be with the horse when it gets there!"

Chip Merriwell leaped across the road, Billy close behind him. They vaulted the rail fence on that side, and set off across the marsh land at the best possible speed.

It did not seem that Billy McQuade's hope would be fulfilled. The runaway had by this time reached the central point of the curve, and the driver's efforts seemed to have no effect, for the buggy was careering and bouncing as if ready to smash up at each wild leap.

Merriwell took a glance over his shoulder, and increased his speed. But it was difficult to cover the ground rapidly; pools of water lay here and there, the soft grass and soaked soil sucked at every step, and only by jumping from tussock to tussock could progress be made.

The two runners made it, however. They were nearly across the neck of sunken land when Merriwell heard a startled cry from his friend, and glanced around.

He was just in time to see the driver flung from the buggy!

With a thrill of fear that his carelessness had brought about an irreparable injury, Chip Merriwell dashed forward. The horse was almost upon him as he scrambled up and swung himself across the fence, but the frightened beast had no time to swerve. Taking a few long running steps, Merry flung himself sideways and caught at the bridle.

Almost directly, the horse stopped, trembling and heaving. With a breath of relief, Merriwell began stroking his muzzle, patting his neck, and uttering soothing words. The animal perceived that he was a friend, and stood quiet.

One swift glance showed that the buggy was uninjured, then Merriwell looked around for the driver, stepping back from the horse to get a clear view.

He saw Billy McQuade meeting the driver, who had risen to his feet. It was evident at once that he had suffered from nothing worse than a severe shock, for, as Merriwell turned and approached the two, he heard the driver cursing furiously. With a feeling of distaste, he inspected the man, whose clothes Billy was hastily brushing.

The driver of the rig was a tall, spare, stoop-shouldered man. He was very well dressed, and wore a gray mustache and goatee. There was a hard set to his face, and a pouchiness beneath his black eyes, that denoted self-indulgence, and a life that was anything but what it should be.

"You good-for-nothin' loafer!" he roared, turning furiously on Billy, as Chip Merriwell came up. "You done this a-purpose! You———"

"It was not Billy's fault at all," broke in Merry warmly. "I was the first one over the fence, and your horse shied at me."

The driver whirled on him, his rage becoming a cold fury as he met Merriwell's firm, steady gaze.

"What are you doin' in them duds?" he demanded. "So it was you, hey?"

"Yes," and, although Merry's eyes flashed at the tone of the man, he kept his voice cool. "Yes, and I'm very sorry about it. Of course, I'll be glad to settle for whatever damage was done."

"Lot o' good that'll do!" growled the other, who seemed to be eying him with anything but liking. "What you chasin' around in them duds for?"

"We were doing a bit of cross-country running," Merriwell said quietly. Billy McQuade was flashing him queer looks which he interpreted as warnings, but he took no heed of them. "As I said, I'll expect to make good any damage, and I'm very sorry the accident occurred. My name is Frank Merriwell, junior, and you'll find me at the McQuades' residence, if you want me."

The man flung Billy a hard look, then laughed sneeringly.

"Mebbe I will and mebbe I won't," he jeered. "They ain't goin' to have a residence very long, I reckon. I s'pose he put you up to scarin' that hoss, eh?"

"He did not!" cried Merry indignantly. The insinuation made him angry clear through. Billy flung him an imploring glance, but he was a chip of the old block, and showed it in his next words.

"I don't know who you are, my friend, but you've got a disposition that I wouldn't like to be let loose with. We've caused an accident, or, rather, I have, and I've apologized and offered to do all in my power to make it right.

"Instead of throwing slurs and curses into the atmosphere, it'd be a whole lot more decent if you'd try to act white. I don't blame you for being mad. I'd probably be mad myself in the same circumstances. But that's no reason for your acting in this way."

The stranger gave him a black look, then moved off.

"Humph!" he grunted sarcastically. "I guess you're like your dad, if all I've heard say is correct. Let's see what damage was done. I reckon the buggy was smashed up."

Merriwell and Billy McQuade followed him to where the horse stood. The man went over the buggy, then examined the horse.

"Ain't nothing busted," he said, almost regretfully, it seemed. "But you kids are too gay, runnin' around the country in them duds. It's goin' to be stopped."

"Don't let our clothes worry you," retorted Merry. "You know where to find me if you want damages. Come along, Billy."

He promptly turned his back. Billy threw a dubious look at the man, then followed slowly. Once more the deep voice reached Merriwell.

"You'll be sorry for this, mind my words! You ain't a-going to talk to me that way and get off with it, you young scoundrel!"

Chip Merriwell's cheeks flamed a little, but he kept a firm grip on himself and walked on. After a moment he turned to see the man climb into his buggy and give the horse a savage cut with the whip.

"The brute!" he murmured indignantly. "What that horse needs is a kind word, instead of the lash. More than likely that fellow had him whipped into such a temper that he would have shied at a dead leaf."

Billy nodded. To his surprise, Merry saw that his friend's usually clear, frank features were overcast and troubled.

"What's the matter, old man? You seemed to know that fellow."

"I do."

Billy cast a worried look at the rig, now disappearing around the curve of the road.

"Here's a go!" he muttered gloomily. "I guess we're all in for it now, Chip."

"Why? That man isn't the sheriff, is he?" asked Merriwell, with a laugh.

"No. He's a whole lot worse. That chap is Colonel Carson, who owns most of Carsonville, and he'll make the old burg plenty hot for us now, believe me!"

CHAPTER II.

WHY BILLY LEFT SCHOOL.

hip Merriwell looked curiously at his friend and host. "Has this Colonel Carson anything to do with your leaving Fardale—or, rather, with your writing that you would not be back?"

"Yes," Billy said, in a low voice. "Let's walk along, Chip, and I'll tell you about it. It might as well come out now as any time, I s'pose."

It was Merry's second day in Carsonville. Billy McQuade, or, as he was more generally known, "Billy Mac," was a plebe at Fardale Academy. During the preceding summer he had shown remarkable ability as backstop on the scrub nine, and it was reported that he was in line to catch for the regular team during the coming season. Billy Mac was also good at first, however, so that Fardale had been in no little doubt.

Shortly before the spring vacation began, Billy had been called home to Carsonville. His father was dead, and his mother had merely written that she needed Billy's presence to settle up some portions of the estate. Then had come a letter from Billy himself—a heartbroken letter, stating that he would be unable to return to Fardale.

He assigned no definite cause, and the reason remained pretty much a mystery. It was a most disconcerting mystery, also. Owen Clancy, Chip Merriwell's regular backstop, was somewhere off in the Southwest. It had been pretty generally settled that Billy Mac would don the mask this season, and his sudden withdrawal was a body blow to Fardale hopes.

These had been swiftly raised, however, when on the last day of school before the vacation Clancy had appeared without warning. He had retrieved his family fortunes, and was ready to pitch into work at Fardale once more. This, none the less, did not throw any light upon the mystery of Billy Mac's dropping out.

Both Merry and his father had been no little worried. Frank Merriwell, senior, had finally suggested that Chip drop around to Carsonville during vacation. Although head over ears in track and field work, Chip had assented gladly. Billy Mac sent him a cordial invitation to come along, and he had promptly arrived.

The McQuade home was a comfortable, old-fashioned residence on a hill near the river, just outside of town. During his first day, Merry had asked no questions, but his eyes had been busy. He noted the worried, uneasy air of hospitable Mrs. McQuade, and the nervousness of his friend. It was not hard to guess that the estate of the senior McQuade had fallen into difficulties, though not a word had been said on the subject.

"Let's have it, old man," said Merry gravely. "Nothing helps a fellow so much as being able to spout out his trouble to some one else."

"I know," sighed Billy Mac hopelessly. "But this is different. I s'pose you remember about—about dad dying just before Christmas holidays?"

"Yes," said Chip sympathetically. "And we were all mighty sorry to hear of it, old fellow."

"Well," went on the other, "things didn't look so bad just then. Mother had a thousand dollars of insurance money, while the house and orchard was ours. We've got some mighty fine fruit trees there, and they promised to take care of things pretty well."

"I should think they would! Those apples you dug up yesterday were something fine, Billy Mac."

"They were the last of the ones we buried last fall, Chip. We shipped off some of them, for with the apples and other things we get high prices from the city. They seem to appreciate getting extra fine fruit."

"Of course they do. The trouble with most farmers is that they don't take pains enough to market their crop right, and take care of it on the way. But go ahead."

Billy sighed again, and glanced heavily at the river.

"This here Colonel Carson," he broke out, "suddenly produced a mortgage on the house and orchard for two thousand dollars. That was just before vacation, when mother wrote for me to come home."

"But you knew that he had the mortgage?" queried Chip, frowning.

"We thought dad had paid it. You see, dad—well, dad was kind of careless about money. Just the same, we knew he had paid that mortgage. Mother could find no receipt, however, and Carson

13

vowed that it had never been paid."

"Somebody ought to teach him something," said Merry warmly. "Hadn't you any proof whatever?"

"Not a scratch, Chip. We couldn't find a single thing. Mother pleaded with him, and he agreed to give us a little time in which to pay it—over again. It hit us pretty hard, you see. We knew that dad had paid it, but that villain Carson only wants to get hold of the place."

"Looks as though the scoundrel had you," said Merriwell thoughtfully. "Can you pay it, Billy?"

"Maybe. Mother has that thousand insurance money, and—well, to tell the truth, I've arranged to get a job as clerk in the Carsonville general store. If we can hold the colonel off a while, I guess we can fix it."

"Pretty hard lines, just the same," commented Merry. "So that's why you wrote that you wouldn't be back to Fardale, eh?"

"Yes," said Billy Mac miserably. "It's all off, Chip. And now, after what's happened this morning—well, you can guess that Carson won't have much mercy."

Merriwell whistled softly. Now he began to see the possible disaster he had brought upon the McQuade family through scaring Colonel Carson's horse. Recalling the man's face, he was forced to admit to himself that he could not see much hope in it. Every line spelled hardness, cold unscrupulousness.

There was good cause for Billy Mac's worry—yet he had cast no word of blame on Chip, whose lack of caution seemed to have brought wreck upon him. Merry appreciated this fact. It was only another indication of the sterling qualities of his friend.

At the same time, it gave him serious food for thought. If Colonel Carson did come down upon Mrs. McQuade, in his rage, Chip knew that he would be morally responsible for it.

"I'm mighty sorry about this, old man," he exclaimed soberly, "What kind of a fellow is this Carson? Is he well off?"

"Got slathers of money," said Billy Mac, with added gloom. "The burg was named after his family, and he owns most of the main street, the bank, and everything else, even the baseball team."

"Baseball team?" inquired Merriwell sharply. "A professional team?"

"No, the Clippers are made up of amateurs, and stand pretty high in the Amateur League. But it's like everything else, Chip. The colonel is said to be mighty careless about methods in everything he does, so long as he gets what he wants. The Carsonville Clippers are amateurs, all right, but I notice most of 'em have jobs in Colonel Carson's bank, or on his farms, or somewhere. And the jobs don't need much attention."

"So that's it, eh?" Merriwell looked thoughtful. "Are they a good bunch?"

There was no doubt that the Clippers could play ball, and play it well enough to win most of their games. Carsonville, of course, was not a large-enough place to support such a team, but, where his one great hobby was concerned, Colonel Carson was willing to spend money like water.

One reason for this was that his own son was the star pitcher of the Clippers. Another was that Colonel Carson had a consuming ambition to make such a showing with his amateur team, that he could buy into one of the larger professional-league teams as a well-known follower of the sport.

To this end, it was necessary that his team should win games. The Clippers did so. But—and this point Merry dragged by sheer force from the reluctant Billy—it was whispered that Colonel Carson did not care much how they won, so long as they did win.

"I don't believe in repeating calumnies," went on Billy, "whether you like a man, or don't. I believe that Colonel Carson is a scoundrel and a liar where my family is concerned, but I don't like to repeat things that have no foundation."

"Right you are," exclaimed Chip. "But in a case of this kind, rumor is apt to hit pretty close to the mark, Billy Mac. Is there a good diamond here?"

"You bet!" cried Billy enthusiastically. "Almost as good as the Fardale grounds, Chip. It's laid out down below the milldam, by the river, with concrete stands and all that. Colonel Carson certainly does things up brown!"

"That's what he wants," agreed Chip. "It'll help his reputation with the league magnates. But if he builds his reputation on secret chicanery and dirty work, he isn't going to get very far, and, judging from your own case, it looks as though Colonel Carson had a tricky streak right through him."

He could not help feeling sorry for Billy Mac, even while admiring his sturdy pluck. To throw up school, athletics, and everything else in order to take up a hopeless undertaking was a stiff proposition. And Billy's task looked hopeless.

His salary as clerk in the Carsonville general store would certainly be small. It would take him a long time to get together a thousand dollars, to add to the thousand his mother already possessed. Yet it had been the only chance, and Billy Mac had plunged desperately at it without a squeal for help.

Merriwell knew better than to offer financial assistance, though he knew that his father would be glad to help the McQuades. He had seen enough of Billy's mother to guess at her pride, and, as though Billy had read his secret thought, he turned to Merriwell.

"Don't say anything to mother about my telling you this," he said quietly. "It may come out other ways, or she may tell you herself——"

"I understand," interrupted Chip. "She wouldn't like to think that her guests had been bothered with family troubles. She's a mighty fine mother to have, Billy."

"You bet your boots!" and the other's eyes lighted up. "She didn't want me to quit Fardale, of course. But it was the only chance there was, and she had to give in at last."

"Well, the place isn't lost yet, so brace up," advised Merriwell.

By the time they had finished this heart-to-heart talk, they were at the outskirts of the town, and nearing the McQuade home. Billy pointed out a large white house set in from the road as the Carson residence.

They had just passed this point, when, from a bend in the road, came a shrill cry in a boyish voice. An instant later they sighted two figures. One was that of a rather small young fellow, crouching; over him stood a tall, heavy-set figure, striking at the smaller chap, and paying no attention to his cries for mercy.

"My eye!" cried Billy Mac hotly. "Trail along, Chip. I'll give that brute something else to think of!"

And Billy broke into a run, with a yell of anger.

CHAPTER III.

LIKE FATHER, LIKE SON.

"Bel-l-lup!"

At sight of Chip Merriwell and Billy Mac, the smaller of the two figures uttered a shrill appeal. As the bully straightened up, the little fellow writhed away and danced over to the side of the road.

"Hello, Chub!" cried Billy, pausing. "What's the trouble? Were you playing?"

"Pl-l-laying nothing!" returned Chub shrilly, dancing about in his rage, and pointing at his tormentor. "That big stiff said I rooted too much for the visiting team l-l-l-last Saturday! He caught me and was l-l-lambasting me!"

Chip saw that his friend was fully competent to handle the situation, and stood back. There was something comical about the helpless rage of Chub, and about his manner of stumbling speech, that amused Merriwell.

"You're a fine sort of sport, I don't think!" exclaimed Billy Mac, addressing the bully. "Just because a fellow doesn't root for you, you want to punish him—and a little chap like Chub, too!"

The bully glowered at Billy Mac in a threatening fashion. He was a hulking big fellow, wearing a sporty necktie of flaming red, and a loud-checked suit. His features were heavy and overbearing, with deep-set black eyes, that gleamed maliciously, and from one corner of his mouth drooped a burned-out cigarette.

"What's it to you, Billy Mac?" he growled menacingly. "You'd better not try to show off around here, just because you been to a military academy fer a few months!"

"There's no one showing off around here except that necktie of yours," snapped Billy Mac. "It's a wonder you couldn't find a baby to lick, you coward!"

It became evident to Merry that the two knew each other, and that his friend cherished a thorough dislike for the bully.

"Give it to him, Bil-l-ly!" chirruped Chub, who was well out of danger by this time. It seemed impossible for the little chap to pronounce the letter "l" without spilling it out by degrees. "L-l-l-lam him for me!"

The big fellow sneered.

"I suppose you think you can run the place, Billy Mac, now that you've been away to school, hey? You think you are a real athlete, with them underwear things on, don't you?"

Seeing that his friend was speechless with rage, Merriwell interfered.

"It's quite evident that you're not fitted to pass on athletes, my friend," he broke in ironically. "I've always found that the fellow who goes around with a coffin nail sticking in his face is the one who sticks in the bleachers. He doesn't get out and toss the ball very much."

For some reason, this speech seemed to infuriate the bully. He whirled on Merry with a snarl of anger.

"Smart guy, ain't you? I suppose you're that Merriwell kid that Billy's been blowin' about so much?"

"It seems that you have some brain left, in spite of cigarettes," returned Merry dryly. "You're supposing a lot of things, my friend. It might strike you to suppose that your absence is better than your company."

"Oh, is that so?" The big fellow clenched his fists, glaring. "Say, fer about two cents I'd take you down a peg, Slim-shanks!"

Billy Mac turned quickly.

"Look here, Chip, you butt out of this!" he demanded. "Chub Newton's a friend of mine, and this isn't your quarrel."

"All right, old man," said Merriwell, waving his hand. "I'll gladly turn over our genial friend to you. He looks as if a dose of McQuade compound would improve his health a good deal."

"Yah!" shrieked Chub Newton, in wild delight. "That's the way to talk! L-l-listen to that, Bul-l-ly! You're goin' to hear things, al-l-l right!"

Bully favored Chub with a black look.

"I've give you one lesson about closin' that jaw of yours, Chub," he grated. "You'd better lay mighty low, mind my words!"

There was something in the tone and aspect of the fellow that struck a responsive chord in Merriwell's memory. What the familiarity was, he could not fathom. However, he was sure that there was a familiarity.

"L-l-light into him, Bil-l-ly!" pleaded Chub, his shrill voice appearing to irritate Bully like the buzzing of a mosquito. The latter shook his fist threateningly.

"You heard what I said!" he roared. "Shut that jaw, or I'll show you what a real lambastin' is, you tow-headed little rat!"

"I don't think you will, Bully," said McQuade. Merriwell had thrown him a warning look, and he had curbed his temper.

"Hey? Why not?" The big fellow turned on Billy, seeming to comprehend for the first time that he was being actually interfered with. "I suppose you'll stop me, hey?"

"Well, I've been thinking it over quite a while," admitted Billy, with a grin. "Try a fresh cigarette, Bully. It might help you to get ideas faster."

Chub Newton waved his arms in delight. A few passers-by were pausing to listen to the altercation, and the little fellow turned to them eagerly.

"Watch Bul-l-ly catch it!" he sang out shrilly. "He's going to get a fal-l-len on harder than the Sprucetown batters fel-l-l on him l-l-l-last Saturday!"

At this the big fellow's face went positively black with rage. It was clear that he could think of no taunts to fling back at his diminutive foe, so he did the next best thing that occurred to him. He took a swift step toward Chub, his fists clenched.

"No you don't!"

Billy Mac leaped forward and caught his shoulder, twirling him around.

"Look out!" roared Bully furiously. "I'll mash that smart-alec mouth o' yours, you fool! Go home an' dress yourself!"

"I'd make a better job of it than you've done," retorted Billy, with contempt.

Among the gathering array a quick smile passed, with significant looks at the loud attire of the big fellow. This only served to infuriate him the more. It was clear to Chip that Bully was by no means a favorite, though for some reason no voice was lifted against him, save that of Chub Newton.

"Go for him, ol-l-ld scout!" Chub shrieked. "You can l-l-lick him easy! He's got a yel-l-ler streak!"

"And you've got a yelling streak," observed Merry, with a laugh.

Glaring from his deep-set eyes, Bully stepped toward McQuade.

"I guess you need a lesson," he growled. "You're gettin' too all-fired smart around this town, for a pauper."

Billy went white.

"I'd sooner be a pauper than the son of a crook," he snapped. "And I'd sooner be the son of a crook, than a crook myself, Bully!"

A murmur of applause went up from the crowd. It was cut short by a roar from the big fellow.

"Call me a crook, will you!"

With a quick lunge forward, he aimed a vicious blow at Billy Mac. The backstop did not appreciate the compliment, however.

Catching the blow on his arm, he took a quick step in, and there was a dull smack. Bully went staggering back.

"Yah!" chirruped Chub, in great glee. "I tol-l-ld you! L-l-lam him again!"

The big fellow hesitated, with a surprised expression on his face. Evidently concluding that an accident had happened, he rushed at Billy with a shout.

"Here's where you get yours, smart alec!"

Billy Mac did not seem at all disturbed over the prospect. He waited the rush quietly, and, as the big fellow drove in another blow, Billy caught the arm. He turned, jerked the other's wrist over his shoulder, and Bully flew over him into the dust. This brought a shout of applause from the spectators.

It was a simple jujutsu trick. Billy Mac had not learned it very adroitly, but he had learned it well enough to spill his adversary head over heels. Bully was unhurt, and was up instantly, brushing at his gay attire.

"Got some luck, ain't you!" he sneered furiously.

"Better not try my luck again," said Billy Mac, with a laugh.

Chub Newton let out a shrill yell.

"L-l-look at the l-l-loud guy now! Yah! Why don't you cl-l-laim you stubbed your toe, Bul-l-ly Carson?"

Merriwell started. Could it be possible that this fellow was the son of Colonel Carson, of whom Billy Mac had spoken—the baseball player? Yes, he placed the chap now. The features and voice were not unlike those of Colonel Carson.

However, he had no time to conjecture further. Bully went at Billy Mac with a second rush, this time exercising more caution. McQuade had to depend entirely on his quickness, and proved that it was quite dependable.

He slipped aside, raising a cloud of dust as he did so, and tried to trip his opponent. Bully staggered and lost his balance, and, as his arm flew out wide, Billy Mac stepped in and his fist went out.

Again there came a sharp crack as the blow landed. The big fellow, struck fairly on the angle of the jaw below the ear, shivered, and then went reeling across the street. He pulled up at the fence, clinging to it desperately.

"Yah! He's scared out!" cried Chub.

So, indeed, it seemed. The blow had not been hard enough to knock him out, yet he made no offer to return to the fight. Instead, he raised his fist and shook it menacingly.

"You'll suffer for this!" he exclaimed. "You wait till I see dad!"

"Yah!" shrilled Chub Newton, dancing wildly. "Go put a muffl-l-ler on your new cl-l-lothes, Bully Carson!"

Bully moved off, evidently sick of the encounter. Since it was plainly over, the spectators drifted away, and Chub Newton thanked his rescuer. Billy Mac introduced him to Frank Merriwell, junior, but seemed to have little delight in his victory.

"Now I am in for it, and no mistake!" he exclaimed, looking after the big fellow.

"Why?"

"Didn't you notice the resemblance?"

"Well, yes. And I heard Chub call him Bully Carson——"

"Yes, that's his usual nickname. He is Colonel Carson's son, Chip. And I guess you can see that I've done a pretty bad morning's work for the McQuade family."

CHAPTER IV.

COLONEL CARSON'S REVENGE.

"I'm awful-l-ly gl-l-lad to meet you! Bil-l-ly's tol-l-ld me a l-l-lot about Chip Merriwel-l-l!"

"We seem to have come along just right," said Merry, shaking hands with Chub. "But we'd better get home, Billy Mac. We seem to attract a good deal of attention in these running togs."

Billy Mac nodded.

"Sure. You'd better come with me, Chub. We'll go down to the swimming hole near the house and have a plunge."

Chub looked disappointed.

"I'm sorry, fel-l-lows, but I can't. I'm workin' at the grocery, you know, and I got to get orders this morning. I'l-l-l see you l-l-later, though."

"You come down to the swimming hole," offered Billy quickly, "and I'll help you make up for lost time by covering this street and taking orders."

"Wil-l-l you, honest!" cried Chub! "Oh, hurray! Watch me go!"

"Well, chase along to the river, then. We'll get our duds and be right down."

Chub went capering off at full speed, while Chip and Billy trotted off to the McQuade home.

Here they secured their clothes and towels, saying nothing to Mrs. McQuade of what had happened that morning. Billy was full of fears, but he forced them down in her presence. He did not want to worry his mother unnecessarily.

When they left the house to get to the river, they passed a corner of the orchard. It was bright with blossoms, whose scent came sweetly on the breeze, and Billy jerked his head toward the gnarled trees.

"I'd hate to see those trees piling up an income for Colonel Carson, Merry."

Chip Merriwell nodded in comprehension.

"It would be hard, old chap. But that's exactly what they're doing, right now, since you'll have to pay the loan a second time. Even that will be better than letting the place fall into his hands."

"Can't help it," and Billy shook his head gloomily. "The mortgage is overdue, and he could foreclose any time he wanted to, you see. He's going to be sore as blazes over what happened this morning, too."

"He doesn't seem to be very fair-minded, for a fact," agreed Merry. "But it's a bad plan to worry over what hasn't happened, Billy. Just forget about financial troubles, and enjoy your swim."

It would have been hard for the most hardened pessimist not to have enjoyed that plunge into the cool, quiet old river, whose waters were backed up for half a mile by the dam below, forming an ideal swimming pond. The warm air was fresh with the breath of fruit blossoms, for Carsonville was in the fruit belt, and surrounded by orchards.

After twenty minutes of vigorous exercise, the three friends pulled themselves out on the grassy bank and enjoyed a sun bath.

Somewhat to his surprise, Chip Merriwell found that Chub Newton was older than he appeared, and was an expert swimmer. Also, he had no high opinion of the autocrats of his native town.

"I hope the Cl-l-lippers get l-l-lambasted good and proper this year," he announced pleasantly. "Bul-ly Carson has the worst case o' swel-l-led bean you ever saw!"

"He looks like it," said Chip, stretching out lazily. "Can he pitch?"

Chub Newton snorted disgustedly, but Billy spoke up.

"Sure he can pitch, Chip. Chub has a private grouch on, that's all. Bully isn't any great favorite off the diamond, but he has the knack of tossing the ball, all right."

"Yah!" sniffed Chub. "He's got l-l-luck with him."

"That's what he said about Billy," said Merriwell. "What's your private grievance against the colonel's son?"

"Why, I wanted to pl-l-lay on the Cl-l-lippers," bubbled the little chap. Every time he struck the letter "l" his tongue seemed unwilling to let go of it. "I tried out with 'em and made good. Then a bunch o' city fel-l-lers come out here and got jobs whil-le they pl-l-layed bal-l-l. They done me, al-l-l right, and three or four other fel-l-lers, too. I was too short to pl-l-lay third, and one o' them guys was a swel-l-l shortstop. That l-let me out. L-l-lot o' folks think that Colonel Carson ought to 'a' favored home pl-l-layers."

"I don't know about that," said Merry thoughtfully. "Of course, sentiment can't enter into ball games that way, Chub. If the odds were about even, though, he might have done so, I should think. Those city chaps aren't ringers, are they?"

"No, I guess not," spoke up Billy. "I don't think that even Colonel Carson would try that game, Chip. He made quite a bit of bad feeling among the young fellows here, just the same."

"Time we were gettin' dressed," observed Chub uneasily. "I hate to go, but those orders have to be in before noon."

The three took a last plunge into the cool water, had a quick rub down, and dressed. Then Chub and Billy Mac departed to take a short cut back to town along the river banks, while Merry returned to the house in order to write a letter to his father. On the way, however, he reconsidered.

"I think I'll let it wait till to-night," he reflected. "I'll have a talk with Mrs. McQuade first, if I can work it, and see how the idea strikes her."

As he passed the corner of the orchard, and came to the garden patch that stretched below the house, he paused suddenly. A sound of vehement talking drifted down to him, and he recognized the deep voice, with a thrill of alarm.

The next moment he made out a horse and buggy standing in front of the house, in the drive. An exclamation of dismay burst from him, for he recognized it at once as the same which he had encountered at the horseshoe bend that morning.

"It isn't possible!" he murmured. "Colonel Carson wouldn't try such a trick!"

He approached the house, and, as he did so, his alarm increased. There was no doubt that the autocrat of Carsonville was present, and that he was extremely angry. As Merriwell sprang to the wide veranda, he clearly heard the vibrant tones.

"Yes, that graceless son of yours publicly assaulted my boy in the streets, not half an hour ago, Mrs. McQuade. It's the last straw, I tell you! First he tries to frighten my horse, then he assaults my son. If it hadn't been for the spectators, he might have killed the poor fellow. Now, you've either got to pay that mortgage or move out."

Merry chuckled at this version of the incident. Then his face became serious.

"Billy is a good son," faltered the voice of Mrs. McQuade. "I'm sure there's some mistake, Colonel Carson. He's going to start to work Monday at the store, and we hope to pay you that loan before long."

"You'll pay up inside of five days," stormed the angry man. "I'm sick of this fool way of conductin' business, mind my words! You've got till Monday mornin', then out you go, if you don't settle."

Merriwell stepped to the door, his eyes snapping. Colonel Carson stood inside, and Mrs. McQuade was helplessly facing him.

"I think you've made a mistake, sir," said Chip quietly. Carson swung around. "I was present at the encounter in the street, and I assure you that your son was in no danger. Billy hit him twice, and he lost his nerve and started for home."

Colonel Carson's face purpled with fury.

"So you admit it, hey?" he roared. "You can be mighty thankful, young man, if I don't have both o' you arrested for this business! Nice goings on, this is!"

"I guess you won't do any arresting in a hurry," said Chip calmly. "It wouldn't make a very nice story to get out about your son. The 'poor fellow,' as you call him, was brutally beating little Chub Newton, and Billy stepped in to prevent it, that's all. If there's any arresting to be done, it might be the other way around, for your son assaulted Billy first."

Mrs. McQuade gave Merriwell a grateful glance. Colonel Carson sputtered.

"That's a lie!" he broke out.

Chip's eyes flashed.

"I think we've had enough of your brand of politeness," he said quickly. "You have given Mrs. McQuade until next Monday to pay you, and that settles your business in this house, Colonel Carson."

"What's that to you?" shouted the enraged autocrat. "You ain't got any right here neither——"

"I think you had better go, Colonel Carson," and Mrs. McQuade gestured toward the door, with quiet dignity. "I have no legal proof of the mortgage having been paid, although the fact is morally certain. If we are not able to pay you before Monday, we cannot resist eviction, of course."

"Fine chance you have of raising two thousand dollars by then!" sneered Colonel Carson, grasping his hat. "I'll be around at eight o'clock Monday morning, so you'd better be packed up."

And with that he left, still muttering threats.

"I'm sorry about this, Mrs. McQuade," said Merriwell. "But don't give up hope yet. Billy told me about the matter after we met Colonel Carson this morning."

"It's hard to keep up heart," and the good woman looked out

the door, her face strained and hopeless. "You see, we are positive that Mr. McQuade paid off that loan long ago, but we have no proof that would stand in law. It seems hard that such a man as Colonel Carson should drive us out!"

"He's not done it yet," responded Chip cheerfully. "I never knew chicanery to get a man anything lasting, Mrs. McQuade. It may seem to win out, but there are other things more important than money, you know."

"You're a good comfort, Mr. Merriwell," and she gave him a smile, as she dabbed at her eyes with her apron. "Well, I'll have to see about those cookies——"

And she went to the kitchen, leaving Chip in a thoughtful mood. When Billy returned half an hour later, he was wrathful at hearing of the colonel's ultimatum, but could see no hope ahead. During luncheon, however, Merry made a proposition.

"If I could get a thousand dollars to add to your thousand, Mrs. McQuade, would you let me lend it to you? You could pay me interest, of course, and give me a mortgage to that amount, if you liked, as security."

This proposal was argued pro and con., but Chip had made it in such a way that it was a straight business proposition, and in the end Mrs. McQuade assented, providing that Merriwell could get the money.

So that night Chip wrote his father at Bloomfield. He related the situation at Carsonville, told what had happened that day, and stated that since he felt responsible in some measure, he would like to borrow a thousand dollars from his father in order to help out the McQuades. It never occurred to him that his father might refuse the loan.

CHAPTER V.

THE VILLAGE GREEN.

hen are them guys coming?"

"They'll be along pretty quick, Bully. I hear there ain't any game Saturday?"

"No. There's been a flood down the valley, and them Greenville scrubs wired that they wouldn't be up. They're all helpin' flood sufferers. Think o' lettin' a little thing like that interfere with our schedule!"

Bully Carson grunted sarcastically. It was evident that he had little use for flood sufferers.

"Come on, Bully, let's get a little practice right here," suggested one of the half dozen fellows standing around in baseball uniforms. "Bunting practice."

"Might's well, while we're waiting, I suppose," assented Carson.

They were waiting by the schoolhouse, lolling about the village green, and waiting for the remainder of the Clippers to show up for the morning work-out. Off at one side stood a group of young fellows who were watching proceedings with scowling faces.

Bully Carson and "Squint" Fletcher, who covered home plate for the Clippers, stepped out and began to plunk a ball back and forth. Hendrix, the shortstop, seized a bat and began to bunt.

At this juncture; Frank Merriwell, junior, accompanied by Billy Mac, strolled up. They had been having a work-out of their own down by the river, and Billy carried his catcher's mitt. They paused not far from the group of discontented-looking chaps, who nodded to Billy. Merriwell was introduced, and all watched the Clippers at work.

It was the morning after Colonel Carson's ultimatum had been delivered. From the comments which were passed, Chip decided that the young fellows of Carsonville cherished a distinct feeling of dislike for the colonel's son, who was captain of the Clippers.

"Bully gives me a pain," declared one of the group, Bud Bradley. He proceeded to narrate Carson's comment on the action of the Greenville club.

"That doesn't sound extra well," commented Merry. "It'd be more to the point if the Clippers would pile down to Greenville and help out the flood sufferers."

"No chance of that," exclaimed Dan McCarthy, a lanky village youth. "Nobody ever heard o' Bully Carson helpin' any one, nor his dad neither."

"Howdy, fel-l-lers," piped Chub Newton, as he joined the group. "Any one want to order groceries this morning? I hear there's no game Saturday."

"Open date," returned Billy. "Too late now to rearrange things, too."

"Look at that second baseman drop them!" growled Jim Spaulding.

"And talkin' about bushers, watch that feller who tries to play first," added McCarthy.

"Yah!" jeered Chub Newton, prodding Bud Bradley in the ribs and dancing away. "You fel-l-lers are jeal-l-lous, that's what! You're sore because you aren't inside of those uniforms."

"And who wouldn't be sore?" said Bradley hotly. "When that fellow Carson blacklists his own townfolks, and drags in city players, it's enough to make any one hot!"

"'Tisn't as if we wasn't good ball players, either," added McCarthy. "Bully knows he couldn't show off around us, that's all. He wants to be captain, and he'd stand a fine chance of us electin' him!"

Merriwell moved off a few steps, watching the Clippers. The foregoing remarks had indicated clearly the position of things in the town. The group of disgruntled natives comprised several of those who, like Billy Mac, had been ousted from the Clippers by the imported amateurs.

It was not hard to understand the reason for this, and Merry found himself in sympathy with the feeling. Knowing what he did of Bully Carson, he thought it highly probable that the captain of the Clippers doubted his ability to hold that position among the young fellows who had grown up with him.

It was much easier to impress a crowd of chaps who worked for his father. They would be very likely to toady to him, and allow him to lead them. This was plainly the sort of thing that Carson loved.

"Just the same," remarked Chip to Billy, who stood beside him,

"I don't think your friends give him full credit, old man. He looks like a good pitcher, and those other chaps know their business."

"You'd show him up in two jerks, Chip," declared Billy stoutly. Merry smiled, but did not reply.

Carson had noted the arrival of the two friends, for more than once he looked blackly at the group, and passed remarks to his companions that drew their eyes also. They grinned at his words as if they formed great strokes of humor.

Merry saw at once, however, that Carson knew his business. So did the rest of the Clippers. They had spread out over the green, and handled the bunts in fine shape, moving in perfect harmony and whipping over the ball with precision.

Their captain and star pitcher might have a bad case of "swelled head," but he showed that when it came to pitching, he was right there. As a group of girls passed on the other side of the street, he proceeded to cut loose.

And Merry admitted to himself that Bully Carson was a pitcher. He had speed and good control, while his curves broke sharply.

"Aw, cut out the comedy, cap," growled his catcher, Squint Fletcher. "This ain't no stage performance!"

Carson scowled, but kept silent. Perhaps he had already discovered that his husky backstop had little desire to truckle to him.

"Say, I got an idea!" chirruped Chub Newton shrilly. His voice lifted across to the green, and it caused Bully Carson to throw a vicious glance in the direction of the group.

"Be careful of it," grinned McCarthy. "You want to set on it an' hold it gently by the ears, Chub. Don't push it too hard."

"You l-l-listen to me," went on the little fellow eagerly. "We could get a better team right here in town than those Cl-l-lippers! I'd l-l-like to form another one, a cl-l-lub of our own, and l-l-lambaste the spots out o' them!"

At this astounding proposal, the members of the group stared at each other. Carson, who must have heard the words, looked blacker than ever, but continued tossing the ball.

"We couldn't do it," and Bud Bradley shook his head. "We've no money for grounds or uniforms or things, and most of us have to keep close to work."

"I'd like to show that second baseman up, just the same," said Spaulding. "But I guess there's no chance, Chub."

"Why not?" spoke up Billy Mac hastily. "We've got uniforms of one kind and another already, haven't we? We don't need grounds—we can practice up and beat the Carsonville Clippers on their own grounds, fellows!"

"Yah! That's the stuff!" shrieked Chub, dancing excitedly. "Wouldn't that be a scream, though! A bunch of us l-l-lambastin' the town cl-l-lub! Wow!"

It was plain that Chub's proposition appealed strongly to most of those present, but the difficulties seemed insurmountable.

"It'd take down Colonel Carson a heap," muttered McCarthy. "I'd do a good deal to pay him back fer the way he gobbled our pasture lots, when his cussed mortgage come due!"

"Look here," exclaimed Billy Mac, with eagerness. "It isn't near so bad as it looks, honest! We got pretty near a full infield right here in this crowd. We could get to work and practice off days till the ball season gets going, then light into that bunch right."

"Sounds good," admitted Spaulding. "But it won't work, Billy. Those fellows are sluggers from Sluggville. We'd have to have a crackajack pitcher to hold 'em down. And you know as well as I do that we'd have a hard job hitting Carson."

"That's all right," retorted Billy Mac. "Mebbe we could get Chip Merriwell, here, to come down from Fardale and pitch!"

At this proposal, every eye went to Merry. McQuade's eager seconding sent Chub into spasms of delight.

"Yah!" he piped shrilly. "Put Chip in the box, and watch him l-l-lam Carson! See him cl-l-lip the Cl-l-lippers! Yah!"

"What do you think of the plan, Merriwell?" inquired Bud Bradley doubtfully. "Would you be willing to come over and pitch?"

Merry nodded. Before he could speak, however, his eye was caught by a sudden movement on the part of Carson's team.

Three or four members had just arrived. Bully Carson, who must have heard the eager cries of Chub Newton, had immediately ceased practice. He had gathered the Clippers around him, and appeared to be talking vigorously, though his words were lost.

"You'd better put on the soft pedal, Chub," advised Merry. "Seems to me that Bully has it in for you and Billy Mac."

"Let him come!" sniffed Billy. "But what do you think about the idea, Chip?"

The group closed in about Merriwell, every member anxious for his opinion, as Billy had more than once described the diamond wizard's prowess to his home friends.

Merry hesitated, as he glanced around the faces. It did not appear likely that the Clippers could be easily trounced, and, besides this, he did not like to appear to be stirring up ill feeling.

He knew that there was a strong current of dislike against the Carson methods. At the same time, Colonel Carson controlled the town, and could possibly make it hot for those who opposed his son. Merry hesitated to give advice, under the circumstances, but finally nodded.

"Yes, I think the idea's a good one, if you don't carry your antagonism to extremes. As to coming over and pitching for you, I can't promise definitely. I'd be glad to do it, of course, if things shape themselves right."

"Hurray!" went up a general shout of delight, and Billy Mac patted his friend on the back, until Merry almost choked.

"Hurray for you, Chip! I knew you wouldn't go back on us!" he cried.

"By gum, we'll have the first practice this afternoon!" exclaimed McCarthy, in high excitement. "Chub can get off o' the store, I reckon, and we'll go down to the river an' start things! Jim, can we get enough fellers together?"

"I guess so," assented Spaulding, with a nod. "Merriwell might be able to give us some good advice, and he could get a line on our work."

He was interrupted by a sudden cry from Chub Newton.

"Hey! L-l-look out, fel-l-lers! Here they come!"

Merry and the others turned quickly. Bearing down upon them was Bully Carson, a bat in his hand, and crowding around him were the members of the Clippers. One and all looked ugly in the extreme.

CHAPTER VI.

A CHALLENGE.

As the Clippers approached, there was no sign of giving way in the ground around Merriwell. The Carsonville boys were not equal in numbers, but they were plainly anxious enough for battle. Carson paused a few yards distant.

"Well, what do you want?" snapped Merry.

"We're goin' to run you out o' town, see?" retorted Squint Fletcher, his cross eyes glaring savagely. "You're here tryin' to stir up trouble against us, eh? Well, you don't get no chance."

"I think you're misinformed," returned Chip quietly. "No one's stirring up a fuss except you."

"Oh, is that so?" Bully Carson pushed forward aggressively, clutching his bat. "I suppose you didn't try to kill dad yesterday, hey? I suppose you didn't set Billy Mac on me, hey?"

"You're doing a lot of supposing," said Merry dryly. "Your thinking apparatus needs oiling, Bully. Try a cigarette. It may straighten out things."

Merriwell's calm demeanor, and the resolute air of the group around him, rather cooled the ardor of the Clippers. It only angered Carson and Fletcher the more, however.

"So you're the famous Chip Merriwell, hey?" spluttered Squint, shoving his undershot chin forward. "I guess we've heard enough slush out o' you and the rest o' this gang. Let's beat 'em up proper, fellers!"

"Yah!" chirruped Chub, dancing on the outskirts of the crowd. "Try it! Ask Bul-l-ly where he got that bump on his chin. Ask him!"

This sally scored, for Billy Mac's fist had left unmistakable marks on the heavy countenance of the captain of the Clippers.

"You'll get yours, you little runt!" foamed the angry Carson, brandishing his bat at Chub. "We'll make you pretty sick of lettin' off your jaw around here!"

"Well, you're a mighty slow bunch to git started," observed the lanky, bronzed McCarthy, who worked in the orchards, and looked it. He spat on his hands. "I allus did want to paste them lamps of yours, Squint."

"You'll get your wish, all right," added Bud Bradley, shoving forward belligerently. "Let's take Carson down and throw him in the river, fellows!"

This proposal was greeted with high delight on the part of the town group. The Clippers began to move forward, and Merriwell saw that a conflict was imminent.

"You'd better go slow," he advised the Carson crowd. "We're not forcing any battle, remember. Keep back there, Bradley. If they start it, let them take the consequences."

"We've got 'em scared already," jeered Squint Fletcher. "Leave that Merriwell kid to me. I'll handle him!"

"Yes, you won't!" piped up Chub Newton. "Yah! L-l-lambaste 'em, Bil-l-ly!"

Chub's shrill cry was the last straw. Carson emitted a furious roar and raised his bat, while his team began crowding forward. The group around Merry closed in compactly, and it looked as if there would surely be a fight.

At that instant, however, a brawny man shoved in between the two parties. Squint Fletcher was just aiming a blow, and the man seized him by the shoulders and flung him back, sending him into Carson with a thump.

"That's enough o' this!" roared the town constable, for the man was no other. "I been keepin' my eye on you, Fletcher. Clear out o' here, the bunch of you."

"What right have you got to interfere?" cried Carson angrily. "I'll have my father——"

"You shut up, or I'll pinch you!" exclaimed the constable hotly. "I don't care for either you or your dad. I'm constable o' this town. Git out, now, and do it lively, or I'll run the lot o' you in! Jump!"

He pulled forth his club. Seeing that he meant business, Carson flung a sullen look around, nodded to his gang, and they melted away. The constable turned to Merry.

"Much obliged," said Chip, smiling. "We were afraid they meant trouble."

"So they did," growled the constable. "You'd better let 'em simmer down."

"We will," said Billy. The group was just breaking up when Merriwell halted them.

"One minute, everybody. What do you say to getting a game with the Clippers this Saturday? I believe it's an open date; I can pitch, and if you're willing to work between now and then, we can give them a run for their money!"

"Whoop!" A yell of delight burst from every throat.

"Bully for you!" cried Spaulding, grabbing Merry's hand and pumping it.

"No, us fer Bully!" said McCarthy. "You bet we will!"

"Can you get a team together?" asked Chip. "If you can, meet at Billy's house to-night and talk things over."

"We can get everything but a first baseman," said Bud Bradley, thinking quickly.

"Well, maybe I can take care of that," said Merry. He remembered that Owen Clancy was at Fardale, and his chum could be induced to come to Carsonville. "So long, then. Billy and I will get the game, and we'll expect you right after supper. Bring all the fellows you can get, and we'll start practice work in the morning."

This sudden proposal had been simmering in Merriwell's brain for some moments. He knew that it would be hard for him to get away from Fardale later in the season, and if these local players had any talent, there might be a chance of defeating the Clippers at once.

The group broke up. Merry and Billy set off together, while the others spread the news through the town in great excitement.

"We've undertaken a big contract, Billy. Let's go up and see the colonel now."

"I'm willing," said Billy Mac. "But he'll want to bet on the game, Chip."

"He'll—what?"

McQuade explained hastily. It seemed that Colonel Carson was used to plunging heavily on his own team, in common with a number of other men who followed the Amateur League. Some large sums of money changed hands as a result of the games.

"If he only knew it," exclaimed Merry, frowning, "that will hurt his chance of ever buying into a big-league team. That sort of a man is not wanted in baseball to-day. However, we'll see if he's willing to play us."

The two friends wended their way to the large white house occupied by Colonel Carson. They were met at the door by that gentleman, in person, who did not ask them inside, but stiffly inquired their business.

Merriwell stated it, saying that he understood the Clippers had an open date on Saturday, and that he would like to meet them with a pick-up Carsonville team. The colonel tugged at his goatee suspiciously.

"What's your object?" he snapped. "Want to play for the gate receipts?"

"Not at all," said Chip. "We just want to play the Clippers off their feet, and we intend to do it."

"Humph!" grunted the other. "Got a mighty good opinion of yourself, hey?" His face cleared suddenly. "Mebbe you'd like to make a little side bet, you or Billy?"

"No, thanks," returned Merriwell. "I don't gamble, and I don't think Billy does."

"Well, look a-here," went on Colonel Carson wheedlingly, addressing Billy. "I know you've got some insurance money, McQuade. You put it up on this game, and I'll give you odds, two to one. How's that? Ain't that fair?"

"Fair enough," grinned Billy Mac. "Only, I'm not in your class as a gambler, colonel. No, we're in this just to show up that club of yours, and do it proper. That'll satisfy us."

"But if you won," persisted the other, taking no heed of the taunt, "you'd have enough to pay off that mortgage, and some over!"

Billy wavered, but only for an instant.

"Nothing doing," he declared firmly. "If you want to play us, we'll make your old team hump itself. If you're scared of getting beaten, all right. Just say so."

"What! The Clippers scared o'you!" Colonel Carson laughed scornfully as he eyed the two. "Well, I guess not! It's a go. The reg'lar umpires will be here, anyway, so I guess we can use 'em?"

"Certainly," said Merriwell. "We may have the ball park for practice?"

"Not much," retorted Colonel Carson. "Get your own practice ground. Mebbe you had a notion I'd lend you uniforms!"

"No, we'd hate to play in Clipper uniforms," returned Merry gravely.

Colonel Carson was not quite sure how to take that remark, so he let it pass.

"Too bad you're scared to bet on yourself," he said cuttingly. "Got any battery picked out yet?"

"We'll be it," said Billy, with a grin. "Merriwell pitches for Fardale, you know."

"Humph! And you'll do the ketchin', hey? Well, I don't wonder that you fellers don't want to bet, then!"

Merry flushed a trifle.

"You're wrong, Colonel Carson. I don't believe in betting on principle. And especially where baseball is concerned. It's an unhealthy element to drag into the game, and the big baseball men have no use for a gambler, any more than good business men have."

This speech caused Colonel Carson to flush. His hard-lined, unhealthy face took on a most unpleasant aspect.

"Oh, you think you're smart!" he observed darkly. "Young man, I've not forgotten what took place yesterday morning. You're goin' to regret it. I intend to make you so sick of this town that you'll never come back to it."

"Thanks," said Merry easily. "The town looks pretty good to me, though—all except the name. Well, you haven't said whether we'd get that game or not."

"Of course you'll get it," said Colonel Carson. "We'll run up such a score on you that you'll quit before the third inning."

"Thanks again," and Merry chuckled. "Maybe you'll change your mind about that. Anyhow, we'll make you hump."

"Humph!" grunted the colonel, as if to echo the last word. "Two-thirty this Saturday. I'll provide the umpires, and they'll be our regular league men."

"That suits me," said Merry, and the two friends took their departure.

Billy stated that there need be no worry about the umpiring, as that end of the league was in good hands, and the umpires were excellent men.

"That'll help a whole lot, then," said Merry. "To-day is Wednesday, Billy. We will get started to-morrow morning. Two days of practice looks pretty slim, but I guess we can pull through. Want to get out with your mitt for signal work this afternoon?"

"You bet!" cried Billy excitedly. "And I'll catch you in a real game—my eye!"

"Let's hope we don't make exhibitions of ourselves," said Merry.

CHAPTER VII.

CHIP GETS A LETTER.

That evening, the McQuade homestead thrummed with eager voices. Six of the best local players, carefully picked by McCarthy, had gathered. A good many more had offered their services, but most of these had more enthusiasm than baseball knowledge.

"We sure need a first baseman," exclaimed Spaulding. Merry smiled.

"I wired my chum, Owen Clancy, this afternoon," he explained. "He's at Fardale now, and has been out West. He's just getting over a sprained ankle, but I think he can cover first for us all right. Now, let's get down to business and map things out."

Billy Mac, of course, would be backstop. He had been practicing all afternoon with Merry, and Chip had found that he could ask no better partner. The lanky Dan McCarthy would cover third, and looked as if he would do it efficiently.

Jim Spaulding made a bid for the central sack. He was one of the town players who had been ousted by Bully Carson, and was correspondingly bitter against the Clippers. Chub Newton would take care of short.

"We won't be a cl-l-lassy-l-l-lookin' bunch," announced the little fellow, as he inspected the ancient and tattered uniform he had brought along, "but we'l-l-l be right there when it comes to bal-l-l pl-l-l-laying!"

"You bet!" chuckled McCarthy, eying his own faded green shirt and baseball pants. "If I don't bang out a two-bagger, I'll quit tryin' to play ball, by gum!"

The outfield would be taken care of by Moore, also an ex-Clipper; Henderson, who had been a high-school star two years before, and a tremendously built young chap named Nippen. This Nippen was almost a giant in build, possessed of terrific strength, and apparently had the general aspect and intelligence of a cow.

He was the one member of the gathering who did not impress Merriwell as being especially adapted for baseball. Billy, however, reassured his friend in a whispered aside that Nippen would produce the goods.

"He doesn't look up to much, Chip, and he lumbers around like an overgrown puppy. But when he lands on the ball, he kills it, and the way he covers center field is something wonderful to watch. You wait!"

So Merry smiled and waited. Every one present displayed inspiring eagerness to work. There was one thing, however, which troubled Merriwell. This was the ill feeling which they displayed.

"You've got to watch that, fellows," he said. "I noticed to-day that you weren't a bit anxious to avoid trouble. Now, if we start in to win that game, it's going to make the other crowd sore. They'll try to get us into a fight and break up things. I want you to promise me that whatever they say or do, you'll keep your heads and let the scrapping wait till later. We can't afford to get rattled, you know."

All save McCarthy recognized this fact and readily extended their promise. The lanky third baseman held back, however.

"If that feller Squint Fletcher gets gay, I'm goin' to paste him," he declared stubbornly. "I won't take any talk or any dirty work from him."

"All right," said Merry quietly. "We'll have to find another man to cover third, I'm afraid. We can't take any chances that way, fellows."

McCarthy was taken all aback by this. When he found that Merriwell was in earnest, he scratched his head and reconsidered.

"All right," he said, "I'll promise not to start anything like a scrap, no matter what Squint does. But I'm goin' to file my spikes, jest the same. I reckon we'd better make Merriwell captain, fellers."

There was an instant shout of agreement. Chip held up his hand.

"Hold on, everybody! I think that Billy Mac ought to be your captain. I'm an outsider, and I'm only butting in here, anyhow——"

"Not on your life!" yelled Billy.

"Yeh! You're it, Merriwell!" chirped Chub Newton. "I'l-l-l bank on you every time! L-l-let's make it unanimous, fel-l-lows!"

Merry's protests were voted down amid wild enthusiasm, and he was elected captain of the pick-ups. Spaulding suggested that they call themselves the Carsonville Clippings.

"That's it!" cried Chub. "The Cl-l-lippers and the Cl-l-lippings—wow! Won't Bul-l-ly Carson be mad, though!"

The name was adopted with a yell of delight. The meeting was just breaking up when there was a ring at the doorbell, and Billy returned with a telegram for Chip.

"It's from Clancy," cried Merry, tearing open the envelope. "Hello! Listen to this, fellows!"

And, holding up the message, he read as follows:

Coming on the jump. Ankle fine. Bringing your uniform and some balls. Arrive to-morrow noon via Hornet.

Owen Clancy.

"What's the Hornet?" inquired Billy, in wonder. "There's no noon train in!"

"That's Clancy's car," laughed Merry. "It's an old auto that he took off the scrap heap and made into a racer, though it doesn't look up to much. He brought it with him from the West."

"I'd like to put him up," volunteered Spaulding. "We've got lots of room at our place, and he'd be welcome to stay a month."

Billy protested, for he wanted Clancy as a guest himself, but Merriwell knew that two guests would sorely tax good Mrs. McQuade's resources, so he accepted Spaulding's offer gratefully. The meeting broke up with the first practice set for the following morning, Chub Newton stating that he would get off work easily enough, as his employer had no love for the Carsons.

Merriwell rather expected that he would get a letter from his father in the morning's mail, but none came. Though he said nothing of it, this worried him slightly. He had explained to Billy that he had written his father, asking for the thousand dollars, and he began to wonder if his letter had miscarried.

He soon forgot his worry, when the Clippings assembled on an old diamond used by the high school. It was in a meadow beside the river. Three or four old balls were produced, and Merry at once set to work to get an idea of what his team could do.

The results were both encouraging and discouraging. The diamond was rough and uncared for, so that the infield had a tough time judging balls, but the base throws were excellent, and they showed good form.

Merry handed up slow ones, and the batting practice proved that in this quarter his team was lamentably weak. Chub Newton would bite at anything. McCarthy faced the plate wickedly, but his eye was poor on slow ones, and it was said that Bully Carson did his best work with a fadeaway ball.

Spaulding proved to be a fair batsman, while Nippen landed on Merry's first ball and knocked it into the middle of the river. Henderson and Moore did poorly, and, although the three outfielders showed up better on gathering in high ones, Merry was not greatly encouraged when he and Billy went home for lunch.

"We've got a tough nut to crack here, old man," he remarked soberly. "Can the Clippers hit pretty well?"

"That's their strong suit," gloomily returned Billy Mac. "They get a pitcher going, and it's all off with him. They're pretty ragged when it comes to headwork, but they give Carson mighty good support. Yes, they can certainly hit. Squint Fletcher leads the league."

"Slugging doesn't always mean hitting," said Merry cheerfully. "Brace up, old man! We've a day and a half for practice, and we're going to improve a whole lot."

"We'll need to," muttered Billy. He halted suddenly, staring up at the house just ahead of them. "Hello! There's a machine standing out in front!"

"Clancy must have come ahead of time!" cried Merry.

The two burst into a run. Reaching the veranda, they found a red-haired young fellow seated in a rocker. He was talking with Mrs. McQuade. At sight of Merriwell, he leaped up and vaulted the railing.

"Hello, Chip!" he cried, wringing Merry's hand. "Wow! I'm glad to see you!"

"Same here," returned Chip. "I see you've already met Mrs. McQuade, eh?"

"We're old friends by this time," said Clancy. "Hello, Billy! I haven't seen you since last fall. How's everything?"

"Pretty good," stated Billy, forgetting his troubles for the moment. "When do we get some eats, mother?"

"Lunch is all ready," said Mrs. McQuade, who had taken a fancy to the red-haired chap already. "Do you want to bring your stuff inside, Mr. Clancy?"

Merriwell hastily explained that Clan was going to stop with Jim Spaulding, and they turned to examine the load heaped in the vacant seat of the machine.

This was composed of two Fardale uniforms, together with a catcher's mitt, protector, and mask, and a half dozen balls. On these Billy pounced with delight.

"Wait till this afternoon, Chip! We couldn't do much with those old balls this morning, but we'll show you something this afternoon! Say, this looks pretty good to me."

"Something to eat would look pretty good to me," said Clancy. "I've been hitting the high places ever since early this morning. Say, it certainly did feel good to go out and have your mother pump water over me, Billy. Reminded me of days on the farm."

The three settled down about the table, and Merry at once launched into a description of events at Carsonville. Billy and his mother never tired of watching the bronzed young fellow, who had been regaling Mrs. McQuade with tales of his adventures in Arizona, and Clancy polished off the good things before him with astonishing rapidity.

"It listens good to me," he commented, with a sigh, when, at length, he could stow no more away. "I hear at Fardale that Billy has developed into quite a backstop, eh?"

"Sure," said Merry. "He's a wonder, and no mistake, Clan."

"Oh, my eye!" sniffed Billy. "Just because I happen to hold on to your double shoots, you needn't raise my modesty like that!"

"It isn't every one who can hang on to them," said Clancy. "Oh, by the way, Chip, I came mighty near forgetting! Your father was at Fardale yesterday on a flying visit."

And he began to dig excitedly at his pocket, finally extricating an envelope which he handed to Merry.

"Your father asked me to give this to you. He said it would get to you quicker than if he mailed it."

Merriwell nodded. With a word of apology to Mrs. McQuade, he tore open the envelope, half expecting to see an inclosure. None fell out. He ran his eye quickly over the letter, and his cheeks paled a trifle, then he refolded it, and put it in his pocket.

Five minutes later he stood on the veranda with Billy. Clancy was down in the drive explaining the hidden beauty of his car to Mrs. McQuade.

"What's the trouble, Chip? Wouldn't he let you have the coin?" asked Billy.

"I'm sorry, old man," and Merriwell bit his lip. "He didn't think it wise."

CHAPTER VIII.

GETTING DOWN TO WORK.

erriwell drew out the letter and sank into a chair. While Billy listened, he read over that portion of the letter referring to the request for a loan. Chip read as follows:

"I sympathize very deeply with both Billy and his mother, Frank, and I would be glad to have you read this to Billy, and assure him of my best regards and wishes. As to lending you the money, however, I do not think that this would be wise, for several reasons.

"The first and most important is that it seems to me to be a poor way in which to checkmate a scoundrel like this Colonel Carson. I have made inquiries about him, and find that he had a reputation as a plunger on ball games, and is wrapped up in the success of his own team.

"I think you have done well in raising a team to defeat the Clippers, as intimated in your wire to Clancy. I was going to suggest that very thing. If you and Billy can beat his club, it would be an ideal way in which to punish him. I only wish that more of the Fardale boys were here, so that they could come down and help, but vacation has scattered them."

"That's all very well," interrupted Billy mournfully, "but licking the Clippers isn't going to save this house for mother, Chip. I wish—I wish we'd taken a chance on it, and taken up that bet he offered!"

"No, you don't," exclaimed Merriwell. "Hold on, Billy. I haven't finished yet."

"Go ahead and whip Carson's team, Frank. You and Billy and Clancy can do it if you try, and remember that I've every faith in all of you. Do it, and I will see that Billy and his mother do not lose the roof over their heads.

Your loving father,

Frank Merriwell, Senior."

Merry looked up to meet his friend's startled gaze.

"What does he mean by that, Chip?"

"Search me," said Merry, as he stowed away the letter. "But you can be sure that father means something, all right."

"I guess he does," rejoined Billy, new hope dawning in his eyes. "My eyes! It's a promise, Chip! I'll bet he means that if we beat the Clippers he'll lend you the coin!"

"No," and young Merriwell shook his head decidedly. "He doesn't think it a good plan, old man, and that ends it. Father doesn't have to say a thing twice. Yes, it's a promise, I imagine. I've no idea what he means by it, of course, but he has some kind of plan up his sleeve. You quit worrying."

"I'll try," said Billy, with a sigh. "But I wish he'd said something a little more definite than that."

"So do I, Billy," confessed Merry. "He didn't, so there's no use wondering. I'm not going to say anything to Clan about this business, so now let's go around to Jim's house with him, then we'll get out to the ball field again."

Merriwell decided that the McQuades' trouble was a personal affair. He had entered into it largely through accident, and he did not consider it a matter to share even with Clancy. So all three of the friends piled into the Hornet, Billy standing on the running board, and they made a triumphal progress to the Spaulding residence.

Despite his unbounded confidence in his father, Chip could not help feeling disappointed over that letter. However, the definite promise at the end served to relieve his anxiety, to some extent, but he could see no light upon the subject. How could his father prevent Colonel Carson from carrying out his threats?

As he obtained no answer to this mental query, Merriwell tried to forget the whole thing, and trust that his father knew best. But it was no easy matter.

That afternoon they met the other Clippings on the village green, going from there to their practice ground. Chub Newton had been given a vacation until Saturday night, and his employer had promised that if the Clippers were beaten, Chub would get full pay.

In fact, the entire town was already plunged into excitement over the sudden contest. Public disapproval of Bully Carson had long simmered beneath the surface, kept under cover by the influence and general fear of Colonel Carson.

It was not yet daring enough to show itself openly, but it peeped forth in minor ways. Every one knew that Billy McQuade, prompted by his guest from Fardale, Chip Merriwell, had dared to defy Colonel Carson. Also, that half a dozen of the town's best local baseball talent had joined the two friends.

Consequently, the grocer's son, who was taking Chub Newton's place behind the counter temporarily, ran out with a bag of apples and deposited them mysteriously on the ground by the astonished Clippings. A little later, as they passed the one ice-cream parlor in the place, the proprietor appeared suddenly and thrust a paper bucket of ice cream into Spaulding's hand, then vanished without a word.

By such tokens as these, Frank and his friends soon discovered that they were not without secret good wishers, though none of the latter dared come into the open.

"Talk about a scared town!" laughed Clancy, munching an apple vigorously. "Looks like your friend Carson had this place buffaloed for sure, Chip!"

"Well, there's good reason for it," explained Spaulding. "The colonel owns the bank here, and pretty near half the farms and orchards around. If he said to smash a merchant, that merchant would be apt to smash. I know, because he's done it before this, and he'd do it again."

"It's a pretty poor kind of influence to hold over people," declared Frank. "I'd hate to walk down the street and know that nine out of ten people hated me in their hearts."

"The colonel doesn't know it. He's got too much vanity. And he wouldn't care very much if he did realize it, I guess."

"Somebody ought to l-l-lam him good," piped Chub. "I'd l-l-like to see him run out of town!"

"Maybe you will some day," growled McCarthy ominously.

"Don't forget your promise," said Frank, in a low voice.

"No danger o' that, Merriwell. I filed them spikes o' mine, though."

"See here, Dan, I don't want to have any of that work——"

"I ain't goin' to start anythin', I said," broke in the lanky youth doggedly. "And I won't. But I ain't goin' to let trouble hit me over the ear, you bet. I'll be jest as meek as a lamb until they try dirty work on me, only I want to be ready."

Frank nodded. After all, he did not greatly blame McCarthy for distrusting the caliber of Squint Fletcher, or, for that matter, the rest of the Carsonville club. He did not believe in fighting fire with fire, but he saw that it would be useless to try argument with Dan McCarthy.

So he let the matter drop, confident that the lanky third baseman would not be the first to start any "dirty work." The general sentiment of the Clippings was that the Clippers would not stop at anything to win, but that the umpiring would be fair.

"I want you to help me out, Clan," said Frank, as he walked along beside his old chum. "These chaps are just aching for a good chance to start a scrap with the other team. They've all promised me that they'd go slow during the game, but I want you to get after 'em during practice."

"In what way, Chip?"

"By showing them how necessary it is that they keep their heads. That's our only hope. If our boys get rattled, the Clippers will walk away with us. Impress on them, Clan, that, no matter what provocation they get, they have to keep quiet while the game is on. What happens later doesn't concern me."

Clancy grinned. "All right. Count on me, Chip."

Upon reaching the practice grounds, Merry at once sent the men to their positions. He took the bat, and for half an hour gave the entire team a driving practice work-out. The new white balls seemed, oddly enough, to put new heart into his team.

It showed them that Frank and Clancy meant business. It was a little thing, but it is just such little things that count tremendously. The red-haired chap covered first like a demon, scooping up everything that came his way. His example fired the others.

As Billy had foretold, the Clippings seemed like a different set of players. They went after the ball with a vim. Spaulding, Chub, and McCarthy tackled anything, and managed to smother the stiffest ones Frank drove at them.

In the outfield, the marvelous fielding of Nippen astonished Merriwell. The gigantic, overgrown fruit picker, in his lumbering fashion, fairly ate up the ground. When he went after a high one, he seemed never to know where it would fall, but when it came down, it invariably plunked into his mitt. He had no science, but he seemed to have luck.

"How do they strike you?" inquired Merry, as he and Clan conferred during a brief rest.

"Pretty promising bunch, Chip. But when they get up against those Clippers, it'll be a whole lot different. Those fellows can do in their sleep what this crowd has to break their necks over."

"That's true, but, just the same, they'll improve a lot by Saturday."

Clancy shook his head doubtfully. It was clear that he was not greatly impressed by the Clippings.

The batting practice that followed served to back up Clancy's opinions. Calling in the outfielders, Frank kept putting over nothing but outs and ins and straight fast ones, yet the batters could not seem to connect.

His coaching helped them a good deal, but nothing wonderful resulted. Nippen seemed to have spent all his energy on the one ball he had struck that morning. Chub Newton could hit nothing. Henderson was afraid to stand up to the plate, and Billy McQuade seemed to have lost his batting eye.

McCarthy, however, fell on the ball, and pounded it viciously until Frank served him up slow floaters, when he failed lamentably. Then Merry put Billy through his paces as backstop, using everything from the double shoot to the jump ball; and the workout was over.

"It's a bum lookout," observed Billy, when they were walking together past the orchard to the house. "We did pretty rotten at bat to-day."

"Oh, not so bad," said Frank encouragingly. "We'll all be nerved up more on Saturday, for one thing. Then remember, Bill, it isn't the sluggers who win."

"That's right, Chip. Do you honestly think we've got a show?"

"I do," replied Frank earnestly. "Our fellows are fine on base-throwing, and when they get to work on a decent diamond, the results will be astonishing. I really think we've an excellent chance, old man."

"Then that takes a load off my mind," said Billy, with a sigh. "I thought you'd be pretty disgusted with us."

Frank smiled and patted him on the back cheeringly. But in his heart he felt that, while the Clippings might have a chance, it was a terribly slim one.

CHAPTER IX.

COLONEL CARSON MAKES A BET.

On Friday morning, the day before the game, Colonel Carson was standing in the lobby of the Carsonville Bank. He appeared extremely discontented.

"Not a one," he said disgustedly. "Everybody in town is scared to bet on them Clippings."

"I don't wonder," sneered Bully Carson derisively. "They're a bunch of pick-ups."

Bully Carson wore his most flamboyant attire, for he would not go to work-out with the Clippers for another hour. From one corner of his mouth drooped a limp cigarette.

"Too bad you can't place a few dollars," he went on. "It'd be easy money."

"Is your arm all right?" inquired the colonel.

"Never better. Hello, who's that gink?"

The two turned to gaze at the doorway. The bank had just been opened for business, and, as things were not very brisk in Carsonville, this was the first customer of the day. And he was evidently a stranger.

"Must 'a' come in on the mornin' train," observed Bully.

He was a well-set-up, quietly dressed man, and would have attracted little attention save for his remarkably fine build. A soft crush hat was pulled down over a pair of very keen but pleasant eyes, and the lower portion of his face was hidden by a curly dark beard.

The stranger gave a single glance at the two, and walked to the teller's window. With a nod and a cheery "Good morning," he drew out a long bill book and opened it. Colonel Carson gasped and clutched at his son's shoulder, for the bill book appeared to be crammed with yellowbacks.

"I have a couple of certified checks I'd like you to cash for me, if you will."

His voice was quiet and self-restrained.

"Certainly, sir," replied the teller.

The stranger shoved the two checks he had taken out through the window. The teller glanced at them, and his jaw fell. He excused himself, then beckoned to Colonel Carson to come over.

"These are pretty large checks, colonel," he said apologetically.

"Humph!" grunted Carson, and turned to the stranger. "Made out to John Smith! Is that your name?"

"Aren't those checks sufficient warrant?" smiled the stranger. "They're certified, and ought to be as good as gold, Colonel Carson."

"You know me?" The bank owner looked surprised.

"I've heard of you," returned John Smith pleasantly. "You see, I'm quite a follower of baseball, though I don't often get away from home. I've heard a good deal of the Carsonville Clippers, and came over to have a look at them."

Bully Carson swelled visibly. His father turned to the teller.

"It's all right, I guess. Two thousand is a big sum, but they're certified. Mr. Smith, meet my son. He's the pitcher o' the Clippers. Goin' to stay for the game to-morrow?"

"Perhaps," smiled John Smith. "I'll see what the chances are for placing a few bets around here."

He winked knowingly, and Colonel Carson flung Bully a warning glance.

"We got an awful tough team to go up against," he said, tugging at his goatee. "I'd like to bet on the Clippers myself, but durned if I don't think we'll get beat."

Bully had caught that look.

"Yes, they got a feller named Merriwell," he said dolefully. "I dunno's I'll be much good against him, either."

"Oh, Merriwell! I've heard of him often," exclaimed the stranger. "By Jove, I'd like to get a bet down on his team, whatever it is! I suppose I could see the two teams at work, couldn't I?"

"Sure, I'll take care o' you, Mr. Smith," volunteered Bully.

He went off arm in arm with the stranger, and Colonel Carson turned to his teller.

"There's an easy mark! When Bully gets through with him, he'll be ready to put up some real coin on them Clippings, mind my words!"

Colonel Carson's confidence in his son was well placed. Indeed, Bully had no easy task, for not a soul in Carsonville had any great belief that the Clippers would be defeated the next day.

The stranger went out to the park with them, and was pleasantly astonished by the concrete stands and excellent diamond.

"You have quite a place here, eh," he observed. "Go ahead, boys, don't mind me."

The Clippers did not appear to mind him in the least. They went to work, and, after watching them a little time, the stranger was evidently well satisfied. Bully Carson seemed to have difficulty in finding the plate. His infield gave him wretched support, making wild throws, and letting the ball tear through them.

His outfield did little better. On the whole, the stranger was anything but well impressed by the Clippers, and did not hesitate to say as much on the way back to town. Bully Carson agreed that they were in poor shape, but when the stranger had left him, he congratulated his team warmly.

"I guess that feller's hooked," he observed sagely, and hastened home.

After casual inquiries about town, John Smith found his way to where the team captained by Frank Merriwell, junior, was working out during the afternoon. As this was their first visitor, the Clippings displayed no little curiosity, seeing that he was a stranger to them, but he held aloof from the diamond.

"Who is he—one of the umpires?" inquired Frank.

"Search me," returned Billy Mac. "He's a new one in this burg."

"It's a scout for the Phil-l-ladel-l-lphia Ath-l-letics," chirruped Chub Newton from second. "He's l-l-lookin' for recruits."

"What's that?" cried McCarthy excitedly, taking Chub seriously.

"Sure, he's goin' to sign you on, Dan," grinned Spaulding.

McCarthy did not see the joke. He advanced to take his turn at batting, and, when Frank handed him a stiff inshoot, he fell on it and knocked the ball through Chub's hands. Then Merry began teasing him, but he refused to bite, until he caught one on the nose and lined it out.

"Wow? Mebbe that'll show him what Dan McCarthy can do!" he yelled, as the ball zipped.

When he discovered that he had been victimized, he turned on Chub.

"You blamed little yapper!" he said. "You'd be a whole lot s'prised to find that he was a big-league scout, wouldn't you?"

"Yah!" piped Chub jubilantly. "L-l-line her out again, Dan!"

The stranger hung around for an hour, speaking to no one, but watching the practice intently. Finally he drifted off in the direction of town.

Once back in the town, he began inquiries as to Colonel Carson's whereabouts. That individual was not hard to find. In fact, he was on a still hunt for the stranger, and finally encountered him near the bank.

"Well, Mr. Smith, how'd the two teams strike you?"

"The Clippers didn't look up to much, to my mind," said the stranger easily. "Of course, I may be mistaken, but Merriwell's crowd seemed to be pretty good. Why, one of those fellows lammed the ball a mile, Carson!"

"Yes," and Colonel Carson fingered his goatee, "them fellers can hit, Smith. Placed any bets yet?"

"Well, no," replied the stranger. "I rather thought I might induce you to put up a little money."

"I ain't very flush right now," said the colonel cunningly. It was not the first time that he and Bully had worked together to good advantage. "Still, I dunno as I'd mind placin' a little on the Clippers, seeing's they belong to me."

"Ah, you're a true sport!" cried Smith heartily. "Oh, by the way—I have some friends here by the name of McQuade. Perhaps you know where Mr. McQuade lives, colonel?"

"Well, yes. He lives in the cemetery, right now, Smith. He's been dead quite a spell."

"Dead! You don't say!" The stranger was visibly perturbed. "Poor McQuade! He never had much head for business. I suppose he died poor?"

"He died owin' me two thousand," said Colonel Carson grimly. "I got a mortgage on his place over by the river, right in my safe. I'm goin' to foreclose, too."

"Well, well! Did he leave any family?"

"Son an' widder," jerked the other. "Son's ketchin' on Merriwell's team."

John Smith glanced around. The town constable stood at a little distance, and the stranger pointed at him.

"That's the constable, isn't it, Carson? Well, let's bring him into your office, and if we can make a little bet, he could be stakeholder. Eh?"

Colonel Carson grinned to himself, and agreed with some show of hesitation. With the constable following, they entered the bank and sat down in the owner's private room.

"Look here, Carson," said the stranger affably. "I've been thinking this thing over. McQuade used to be an old friend of mine, and I hate to think of his widow and son being left out in the cold. I tell you what I'll do. I'll set two thousand dollars against that mortgage you hold.

"If you win, the money's yours. If the Clippers are beaten, then

I get the mortgage. How does that sound?"

"No good," stated Carson firmly. "The McQuade place is worth a heap more'n that sum, Smith. I got that mortgage cheap."

The stranger looked disappointed.

"Well," he remarked, replacing the bill book which he had taken from his inner pocket, "I don't know that I'm very anxious to bet against the Clippers, anyway. I'd risk the sum for the sake of McQuade's family, out of pure sentiment, but—— Well, I'll hang about town and see if I can't get a bit of money down on your team. After all, it's safer."

He rose, with a gesture of dismissal to the constable.

"Hold on!" cried Colonel Carson. "You ain't in earnest, Smith?"

"Why, of course!" said the stranger. "Merriwell's team is untried and green. After all, I might be foolish——"

"Set down, set down," and the colonel reached out to his safe. "I've got that mortgage right here. I reckon I'll take a chance, Smith."

And once more he grinned to himself.

CHAPTER X.

HOW THE GAME OPENED.

Carsonville was emptying itself.

Every person in town, young and old, was a baseball enthusiast. The grand stand and bleachers of the club grounds were invariably crowded every Saturday. But on this one Saturday it seemed as though the town had gone crazy over the game.

So, after a fashion, it had. Despite its support of the Clippers, Carsonville turned out to see baseball, rather than to see the Clippers play. It loved the game for itself. Down underneath the surface, however, it cherished a warm dislike for the Clippers and their captain.

This dislike had been, perforce, hidden, for fear of antagonizing the autocrat of Carsonville. When the home team had been playing, all personalities had been forgotten in the game itself. On such occasions, even Bully Carson had become popular for the moment, if he won a game.

It was quite different on this Saturday, however. The Carsons had been defied, and when the crowd had streamed into the park, it forgot all about its fear of Colonel Carson's power.

"I hope them Clippers get trounced! I hope Bully Carson gets knocked out of the box!" cried old Abner Powell, on whose forty acres the colonel held a heavy mortgage.

"So do I! Hurray for the Clippings!" yelled the teller of the Carsonville bank.

"Here's where the colonel gets took down!" shouted the Carsons' hired man.

Every one had forgotten their fears, under the magic influence of the ball park. And every one had raised the price of a seat. By general consent, it was the largest crowd that the Carsonville park had ever held.

Every man on the two teams was known personally to the fans, except Merriwell and Clancy. Even they were known by reputation, though few of the townsfolk had dared to show support by watching the Clippings practice.

The line-up of the two teams was announced that morning by bulletin:

CLIPPINGS.

McCarthy,	3d	b.
Nippen,	c.	f.
Clancy,	1st	b.
Merriwell,	p.	
McQuade,	c.	
Spaulding,	2d	b.
Moore,	l.	f.
Henderson,	r.	f.
Newton,	ss.	

CLIPPERS.

Fletcher,	c.	
Burkett,	1st	b.
Bangs,	3d	b.
Ironton,	ss.	
Johnson,	r.	f.
Murray,	2d	b.
Carson,	p.	
Runge,	l.	f.
Merrell,	c.	f.

The diamond was in perfect condition, its caretaker having spent all morning getting it in shape. Every line was freshly marked, every inch carefully raked free of hindrances. The very sight of it was a joy to the fans, empty though it stood.

And it was joy to Merriwell and Clancy, also, when they arrived at the clubhouse beneath the grand stand. Both had been too busy to look at the place, but they were instantly delighted by it. Meantime, the Hornet proceeded around to the field with Mrs. McQuade and Jim Spaulding's young brother.

"It's a peach of a place, Chip!" cried the red-haired chap.

"Yes—look at that diamond! I don't remember when I've seen a better cared-for place."

Merry continued his inspection as the rest of his team poured in to dress. There were bleachers behind first and third, all well filled, and the only symptom of neglect was in the high board fence. Directly behind second, in the center fielder's territory, there was a strip of fence ten feet wide that had been leveled.

This, it appeared, had been cut out to erect a large score board, but there had been delay in the shipment of materials, and the gap was unfilled.

Billy Mac pointed to the river, which ran about a hundred yards behind the fence.

"No home runs in this field," he said, "unless the ball goes into the river. You see, the diamond inclosure is a little small, Chip. Outside of the fence it's marshy, and it would have cost a lot to fill in. So they compromised on that ground rule. If the ball goes into the river, it's a home run. It's never yet gone in, though."

"Queer kind of ground rule," growled Clancy. "But there's no accounting for tastes, so let's try to put the ball in the water, fellows!"

"We'l-l-l try," piped Chub resolutely. "When do we practice?"

"Right now," exclaimed Frank. "We're a little early, so we'll get to work and let the Clippers howl, if they want to."

When the Clippings walked out, they were greeted by a long yell from the fans. Then there rose a buzz of voices as the players trotted out to their places, and Merry began to drive hot ones along the infield.

Every one was wondering how the home talent would show up. No sooner had the ball begun to snap around the bases than shout after shout pealed up. Despite their rare and wonderful uniforms, the Clippings showed form!

Even Frank was surprised. On the level diamond his team proved that they could do something, after all. They went after the ball with ginger, and the way they snapped it up was astonishing.

The Clippers now produced themselves, and promptly spread out behind the foul lines to inspect their opponents. They delivered themselves of comments, which were audible over most of the field.

"Look at the uniforms!" yelled Squint Fletcher. "They used them kind fifty years ago! Pipe the Irish third baseman! Wow!"

"Who's that scrubby runt playin' short?" cried Ironton, waving his fists. "Wait till I land on him!"

"I'l-l-l show you!" chirped Newton angrily. "Wait til-l-l——"

"Listen to him!" cried Ironton. "Wow! He talks like a washing machine!"

Even the crowd laughed at that, for every one knew Chub. The little fellow lost his temper, and sent the ball far over third.

"They're easy," commented Bully, in contempt. "We got their goat already. You watch when that Merriwell gets up to the plate.

I'll lam him in the head."

"You'd better try it!" retorted Clancy heatedly. Merry signed to him to walk up toward the box, with Chub.

"You fellows keep quiet," he said. "Pass the word around not to give any back talk unnecessarily. First thing we know, this will be a free-for-all, and we have to avoid that if possible."

The Clippings tried to restrain themselves, but it was hard work for them to keep from answering the taunts that poured in from Bully Carson's men. At length, Frank signed to his team, and they trotted in. The Clippers spread out on the field, and began to amuse themselves with threats of what they would do to their opponents, while they tossed the ball around.

In Colonel Carson's private box, square in the center of the grand stand, sat the colonel and his new acquaintance, John Smith. The latter had accepted the proffered seat gratefully, though he refused the proffered stogies, pleading that his health did not permit smoking.

As the Clippings came in to their bench, they looked up and saw the stranger.

"There's your scout, Dan," chuckled Billy. "Only it looks like he was friends with the wrong side."

The stranger waved a hand at them.

"Go in and win!" he cried. "You've got 'em licked, Merriwell!"

"You bet!" returned Clancy quickly. "Just watch our smoke, Whiskers!"

The stranger's white teeth flashed through his beard, and he turned his attention to the Clippers as they fell to work.

"They seem to do better than they did yesterday," he remarked suddenly.

Colonel Carson leaned back and grinned complacently.

"I reckon they slept well last night, Smith," he drawled. "Any team is liable to an off day, you know."

"Yes, I know," returned Smith sharply. "It looks to me as if you had let me in for a bit of sharp practice, Carson."

"Sport is sport," observed the colonel, with a grin. "You risks your money, and you takes your chance."

"I've a good mind to call the bet off!"

"No, ye don't! The constable's down keepin' order in the bleachers, and you can't locate him 'fore the game starts if ye want to. 'Sides, I reckon you ain't a welsher."

The stranger allowed himself to be soothed down, and settled himself to watch the progress of things.

Frank and Bully Carson met with the two umpires, and went

over the ground rule regarding a home run.

"No chance o' your scrubs gettin' the ball in the river," jeered Carson. "Don't need to worry over it. Ain't never been done, anyhow!"

"That's no sign it can't be done," said Frank, with a smile.

A gong rang out. Merry and Carson quickly discussed the question of outs and ins, while the umpires were announcing the batteries.

"I'd like to git in the box first crack, an' knock your block off," growled Bully. "But I dunno's I wouldn't jest as soon knock you out o' the box. Take your choice."

"Thanks," said Merry easily. "Since you're so kind, I think we'll give you a chance to get a home run, Bully. According to the batting order, I'm afraid you won't get a crack till the third inning, though."

Carson, whose name stood seventh on the list, glowered derisively.

"Huh! We'll prob'bly bat around twice in the first inning, you joke! You'd better get another pitcher warmin' up."

"Come on, Bully," cried Squint Fletcher. "Leave that poor simp alone!"

No one had any need to hear the umpires' announcement, and it was drowned in a roar of cheers as the Clippings went out to their positions. Colonel Carson glowered and tugged at his goatee, then smiled as Squint Fletcher advanced to the plate amid a mingling of hisses and cheers. Squint had his backers, who liked him for his rough-and-ready tactics.

Indeed, it soon developed that the Clippers were not without friends. The general sentiment was against them, but there were plenty of hoodlums and toadies who were willing to cheer them. Also, many farmers had come in, who were used to yelling for the Clippers.

The umpires took their positions, and Merry whipped over three balls to Billy. Squint stepped up to the plate, with a sneer, and balanced himself aggressively. Billy Mac signed for the double shoot.

Frank nodded, took his time, and, amid a wild shriek of delight from the crowd, delivered the first pitched ball. Squint Fletcher pulled down his bat—and there was a crack like a pistol shot.

Squint had landed square on Frank Merriwell, junior's, famous double shoot!

CHAPTER XI.

THE CLIPPINGS GET WILD.

The connection, however, was so plainly an accident, and Squint himself looked so bewildered, that every one roared with laughter.

The ball went almost straight up in the air over first, until it seemed to lose itself in the sky. Fletcher came pounding down the base line, while Bully Carson, behind first, sent a roar at Clancy.

The red-haired first baseman was not rattled, however. He calmly stepped back, pulled down his cap, and waited. The ball came down like a bullet and stuck in his glove.

"Out!"

Roar after roar of applause went up. The Clippings, who had been nervous and unsettled, instantly regained their poise and confidence.

"Take your time, Chip!" snapped Spaulding, from second.

"That's the ticket, old man!" cried McCarthy encouragingly.

"L-l-lam into 'em!" piped up Chub.

Frank smiled. Burkett, who covered first for the Clippers, advanced to the plate, pulled down his cap, and waited.

"We're all behind you, old-timer," chirped Clancy.

"Let him hit it, Chip!" cried Billy. None the less, he signaled for an inshoot.

Burkett was plainly anxious to hit. Frank put over a fast inshoot. The ball fairly smoked with speed, and Burkett swung too late.

"Strike—uh—one!"

"Land on him!" yelled Bully Carson. "All he's got is speed!"

Billy called for another of the same, but Merry shook his head. He guessed that Burkett wanted speed, and would be looking for it, so he put over a fadeaway that drew Burkett for another strike.

"This fellow's a cinch!" cried Billy. Burkett looked determined.

Studying him for a moment, Frank nodded at the signal for a jump ball. He sent the sphere down to the plate waist-high. Burkett brought down his bat, but the ball seemed to jump over it, and plunked into Billy's mitt.

"Out!"

Cheer after cheer rolled up, as Burkett sullenly retreated, and was replaced by Bangs. The Clipper third baseman was a wiry, alert fellow, and he chopped down his bat as if ready for anything that could come along. Merry determined to let him hit.

So, without pretending to pitch, he merely tossed over the ball and waited. Bangs gasped, then struck viciously. Another crack, and the ball went on a bee line to McCarthy. And Dan fumbled it.

A groan swelled out from the crowd, but it changed instantly to a cheer. For McCarthy had picked up the ball and slammed it over to Clancy a yard ahead of Bangs.

"One, two, three!" yelled the crowd, confident now that it would see a real game of ball. A storm of applause greeted the Clippings as they walked in.

"Rotten fumble," grunted McCarthy.

"Don't you believe it!" cried Clancy, slapping his shoulder. "You retrieved it before it had a chance to work, Dan. Fine business!"

"You're up first, Dan," said Merry. "Now go in and repeat!"

McCarthy grinned happily, and strode out to the plate. He waited while Carson tossed over his warmers-up.

"This pie-eater's pretty soft, Bully," snarled Squint. "Let him hit. He ain't worth fanning."

The lanky chap opened his mouth, then snapped it shut again, and stepped into the box. Carson eyed him a moment, and the bleachers fell silent in suspense.

"Speed fer him, Bully," cried Fletcher. "He's scared already."

Carson nodded and wound up. The ball seemed to come with startling speed. In reality it was a slow fader, and it fooled McCarthy completely.

"Strike—uh—one!"

Squint returned the ball. Almost without a pause, Carson snapped over a hot one across the inside corner. Dan was taken by surprise, and a second strike was called. It was followed by a third.

"This bunch of rubes is soft!" chirruped Bangs from third.

"Whoop! Down they go!" cried Ironton, as the big Nippen stalked out.

"Who's the cow?" inquired Murray, from second. Carson grinned.

"This is an animal show, Bully," snapped Squint. "Watch the elephant fan his ears!"

The crowd could not help laughing at the awkward figure of Nippen. Carson burned a hot one across. Nippen swung, after it had plunked home.

"Gone to sleep at the switch!" grunted Squint, while the bleachers roared a storm of advice and criticism. The big fellow flushed angrily.

"Hit him in the ribs and wake him up!" cried Murray.

Carson grinned again. He sent over a smoking-hot ball that forced Nippen to leap back. The huge fruit-picker looked at him furiously.

"You watch out!" he cried warmly.

"Shut up, Nippen," exclaimed Merry. "He doesn't dare hit you."

As if to disprove this, Carson launched another in the same place. Nippen jumped back, and, as his bat fell, the ball struck against it and rolled out into the diamond.

The big fellow leaped out toward first. Bangs darted in to secure the ball, laughing as he did so. He straightened up with it, and slapped it to Burkett, but a cry of amazement went up. Nippen had beaten out the throw!

"Watch the elephant run!" shrieked the fans.

Clancy walked out to the plate, while Chub went down to coach at first.

"Hello, carrot-top!" growled Squint. "Watch out you don't scorch the ball on his thatch, Bully!"

Carson knew that Clancy was dangerous. He put over a fast drop, but Clan refused to bite. Then came a slow fadeaway, and the red-haired chap took it on the nose.

There was a groan of dismay. The ball soared high, and Merrell raced back toward the fence. Then he stopped, and waited, and the ball came down into his glove.

Nippen, showing poor judgment, had dashed for second as soon as the ball settled softly in Merrell's glove. The center fielder did not wait an instant, however, and threw the ball to Murray, who made Nippen an easy out.

The Clippings were retired. The inning was over, without a run.

"We're holding them, fellows," said Frank quietly, as they walked out. "Keep up the good work, and we'll win, sure."

"We'll do it, Chip," cried Spaulding.

"L-l-look out for Ironton," snapped Chub, as the Clipper shortstop walked out. "He's l-l-like-l-ly to start something."

Billy Mac evidently thought the same thing, for he signaled for the double shoot. Merry shook his head, and compromised on the jump ball. Ironton struck vainly.

"Hoop-a-la!" sang out Clancy. "He's going!"

"Let him soak it," pleaded McCarthy. "We're all behind you, old scout!"

Billy called for a fast drop. Although doubtful of its wisdom, Frank put it across, and Ironton murdered it. With a clean crack, the ball began to soar toward center field, and Ironton went racing toward first.

"Wake up, Nippen!" roared the fans. "What's the matter with the elephant?"

The huge fruit-picker stood staring up at the ball. Suddenly he turned and began lumbering toward the fence. He did not even look over his shoulder at the ball, but continued through the ten-foot gap, while the crowd sent a storm of catcalls after him.

"He must be going for a swim!" gasped Merry.

"Whoop!" yelled Dan McCarthy. "Look there!"

Nippen had turned abruptly. The ball was seen to fall squarely into his glove—and stick! A wild roar rose from the crowd, then it died away into a groan, as the base umpire motioned Ironton to hold third.

"What does this mean?" exclaimed Frank, walking back. "That ball was caught!"

"Outside the fence," said the umpire. "That gap shouldn't be there by rights. It went over the fence, and Ironton is entitled to his three-bagger."

"By gum!" yelled McCarthy wrathfully. "What kind of——"

"Quiet!" snapped Frank.

He turned and waved back his angry players, who were crowding forward.

"That's a mighty queer decision," he said, forcing himself to calmness. "Does it go for every ball that drops outside the fence?"

"Yes," said the umpire.

Frank saw that the umpire regretted his hasty decision, but would not change it.

"All right," he said.

The crowd looked at it otherwise, however. One howl of indignant surprise went up as Ironton was seen to be safe. The mob threatened to pour out on the field, and only when Frank was seen to be taking up his position again did the fans restrain themselves.

As for the Clippings, they could not understand the decision. It looked to them like foul play, though Merry saw that the umpire had not meant to be unfair. Nippen started to bellow out his rage, Spaulding managed to quiet him, and the game proceeded. But the Clippings had been demoralized.

This became evident when Johnson popped up a foul. McCarthy went after it, and let it drop. He made a throw to catch Ironton at the plate, and sent the ball into the grand-stand wiring. Ironton scored and Johnson stopped at second.

Frank saw that the balloon was going up, and wasted no more time. He struck out Murray with three pitched balls, and then Carson slouched up to the plate with a wide grin.

"Good-by!" he called cheerfully. "Here's where we knock the Fardale wonder out!"

His hopes were not realized, however. Frank handed him a fadeaway, and Carson swung vainly. Billy called for the double shoot. Carson saw the ball break for an in, and brought down his bat, but the sphere suddenly curved away from him.

"Strike—uh—two!"

Mindful of the fellow's threats, Frank put all his speed into the next ball. It was a shoulder-high, straight one, that nipped the inside corner of the plate. So fast was it, that Carson instinctively jumped back, then flung down his bat with a curse. As he did so, Johnson leaped toward third.

Billy whipped off his mask and slapped the ball to Dan. The lanky chap took it and slammed it down on Johnson in a cloud of dust. The Clippers were retired.

"See here, fellows," pleaded Merry, as he picked out his bat, "this has to stop right now! Cool down, everybody. Billy, you work Carson for your base. Clan, get down to first and coach. We've got to break their streak."

And Merry went out to the plate, with a badly demoralized crowd on the bench behind him.

CHAPTER XII.

CLIPPING THE CLIPPERS.

ere's the boy wonder!" announced Squint Fletcher. "Soak him in the bean!"

As Carson began to wind up, a voice pierced the roar of cheers that startled Frank. It seemed like a voice that he knew well.

"Fardale forever! Hurrah for old Fardale!"

Merry could not tell whence that voice came, but he gripped his bat hard at the sound of it. Carson unwound, and a white streak shot toward the plate.

Whether he intended it or not, the ball came straight for Frank, who was forced to step back. Squint grinned.

"Look out for your bean!"

Again Carson sent the ball whizzing down, but this time Merry connected. There was a crack, and the sphere went sailing over second, and Frank went to first.

"Hold it!" cautioned Clancy, as Billy came up to the plate.

"Here's the champion human mistake, Bully!" sang out Squint.

Carson gave Billy a black look and whipped over the horsehide.

"Ball—one!" announced the umpire. A storm of cheers floated across the field.

The next ball broke sharply. It struck Billy on the arm, and the backstop at once flung away his bat and took first. He gave Frank a grin as the latter advanced.

Spaulding came up, and Carson fanned him. The Clippers were evidently waking up.

Moore managed to pop up a weak fly, which Ironton gathered in easily. Henderson followed, and struck out, leaving Billy on first and Frank marooned on second. Two innings were finished, and the Clippers were one run to the good.

In the third, Merry shut out the Clippers, but, although McCarthy connected for a long drive, he was caught trying for third.

In the fourth the heavy end of the Clippers was up, but Burkett, Bangs, and Ironton fanned in beautiful harmony. Clancy was up for the Clippings.

"Lay out a soft one, Clan," said Merry. "This has been an old-time slugging match so far. Get to first, and work the hit-and-run."

The red-haired chap nodded and stepped to the plate. Carson sent over a wide one, and Clancy swung viciously, drawing a chuckle from Squint. Again he swung at a poor one, then Carson lashed a fast high one across.

To the surprise of the Clippers, Clancy choked his bat and laid a neat bunt down the third-base line. So astonished was Bangs that Clancy beat his throw easily, and Frank came up to bat, smiling.

Carson paused, scowling. He did not like Merry's smile, and knew that his speed had not fooled Frank before. So he wound up as if delivering a fast one, and his famous slow fadeaway floated down toward the plate.

Instantly Clancy was sprinting for second. Merry was not altogether fooled by that delivery, and he fell on the ball for a short, choppy stroke that sent the sphere zipping along the ground to Carson.

The pitcher tried to stop it, but it went through him. Murray was backing him up, but before the ball reached first, Merry was standing on the bag, and Clancy was safe. Roar upon roar swelled out from the fans; but Frank did not again hear the voice which had startled him.

Billy McQuade strode out and pounded the plate with a determined air. Carson fooled him twice with a slow fader, and, at the second strike, Merry gave Clancy the signal for a double steal, doubting whether Billy could connect.

As Carson unwound, the two sprinted for third and second. Billy saw the movement, and stepped forward desperately. He managed to bunt, and, although he was nailed at first, Clancy and Frank were safe.

It seemed as though they would remain safe, however, for Spaulding put up a foul tip that was easily smothered by Squint Fletcher. Moore came up, and as he was a notoriously weak batter, Frank gave his chum the signal to steal.

Clancy grinned, ready for anything. Carson kept him close to third, but, as the big pitcher wound up again, Clancy went toward home like a streak. Instantly Carson let the ball fly.

Moore, however, knew his business. He was in his box, and, although Squint yelled at him to get out of the way, he stepped forward and bunted the ball along the first-base line. Clancy came sliding to the plate in a cloud of dust, and the umpire motioned him safe, Moore, in the meantime, getting to first.

Squint at once moved for a new trial, but the umpire denied the motion, and the Clippings and their admirers sent up a shrill yell as they knew the score was tied. During the argument Frank stole third, but an instant later Moore was caught off first, and the inning was over, with the score tied.

The fifth, sixth, and seventh passed without another run. In the eighth, Runge took third on a long fly, which Henderson dropped, but he died there. Henderson made good his error by a hit in the next half, and Chub Newton astonished every one by getting another, but the Clippers woke up and effected a beautiful double play that retired the side.

The ninth opened with the heavy end of both sides at bat. The crowd was now silent and tense, for the game was apt to jump either way without warning. Merriwell seemed airtight, and Carson had superb support behind him.

Squint Fletcher strode up to the plate, and came down on the first ball Frank put over. The hit was a clean one, the sphere flying out between Moore and Nippen for a Texas leaguer, but Squint was not content with this. He tore around first and went on to second like a whirlwind.

Moore sent the ball in to Spaulding perfectly. The second baseman stood off the line, and, as he stooped for the catch, Squint came slamming into him in a whirl of dust. The ball was seen to drop, and, when the dust cleared off, Spaulding was fiercely addressing the grinning Squint, whose spikes had gone into his leg.

"Rotten! Murder him!" went up the yell.

"Dirty work! Smash him, Jim!" cried McCarthy.

Spaulding was about to obey, when Chip Merriwell leaped on him and restored him to sanity. Muttering, the angry Spaulding wiped the blood from his leg and limped to his place. Frank returned to his box, glad that trouble had been avoided.

Burkett fanned, but Bangs clipped a high one that Moore misjudged. Squint was halted at third, while Bangs took second on a close decision, with one out. Ironton came up and deliberately stepped into Merry's double shoot, but did it so cleverly that the umpire was deceived into giving him a base. The sacks were filled.

The next man up was Johnson. Frank fooled him once, then snapped the ball to Clancy in an endeavor to catch Ironton. The effort failed, but Squint Fletcher took a chance on reaching home.

Clancy sent in the ball far ahead of him, and Squint turned to get back to third. As he did so, Billy put the ball into McCarthy's hand. Squint gave a yell and flung himself at Dan feet first, in an undoubted effort to spike.

A shout of anger burst from every man on the field. The lanky McCarthy was not so easily caught, however. As Squint came at him, he writhed aside and drove down his fist with the ball into Fletcher's face.

Squint was knocked a yard away, and rose with a yell of wrath, blood streaming from his nose. McCarthy was only too ready to pitch into him, but Bully Carson dragged his backstop away, and Merry caught Dan by the shoulder.

"You paid him out for spiking Jim," cried Frank. "Now simmer down, Dan."

Squint was greeted with howls and catcalls as he came in. But, during the storm, Bangs had stolen third, and Ironton had taken second. Frank gave Johnson a fast high one, and Johnson hammered it for two sacks.

Murray fanned, but the evil was done. The score stood three to one, and the Clippings seemed lost when McCarthy came out to the plate and went out on a high fly. The crowd began to stream away from the field.

Nippen lumbered up to the plate, and, with a grin, Carson handed him an out. A shriek of astonishment went up as the huge fruit-picker connected. The ball went up and up, and the Clipper outfield raced back. Then they halted in dismay.

Silence fell on the crowd—broken by a gasp. Nippen passed second, rounded third, and held on home. The ball not only cleared the fence, but—dropped into the river! The huge outfielder had knocked a homer!

When the fans understood what had happened, they went wild. Amid the confusion, Clancy came to bat and rapped out a single. The field became a bedlam. Shrieks and wild yells rose on every side, and the thump of feet rose into a dull thunder. When Merry came out to bat, the entire crowd went crazy all over again.

As for the Clippers, they were thunderstruck. Carson tried to gain time, but the umpire commanded him to play ball, and he threw a vicious one straight at Frank's head. Merry calmly stepped back and bunted it toward first.

Carson leaped for it and fumbled. Clancy sprinted down to second, and, before the big fellow could decide where the ball ought to go, Merry was safe on first and Clancy was taking third.

"Wake up, you bonehead!" growled Squint, as he walked out and met his captain. "Say, you're the limit!"

"He's l-l-limited, al-l-l right!" chirruped Chub, from behind third. "The bal-l-loon's gone up, fel-l-lows! Tag al-l-long!"

Carson scowled as Billy Mac faced him. Frank seized his chance and went down to second. Again the crowd lost its head with delight, yelling and stamping in a frenzied manner.

"Finish it up, you bonehead," grated Squint. "Fan this man and we have 'em."

Billy laughed. A moment later the ball came down, and he cracked it squarely. It shot back at Carson like a bullet. The big fellow leaped aside amid a yell of derision, and, before Murray had fielded it, Clancy and Merriwell had crossed the plate.

The Clippings had clipped the Clippers!

Merry and Billy reached the shelter of the dressing room first, but the rest of the team was caught by the frenzied crowd. As the two entered, they found the black-bearded stranger waiting for them. He held out a paper to Billy.

"Here," he said, with a laugh, "is something for your mother, Billy. I think you won it pretty fairly, old man!"

The stranger caught at his beard, and it came off in his hand. Chip took one glance, then leaped for him with a yell.

"Father!"

And Frank Merriwell, senior, smiled quietly as he took Chip's hand.

CHAPTER XIII.

BEATEN AT HIS OWN GAME.

ow, boys, I owe you a word of explanation."
Frank Merriwell, senior, faced the victorious Clippings, who were lined up around Mrs. McQuade's extended dinner table.

"I want you to know why I did this. It wasn't to gamble, as most
of you know that I don't countenance that so-called sport for a
minute. It wasn't to fight Colonel Carson with his own weapons.
That's another thing I don't believe in.

"But I do enjoy beating a man at his own game, when I can do it
cleanly and make him learn a lesson. Now, in plain words, I knew
that Colonel Carson was little short of being a crook. When he
gambled, he wanted to gamble on a sure thing."

"That's right," went up a murmur.

"But I did not make this bet with him in the prospect of winning
money. I made it in order to get that mortgage from him—that
mortgage which my good friend, Mrs. McQuade, had the pleasure of burning just before dinner. He had obtained it legally. Then
he had been paid for it. By some mischance, Mr. McQuade had
not obtained it, and had no receipt to show.

"Colonel Carson produced it after his death, and claimed that
he had never received payment. He intended to oust Mrs. Mc-
Quade from this house on Monday. If she had borrowed the money and paid it off the second time, Carson's villainy would have
triumphed. This I did not want to see."

He paused, his grave eyes sweeping from face to face.

"As I wrote you, Frank, that would be a poor way to defeat him.
So I came to Carsonville myself, in disguise. The worthy colonel
tried to entrap me into betting against his team. I appeared to fall
into the trap, and wagered my money against his mortgage. He
tried to induce me to bet against his money, but this I would not
do. I want you to get the difference, and get it clearly."

"I do, father," exclaimed Chip quickly.

One after another the rest nodded assent.

"What would you 'a' done if you'd lost?" queried McCarthy.

Frank Merriwell, senior, smiled.

"I watched you at practice work, Dan, and felt sure that I couldn't lose."

At this retort a yell of delight went up, and Dan flushed and wriggled in his chair. The speaker went on quickly:

"Are you sure, all of you, that you get my point? I'm not defending betting, even in a righteous cause, mind; it is demoralizing, and every sport in which it is allowed is sure to suffer. Colonel Carson is doing a great injury to baseball to-day. But in this case I might plead extenuating circumstances. I was not betting in order to win. I would cheerfully have let Mrs. McQuade borrow the money, except that this would have been knuckling under to a scoundrel. I won nothing for myself except the satisfaction of having been of service to a lady whom I am proud to number among my friends, and to her son, whom I am proud to number among my son's friends."

And he leaned forward, took up his glass of water, and, with the warm smile which had endeared him to so many hearts, proposed a toast.

"To Mrs. McQuade and her hospitable roof-tree!"

A resounding cheer shook the rafters, and the good lady herself, between tears and laughter, was unable to respond. But she could not have made herself heard.

"And here's another to Frank Merriwell, senior!" shouted Billy McQuade. Another roar went up.

"And another to the 'Chip of the old block'!" yelled Clancy frantically. Chip held up his hand for silence.

"I guess," he said, looking around with the smile that was so much like his father's, "I guess we'd better call off another to the Carsonville Clippings—the picked-up nine that clipped the Clippers!"

CHAPTER XIV.

"SOUR GRAPES."

Too bad about Ted Crockett," said Garding, pulling on the weights.

"For Fardale, you mean," returned Lee Chester. "Fine for Ted."

"Uh-huh," Hunt Garding paused with a sigh. "Going around the world with his dad, eh?"

"He's foolish! I'd sooner be captain of the Fardale nine than go around the world a dozen times! When does he leave, Hunt?"

"Monday night—right after the Franklin Academy game. Say, Chesty!"

"Huh?"

Garding dropped his voice with a glance around. No one appeared to be in hearing, and he leaned forward.

"Do you think Chip will get it?"

"Get what?"

"The captainship. Ted's going away leaves it vacant, you know."

"Holy smoke! That's right! By golly, we've got to root for Chip!"

Hunt Garding nodded, but looked doubtful. He and his brother plebe were among Frank Merriwell, junior's, stanchest supporters at Fardale. In common with many other students, they had remained at Fardale during the spring vacation.

It was Saturday morning, the last day of the vacation. Owing to a conflict in the schedules, a postponed game with Franklin Academy was to be played off on the following Monday, a half holiday having been declared by the two schools. Franklin was Fardale's ancient rival, and as it was the second game of the season, feeling was running high.

Unfortunately for the Fardale team, its second baseman and captain, Ted Crockett, was leaving school. He had been called away suddenly to take a long trip with his father, but had managed to postpone his leaving until after the Franklin game.

His abrupt departure would leave vacant an important office, that of captain of the nine. It was of this that the two plebes were talking in the gymnasium. They did not observe a figure which stood just around the corner, and which was that of Bob Randall. He had just emerged from the locker room, had caught their words, and was listening for the remainder.

"I'm not so sure, Chesty. Chip isn't certain to get the place, you know."

"I'd like to know why not!" broke out Lee Chester indignantly, glaring at his chum. "Why, he's the best pitcher Fardale ever had, barring his father and uncle!"

"Of course," said Garding. "Best all-around athlete, too."

"Well, what's the matter with you, then? All we've got to do is to get the fellows on their toes, and——"

"There are several things the matter. First, there's another chap on the team who's a mighty fine tosser."

"You mean Bob Randall?"

"Yes."

The silent figure around the corner drew back, with a little smile playing about his clean-cut mouth. Randall was a handsome, dark-eyed, fiery-tempered Southerner, who could play ball like a fiend, when he wanted to.

He was full of pride, and his greatest fault was his temper. Despite this, however, he was a prime favorite. At Lee Chester's next words his face flushed darkly, and his smile changed to a quick scowl.

"Randall? Nonsense, Hunt! He's a dandy fellow, and is a peach of a pitcher, but he's not in Chip's class."

"Naturally not, since Merry is a chip of the old block," said Garding, with a chuckle. His face instantly became serious, however. "You're wrong, Chesty," he went on. "Bob Randall is popular."

"So's Chip, according to my notion."

"Sure. There'll prob'ly be an election right after the game on Monday. But Chip, Clancy, and Billy Mac are over at Carsonville, and who'll look after their interests? You can bet that Chip will not try to get the captaincy, but he ought to."

"I s'pose there will be some campaigning done," admitted Chester. "But I don't think Randall has much show. He's too hot-headed to work as captain. Now, look at Chip Merriwell. Did you ever see him rattled? Not enough to notice it. He can pitch rings around Bob Randall, too. Wait till Monday, and you'll see."

"Well, you wait yourself. Randall doesn't think a heap of Chip, I guess——"

"You're wrong there, Garding."

The two plebes whirled in surprise as Bob Randall stepped out. With an effort the latter had wiped the traces of discontent from his dark, good-looking features.

"You're wrong," he repeated easily. "I do think a good deal of Chip Merriwell, but since you seem to be discussing the subject frankly, I'll say that he hasn't any more chance of being elected captain than you have."

The two plebes were inclined to be angry at being overheard by Randall, of all persons, and much more so by his words.

"Who gave you any license to butt in?" snapped Chester.

"I happened to overhear what you said, that's all. This is a public place, isn't it?"

"Generally considered so," said Hunt Garding, with a grunt.

Randall saw that he had hurt himself with these two plebes, and he quickly tried to regain lost ground. He was not the kind to do any disguising of his true sentiments, however, and stated his ground bluntly.

"Look here, fellows, you seem to have the idea that I'm sore on Merriwell. I'm nothing of the kind. But there's no use beating about the bush, after what's been said, and I'm quite willing to admit that I want to be captain."

"We guessed it," retorted Chester dryly.

"Well, there's no harm in that, is there?" Randall began to grow warm. "Can't a fellow contest an elective office with Chip Merriwell?"

"Some fellows could, maybe," said Garding. "But if you want it straight, Bob, you're not the fellow, in this case. He's out of your class as a pitcher."

Randall's dark eyes flashed, but he controlled himself.

"I don't acknowledge that. Who'll go into the box for Fardale when Chip isn't around? Tell me that."

"You will, because you're the next best pitcher," retorted Hunt. "You don't need to get sore, Randall. I'm not decrying your ability when I say that you're not the equal of Merriwell, because you're a blamed good pitcher."

This only added fuel to the flame, however.

"Well, that remains to be seen," declared Randall hotly. "Chip gets away with it because he has luck, that's all. A whole lot depends on this game with Franklin, Monday, and the fellow that pitches and wins the game for Fardale will be the next captain of the regulars!"

"And that'll be Chip Merriwell, for he'll surely pitch," said

Chester.

"He won't!" cried Randall, losing his temper. "I'm slated for that game, and I'm going to show you fellows what a real pitcher can do when he gets started. The trouble with a lot of you plebes is that you truckle to Merry because his father and uncle are old-time diamond stars!"

Lee Chester showed his wrath at this charge.

"I guess that lets you out," he exclaimed angrily. "You're so blamed jealous that your brains are twisted, Bob Randall! Nobody gets truckled to around this school, unless he's got the goods, and you're a long ways from having them."

"Well, I should hope so!" flashed back Randall. "I'd hate to have a crowd of decent fellows thinking that I was a little tin god on wheels! That's what you seem to think about Merry."

"Better take it easy, Bob," advised Hunt Garding, with a frown. "Go out and cool off, and you'll see it differently."

"I see it well enough, thanks," snapped Randall furiously. "It isn't hard to see that a bunch of you fellows toady to Chip Merriwell because you think it's going to get you something. That chap is overrated. He's got ability, but it's your crowd that has given him such a case of swelled head that he thinks he can cop off everything. He's going to find that he can't."

"Aw, go away and sneeze! Your brain's dusty!" jeered Chester.

"I'll tell you two something!" cried Randall, shaking his fist and advancing a step. "We're going to win this game on Monday, and I'm going to do it! Look at the team—it's all shot to pieces! Billy McQuade has left school. Crockett's going to quit. Clancy is off with Merry at Carsonville, instead of being back here practicing to get into shape to cover first. What kind of a captain would Chip make, when he allows this on the eve of an important game, tell me that?"

"He'd make a better one than you would, losing your fool head this way," retorted Chester. "He's at Carsonville trying to persuade Billy Mac to return, and you know it! Say, if I had that jealous disposition of yours I'd hang it on the back fence and throw stones at it! You make me tired!"

Randall's temper lashed out. His face went white with anger.

"Yuh impudent little Yankee!" he roared. Whenever he forgot himself his voice took on a soft Southern drawl, which it now assumed abruptly. "I reckon I'll teach yo'-all somethin' right heah! I'll show yo'-all yo' cain't talk to a Randall like he was a low-down niggah!"

He started for Chester, and Chester started for him with great willingness. Before they could strike a blow, however, Hunt Garding dashed in between with a quick warning, pointing across the gym.

"'Sh-h-h! The athletic instructor's coming!"

Randall flung a look toward the door, then sullenly jammed his hat over his eyes and strode away.

CHAPTER XV.

THREE CHEERS FOR CHIP!

On that Saturday evening there was a momentous discussion under way at the quarters of Colonel Gunn, principal of Fardale Academy.

It was here that Coach Trayne occupied a room, and in his room, was seated Ted Crockett, the present captain of the Fardale baseball team. The two were discussing the future destinies of the nine.

Crockett was extremely popular among his teammates. Coach Trayne knew that his influence would go far toward the selection of a new captain, and had asked him over for a frank talk. He had certain information which was bound to startle Captain Crockett, and which would startle all Fardale when it was made public. The coach did not intend that it should be made public for the present, however.

Meanwhile, Villum Kess had seen Crockett enter Colonel Gunn's quarters, and the astute German lad guessed at once that a consultation was going on regarding the new captain of the nine. He started off hastily, and bumped into a dark figure.

"Who's that?" demanded the voice of Lee Chester.

"Kess," returned Villum, panting.

"Guess?" cried Chester. "Get out into the light, you dub!"

"Kess!" shouted Villum. "Dot iss vot I——"

"Oh, it's you!" said Lee Chester, with a chuckle. "What's your hurry?"

"Vait! You hafe mein vind pumbed avay!"

Villum hung on to Chester's arm for a moment, then straightened up.

"Grogett hass yust gone into der house, yes, no," he cried excitedly. "Dey vos goin' to elegtion a gaptain, Jesty!"

"Whew!" gasped Chester. "Looks like business, eh? Think they're going to make a choice to-night?"

"Yah, aber ve moost hellup oud Chip. I should faint fits oof dey bicked any one else. I bet you've moost get der poys togedder und root!"

"Say, you're not so far off, old scout!" exclaimed Chester. "Come along! We'll settle Randall's hash right here!"

And the two disappeared in hot haste.

The captain and coach of the Fardale nine were engaged in animated discussion, while Villum Kess and Chester were getting to work. Captain Crockett was learning something that carried dismay to his heart, for the success of Fardale was very dear to him, and it looked as though Fardale's hopes were going glimmering for that year.

"I'm afraid I have bad news for you, Ted," said Coach Trayne gravely. "I suppose you know that Frank Merriwell, senior, ran over from Bloomfield last Thursday?"

"Yes, sir," said the perplexed Crockett. "I know he made a hurry visit, and I supposed that it had something to do with Clancy's jumping off for Carsonville."

"Not altogether. He came over to make certain arrangements, and to let me know about something important that has just turned up. Mr. Merriwell gave me permission to use the information at my discretion. I suppose you will regard it as confidential if I pass it on to you, Crockett?"

"Why, certainly, sir!"

Crockett sat up, his eyes beginning to bulge. He knew that something serious had come up, for it was seldom that Coach Trayne used his "business tone" when off duty.

"I hope that nothing really grave has happened, sir?"

"You can judge for yourself, Ted. We're likely to lose the services of Chip Merriwell for the rest of the season."

"Wh-a-a-t!"

Crockett stared at the trainer as if he thought the latter's senses had taken flight. Lose Chip Merriwell, just when Fardale was counting on sweeping all her foes before her! Impossible!

"Are you joking, Mr. Trayne?" he gasped.

"I'm sorry to say that I'm not," returned the worried trainer. He sighed, for he, too, had had visions of what his team would do with Merry in the box.

"No, it's anything but a joke, Crockett. I am not at liberty to say very much, and in fact I'm not aware of the definite reasons myself, but the fact remains that Chip may leave school before long."

"But why?" queried the astounded captain of the nine. "He's not sick or anything, is he?"

"No. As I understand it, his father and uncle are going West, and intend to take Chip with them. Mr. Merriwell did not go into details, but it's easy to imagine that it must be something of importance to necessitate Frank's leaving school at this juncture. It's going to be a hard blow to the team, for he was the mainstay."

Crockett nodded. He was absolutely unselfish, and realized fully that much of the school's success in sports was due to Frank Merriwell, junior.

"That'll be awful news to get out!" he murmured. "It's going to jar things on the campus, all right!"

"Well, don't let it out for a while," went on the coach. "I've told you about it because I wanted to ask you who you had in mind to fill your position when you leave. I'd like to have the election held right after Monday's game, if possible."

"Well," replied Crockett gloomily, "if you hadn't told me this, I'd have said that Chip himself was the man. He'd make a better job of it than I would, in fact. But since he's going to drop out also, I'd say Bob Randall."

"Randall? Yes, he's a good man, Ted. But if Chip does leave, isn't that the very reason why he ought to be elected?"

"Huh! I don't get you," said Crockett, his mind in a whirl.

"It's like this," smiled Coach Trayne: "Frank has done a whole lot for the school, and for the baseball team. It's not settled that he's to leave, remember; but I think that whether he does or not, the school ought to avail itself of the chance to give him honors while it can."

"You're right," assented Captain Crockett quickly. "Yes, I get your angle now, sir. I suppose he'll go in the box for us on Monday? That'll cinch the game, and it'll throw everything his way when I mention to the boys that he ought to be captain."

"I'm glad that such is your opinion," said the coach, with a breath of relief. "I happen to know that Randall is moving heaven and earth to get the election, and—— Hello! What's all this?"

From in front of the house had risen a sudden burst of cheering. Coach Trayne went to the window and flung it open. Instantly a renewed shout went up.

"Merry for captain! Whoop-ee!"

A crowd of students was gathered before the windows. They had been hastily marshaled by Chester and others of Merry's adherents, and more were assembling at every moment. On the edge of the crowd, hidden by the darkness, stood Bob Randall. He was flushed and angry, but he knew better than to give way to his inclinations before this gathering.

"Vot's der matter mit Randall?" shouted the voice of Villum Kess.

A chorus of groans answered, mingled with jeers and catcalls. The dark-haired lad in the shadow clenched his fists and muttered wrathfully, but he kept himself under control. A roar went up.

"Chip Merriwell! We want Chip for captain!"

Coach Trayne slammed down the window and turned to Crockett with a smile.

"Hardly representative of the team, Ted, but they show the trend of public sentiment. But if Merry wins Monday's game, and is elected, what about Randall?"

"That's what I was thinking," said Crockett uneasily. "He's a splendid chap, except for his hot, Southern temper, Mr. Trayne. He really believes that he's as good as Chip on the mound, and I must say that he's the best we have after Merry himself."

"I understand you," nodded the coach. "I think he's a bit jealous of Merry, and it's quite certain that he is anxious to be elected himself. However, he's a bit too quick to pick up grievances. I'd be afraid of him as captain. You understand, old chap, that I'm not trying to dictate?"

"Of course, sir," smiled the captain. "You're dead right, just the same. He has the clear-headed ability to serve as captain, but he's apt to lose it all in a quick flash of temper. A captain has to be a pretty cool sort—I guess the only qualification I had for the job was my coolness. By the way, have you heard from Chip whether Billy Mac will return or not?"

"No word yet," and the coach shook his head. "Things look bad, Crockett. With Billy gone, Clancy will have to catch Merry on Monday. Who'll go to first in his place I haven't decided yet. After you go, the team will be badly disrupted, I'm afraid. When Merry goes—well may——"

And he flung up his hands in hopeless despair. Ted Crockett stared gloomily at the window, and listened to a new burst of cheers that came from the campus.

As if in answer to these, there came a knock on the door. Coach Trayne answered it, and uttered a cry of satisfaction as he received a yellow envelope.

"A wire, Crockett! Let's hope it's from Chip." It was not from Merry, however, but from Owen Clancy.

"Read that, Ted!" cried Trayne, and handed the message to Crockett. It was brief and very much to the point:

Chip won great game in Carsonville. Billy McQuade returning

to Fardale with us. On deck bright and early Monday morning.

"Hurrah!" cried Crockett jubilantly. "Billy's coming back! Say, may I read this to the fellows, Mr. Trayne?"

The coach nodded a smiling assent. The news that the backstop was coming back to school after writing that he would not return, was a great relief to him.

Crockett flung up the window and read out the message. It was greeted with a storm of frantic cheers. Then he held up his hand for silence, and after a moment the crowd fell quiet.

"Three cheers for Captain Chip!" he shouted.

Another roar of cheers welled up through the night as the crowd acclaimed this good news. Then the meeting slowly broke.

With bitter heart and darkening brow, Bob Randall had heard the message read, and had heard the cheers that followed Crockett's shout. He slipped away across the campus and toward the barracks, a fierce anger welling up within him.

CHAPTER XVI.

A WILY PLOTTER.

Randall slowly returned home to the barracks. His heart was hot against Chip Merriwell, and hotter yet against the crowd who had acclaimed his rival.

"Confounded Yankees!" he muttered. "Whatever did I come to this part of the country for, anyway! Just because I had an uncle livin' at Carsonville, I reckon. I wish I had stayed down home an' taken a chance on the Annapolis examinations!"

The cool night air calmed down his heated anger a little, and by the time he reached the barracks it had changed into a dull despair. It seemed to him that no one had a chance to rival one of the Merriwells at Fardale.

Yet Bob was not a bad sort of fellow at heart. His impulsiveness sometimes led him into hot-headed errors, which he bitterly repented later. He had tried to conquer himself, and to some extent had succeeded. None the less, in this case he had given way to his bitterness without restraint.

As he reached the door of the barracks he detected a figure lurking in the shadow to one side. A keen glance showed him that the figure was not in uniform, and was one of the village youths.

"Here!" cried Randall sharply. "What are you doing around here?"

"I'm lookin' for Bob Randall," came the surprising answer.

Randall started.

"You're not looking for him, but at him," he answered. "What's your business?"

The village youth held out a paper.

"Here's a message I was to bring you. And the feller said that you was to keep it under your hat."

Randall took it in some wonder, and the youth darted off. When he reached his room, where his roommate, Harlow Clarke, was busy over his books, Bob opened the paper, and read the message it bore:

Come over to Dobb's Hotel. Must see you and talk with you at once. Don't let any one know you're meeting me.

Your Uncle.

Randall whistled. His uncle! He had had the pleasure of meeting that gentleman on his arrival in the North, and he had not been greatly impressed by Colonel Carson's rather uncouth accents and hard features. Still, Colonel Carson was his uncle, and had come up from Carsonville to see him, it appeared.

He turned quickly to his roommate.

"I've got to go over to town, Clarke," he said. "Will you fix the rope in the window so I can get in without running the guard?"

"Surest thing you know, old man," said Clarke. "Will you get in before taps?"

"I can't tell yet, but probably not."

"Well, get along, then. I'll fix up a dummy that'll fool the inspector when he comes to look at the beds. You'll find the rope out of the window as usual."

Quickly but quietly, Bob left the barracks and the academy grounds. It was not the first time that he and his roommate had wanted to come in after regulation hours, and by the aid of the rope and dummy this was invariably effected without much danger of detection and punishment.

Randall found his uncle waiting for him at the hotel, and was quickly taken to a private room.

"Glad to see ye, Bob, glad to see ye!" he cried effusively, as he pressed Bob into a chair. "Shall I send for a drink, eh?"

"I don't drink, thanks," said Randall. "You must have been in something of a rush to see me, uncle!"

"Well, might's well admit that I was," and Colonel Carson fingered his goatee thoughtfully and eyed his nephew. "I hear there's to be a game here on Monday?"

"Yes," and Randall's face fell a trifle. "Franklin Academy is coming over. It ought to be a pretty good game. Will you stay over?"

"Mebbe. Hard to say, though, Bob. I know about them Franklin fellers. I been keepin' tabs on their pitcher, thinkin' to pick him up for the Clippers next year. I wanted to see ye about that game, Bob."

"I'm glad some one wants to see me about it," returned Randall bitterly. "I thought that I was going to pitch for Fardale. If I pitched and won, I'd probably get elected captain afterward— our captain leaves Monday night, you know."

For some reason Colonel Carson looked perturbed.

"Yes?" he prompted.

"But it seems they've slated Merriwell to pitch. That means he'll do me out of the captaincy. Everybody seems to knuckle down to these Merriwells over here. I can't understand it!"

Colonel Carson looked relieved. He eyed his nephew keenly.

"I s'pose that if Merriwell pitched, it'd be a cinch for Fardale, Bob?"

"It'll be a cinch, anyhow," exclaimed Randall. "If I got in the box I'd draw rings around those fellows."

"Well, I'm talkin' about Merriwell. He'd do considerable more, wouldn't he?"

Randall hesitated.

"Yes," he replied unwillingly. "I'm bound to say that his very name seems to scare Franklin out of its boots. Why?"

Colonel Carson tugged at his goatee slowly.

"Well, I figure on gettin' you in the box, Bob," he said reflectively. "I want to do a little bettin' on that game. If it wasn't for Merriwell, I think that Franklin pitcher might have a chance to win."

"He couldn't do it," exclaimed Randall quickly. "If I got a chance at him I'd show him up!"

The older man's eyes narrowed suddenly.

"I don't s'pose you'd throw the game?" he snapped out.

Randall flushed and sat up. He looked hard at his uncle, but the latter was smiling. Bob sank back, with an uncertain laugh.

"I pretty nearly thought you were in earnest, uncle! Of course, I know you'd never think of such a thing, though. No, if I can win that game I'm pretty sure to get the election that will follow it."

The colonel tugged at his goatee once more. He seemed to get all kinds of inspiring thoughts from that patch of gray hair on his chin. Just at present his thoughts were anything but inspiring, however.

"I've got him placed," he was reflecting inwardly. "He thinks that Franklin feller is no good. Now, if I can keep Merriwell out and let Bob pitch, I can go ahead and place some bets on Franklin. I hate to see Bob get the spots licked off him, but business is business."

Aloud, however, he expressed himself quite in an opposite fashion.

"Well, nephew," he said pleasantly, "I'd like to see ye get a fair chance. It don't seem to me like that feller Merriwell gives any one else a show, does he?"

"You wouldn't think so if you were here at Fardale!"

"I don't need to be here to tell that. If you go on the mound Monday afternoon, you're pretty sure to win, eh?"

"Dead certain," said Randall. "We'll have a bang-up team, and we'll hand it to Franklin pretty hot, uncle."

"Glad to hear it, nephew, glad to hear it. I'll see to it that Merriwell does not do ye out o' your chance."

"You'll—what? What do you mean?"

"None o' your business," and Colonel Carson, with a dry chuckle, pulled out his watch. "I got you placed, Bob. You go right ahead and 'tend to business. I'm a-goin' to help out one o' my kin when I get the chance, that's all."

"But what influence have you with Captain Crockett and Coach Trayne?"

Colonel Carson gave Bob a look of commiseration. Was it possible that his own nephew was so green?

"Not much, I reckon. But I got some influence with Merriwell. There's a train out o' here in twenty minutes, Bob. It'll get me to Carsonville before midnight. I reckon I'd better take it, to make sure. I got a heap o' things to see to."

Randall looked at him in astonishment.

"But I thought you'd be here for the game, uncle!"

"I reckon I will be," laughed the colonel quietly. "Now, you lay mighty low, Bob. Don't say nothin' to any one about seein' me, or about what I said. But as sure's you stand here, nephew," he went on impressively, "you'll be the one to pitch in that game on Monday, mind my words!"

"I'd like to know how you're going to work it!" said Randall, in some wonder. "If you do, you're a wizard!"

"Well, some folks have called me worse'n that," said Colonel Carson, with a chuckle, as he reached for his suit case. "You'll be pitchin', and I'll be here, and I'm a-goin' to lay some whoppin' good bets, let me tell you!"

After Randall had taken his departure, not knowing whether to feel delighted or dejected over his uncle's promises, Colonel Carson laughed softly.

"Oh, yes, I'll lay some bets!" he chuckled again evilly. "But it'll be on Franklin, all right! I guess you're goin' to get a pretty bad lickin', nephew—but business is business. I see where I get revenge on that cussed Merriwell kid!"

CHAPTER XVII.

A NIGHT ATTACK.

here's nothing like being square, fellows. You can't beat it, I don't care what any one says. It's not so much whether you win or lose, it's simply that you feel square inside. That's what Davy Crockett meant when he said: 'Be sure you're right, then go ahead!' Davy didn't care a snap about dying—he knew he was right, and he won out!"

"Lecture on history by Frank Merriwell, senior," laughed Chip. His father smiled as he watched the lights of the train flashing up the valley.

"It's a fact," he went on, turning to Chip and Billy McQuade and Clancy, who had accompanied him to the train. "I'm not preaching, and you know it."

"But Davy Crockett died in the Alamo," interjected Clancy doubtfully.

"Sure," flashed back Frank Merriwell, senior. "That's why he won, that's why he'll live forever, Clancy. He knew he was right—get that? Defeat is no sign of failure, not a bit of it. This Colonel Carson, of Carsonville, has been winning consistently until you fellows turned the trick on him. Now he's started in to reap the whirlwind."

"He reaped it, all right, when Chip pitched to-day," said Billy Mac. "He reaped a few double shoots he didn't expect—or, rather, the Clippers did."

"You've got the idea," said Merriwell, as the train pulled in. "Well, so long for the present, everybody. Good luck to you on Monday, Frank! I'll try to run down from Bloomfield to see that game, but I can't promise. I've got some important affairs on with Dick—you'll learn about them later."

He handed his grip to the porter and sprang up the steps. The eleven-o'clock express was already late, and there was only time for a last wave of the hand before the train began to move, then drew away into the night.

"I wish you fellows wouldn't go to the hotel," said Billy, as the three friends started toward town. "We've all kinds of room at home."

Chip flung his arm over the other's shoulder, smiling.

"Cheer up, Billy! Clan and I haven't had much chance to get together since he came home from the West, you know. We'll have an old-time gabfest, and will get acquainted again before we come up to the house to-morrow. By gracious, these streets are dark!"

"I'm sorry now we didn't come down in the Hornet," said Clancy regretfully. "We could have piled into her somehow."

Late Saturday night in Carsonville was, indeed, a dark time, especially for the Carsonville Clippers!

Quite naturally, Colonel Carson and his son had not taken their beating with a good grace. Bully Carson was an excellent pitcher, but so far did Chip outclass him, that he and his father were furious over the disgrace of being beaten by a pick-up nine from their own home town.

No sooner was the game over, than they put their heads together in order to concoct a plan which would assist them both in humiliating the Merriwells and in winning a few side bets upon the Franklin game. Colonel Carson was fond of gambling, but he usually liked to know beforehand which way the game was going to come out.

As a result of their conference, the astute colonel hurriedly caught the late afternoon train for Fardale, determined to gain revenge on Chip and his father, and recoup his losses at the same time.

He needed only a lever in order to get his machinations into working order, and this lever he found in the person of Bob Randall. Having discovered that his nephew was not cut on his own pattern and merely disliked Chip Merriwell with an open and manly fervor, he had changed his tactics. Obtaining the information he was after, he caught the late train back to Carsonville, passing that which bore Frank Merriwell, senior, on the way. Things were shaping themselves very nicely, indeed, he reflected.

Meantime, Bully Carson had been busy trying to obtain his own revenge. During the evening his team met at the town pool room, which they frequented the greater part of the time, and Bully set to work.

Squint Fletcher, his catcher, could barely walk. Bully passed him up with a scowl, and turned to the rest of the assembled Clippers.

"We hadn't ought to let them fellers get away with it," he declared cunningly. "They put the spurs to us right, then they beat up Squint here."

"If you hadn't blown up they wouldn't have beaten us," growled Ironton, the Clippers' shortstop.

This criticism was quite true. But Bully Carson was loath to admit it, so he merely frowned the more.

"If we'd had a little decent support from you guys," he snapped, "I wouldn't have gone up. How can a pitcher do anything when he don't get any support?"

"How can he get support when his balls get knocked a mile outside the grounds?" snapped back Ironton.

A general grin went up at Carson's expense. It was quite true that when he had started to lose his head, Chip's men had fallen on him and pounded the ball unmercifully, and Bully knew it.

"Well," he insisted surlily, "we oughtn't to let 'em get away with it, just the same. They'd ought to go back home so's they'd know what they'd been up against."

A general mutter of assent went up. On this point, at least, it was evident that the Clippers thoroughly agreed with their captain.

"Well, what's the process?" inquired Murray, the second baseman.

Bully gathered them around him, with a wary glance at the other occupants of the pool room. He lit a cigarette, got it drooping in approved fashion from one corner of his mouth, then explained himself.

"I happen to know that Merriwell's old man is goin' off by the express. I heard 'em say somethin' about it. More'n likely, the kid and that carrot top who played first will come down to see the old man off. It's gettin' along toward train time, and if we went down we'd be liable to meet them two comin' back. If the whole crowd's with 'em, so much the better."

"Count me out," growled Squint Fletcher. "I got both eyes shut."

"It ain't so bad, Bully," said Ironton. "We can beat 'em up proper, eh? Guess there's enough of us without Squint."

Bully Carson's proposal was accepted without any great enthusiasm, but it was decided that Merriwell and his friends needed a lesson, consequently they must be given it without delay.

So, after rolling fresh cigarettes, the party decamped toward the railroad station. There were six of them, all told, for two had remained to help Squint Fletcher home, but it was conceded that six Clippers would be enough to handle Merriwell and as many of his "gang" as might be with him.

While nearing the station, which was situated at some little distance from the center of town, the train was heard pulling out. Ironton had hastened ahead, and a moment later he returned with word that Merriwell and two others were coming. The Clippers hastily disposed themselves in a dark doorway.

CHAPTER XVIII.

THE INITIALS IN THE HAT.

"Why don't you finish the year at Fardale, Chip?"

Billy Mac was distinctly worried. So was Owen Clancy.

"I'm sure I don't know," returned Frank, with a frown. "Dad only hinted that he and I might go West. Looked as though Uncle Dick was mixed up in it, too, but I couldn't get him to say anything definite."

"Looks bad for Fardale if you have to leave," remarked Clancy. "We'll lick the spots off Franklin on Monday, anyhow. With Ted Crockett going away, too, the team will be all bust up for sure."

"I s'pose there'll be a new captain elected," said Billy slyly.

"That's right!" exclaimed Chip.

"I guess there's only one fellow going to nab that honor, Chip."

"Who?" inquired Frank. "Randall would be a mighty good man, and I'd like to see him get it——"

"You old humbug!" cried Clancy. "You're it, of course! Why, Chip, if you didn't get it I'd never set foot on the diamond again!" He broke off abruptly as he stubbed his toe. "Why don't you get some light in your blamed old burg, Billy?"

"We've got shining lights right now if you'd only take your hat off," grinned Billy Mac. "But Clan is right, Chip. Captain Chip, I should say!"

"Nonsense!" said Merry. "Of course, I won't say that I wouldn't appreciate the honor, fellows, but I think that Randall is the one for the place. Besides, remember, dad talked as if he and I would go away. I sure hope it won't come true."

He paused suddenly, for he had detected a dark figure lurking against a wall ahead of them.

"Do you ever have holdups here, Billy?" he went on, in a low voice. "Looks as if that fellow was waiting for a belated traveling man, eh?"

"No danger," scoffed Billy Mac, after a glance at the hulking figure, which remained by the wall in shadow. "This isn't a particularly good residence section, but the constable keeps things pretty clean around here. No, I sure hope you won't leave——"

He was interrupted as the lurking figure slouched out and barred their path. Chip took a keen look, but did not recognize the man at once, for it was dark, and the fellow's hat was pulled down over his eyes. Something about the figure suggested Bully Carson to him, but he dismissed the swift suspicion that flashed over him.

"Where ye goin'?" demanded the fellow, in an obviously disguised voice.

"That's our business," flashed Merry. "Get out of the way."

The figure lunged forward with a swift blow. So rapidly was it done that before Frank could dodge he felt the man's fist strike his breast, flinging him violently back against Clancy. At the same instant the eager voice of Carson rose in a low cry:

"We got 'em, boys! Come along!"

Out from an adjacent doorway poured a group of dark shapes, while Carson flung himself forward with another blow at Merriwell. Before it landed, however, Chip had recovered himself, and he realized the situation in a flash. Darting under the big fellow's lunge, he snapped in a blow that caught Carson full in the mouth and jarred him to an abrupt stop.

"Against the wall, fellows!" he cried quickly. "We'll have to fight them off!"

"It's Carson's gang," exclaimed Billy, as he and Clancy ranged up beside Chip.

"You bet it is," responded a voice, and the dark figures closed in on them.

It seemed that there was no hope for the three friends, as the crowd rushed in at them with furious blows. Chip, however, had hastily pushed back into an angle formed by the union of two house walls, where it was difficult for the Clippers to get at them.

This fact, together with the darkness, rendered the odds somewhat more even. Carson's followers were confused by Merry's quick move, and when they came shoving forward in a mass Clancy stepped out and let fly with his fists.

"Look out!" cried Ironton, trying to get back. "They've got clubs, boys! Watch out for 'em!"

"Quit your crowding," exclaimed Bully Carson, to those behind.

He was flung forward, however, and Merry's fist cracked into his right optic. Unable to see what had hit him, he staggered back with a howl.

"Look out fer sledge hammers!" he cried. "They got some bricks—get back, you fellers!"

Merry was smiling slightly—that old, self-confident smile which spelled danger had the Clippers but seen it. Before Carson could retreat, Chip stepped out and followed up his first blow with two swift punches from right and left. The big fellow was sent reeling back headlong into his own men.

Meanwhile, Clancy and Billy Mac had not been idle. Taking advantage of their opponents' momentary confusion, they had immediately carried the battle into the enemy's camp. Every head was that of a foe, and they struck out with amazing carelessness as to whether they hurt any one.

Taken by surprise at these bewildering tactics, the Clippers tried to shove back from the niche in the wall. Their numbers were against them, however. Those behind were still trying to get into the conflict, and the two or three in the front rank were getting all the benefit of the three friends' flying fists.

A fragment of rock crashed against the wall behind Frank. Flaming with anger at the whole cowardly attack, he leaped forward with a cry to Clancy and Billy. Carson met him with an angry bellow.

The big fellow lacked all science, however. Already smarting under his punishment, his attack was futile. Merry's fists beat a tattoo on his heavy face, while his own vicious blows merely beat the air. Once again Chip's knuckles landed against his puffing eye, and he measured his length in the dust.

One of the Clippers had hurled a rock at Clancy, which had struck the red-haired chap on the shoulder and staggered him. He recovered instantly, however, and as Carson went down the three leaped forward, carrying the fight back into the street.

Ironton went reeling away, clasping his stomach where Billy's fist had located his solar plexus. Clancy floored Murray, while Chip sent another of the assailants staggering. How the battle would have ended was doubtful, had not Bully Carson scrambled to his feet at this juncture and promptly started for home.

Already demoralized by their failure to carry the three friends off their feet at the first rush, the Clippers lost any further desire for combat on seeing their leader streaking his way into the darkness.

Hardly had his flying figure disappeared when the others broke. They attempted no retaliation for the blows they had received, but simply melted off into the night and vanished. Billy McQuade would have pursued, but Chip seized his arm and dragged him back.

"Hold on," he panted, with a laugh. "We can be mighty glad they've decided to go, Billy. No use getting after them, or they might change their minds."

"Bring 'em on!" cried Clancy vigorously. "Hoop-a-la! I'm just getting ready to scrap, Chip!"

"Who were they?" asked Frank, getting Billy calmed down. "Was it Carson and the Clippers?"

"Didn't you recognize Bully's voice? Sure it was."

"Here's a job for the town constable, then," said Clan energetically. "Chip, if this wasn't a cowardly, no-account, low-down assault, then I'll eat my hat!"

"Eat this one instead," laughed Frank. He picked up a soft felt hat which lay on the ground at his side.

Billy struck a match. The hat bore a violent scarlet band, and on the sweatband inside were stamped the letters "E. T. C."

"Who does that stand for?" asked Chip.

"Bully Carson," spoke up Billy promptly. "Edward T., otherwise Bully. Say, fellows, I guess we can land that bunch in the lockup, hey? There must 'a' been six or eight of 'em, and with this for evidence we can maybe jail the whole bunch."

"Seemed to be more like a dozen," said Clancy.

Merry laughed.

"Come along, you two fire eaters. Billy's right, for I counted six."

"You were cooler than I was, then," commented Clancy. "Shall we go wake up the constable, old man? There's no doubt about our being able to——"

Frank shook his head.

"I think they've had enough punishment, to judge by the way they acted. Let it go, fellows. You aren't hurt?"

"Nary scratch," said Clancy. "Somebody hit me with a brick, but it struck my shoulder and didn't hurt. Of course, if you think it's better not to prosecute 'em, I'm agreeable. But I'd like to see that cuss Carson do time for this business."

Frank nodded. He knew exactly how his chum felt in the matter, but the Clippers had received fair punishment, and their attack had failed. When he went on to state that by prosecuting Carson they would be detained in town, the others agreed instantly.

"Sure," said Billy. "We couldn't afford to miss that Franklin game. I wish you two obstinate mules wouldn't go to the hotel, though."

"We'll let your mother get a little sleep," said Clancy. "She got a bang-up supper after the game, and it wouldn't be fair to impose on her, Billy. I'll take you back to-morrow in the Hornet, if you'll sit on the running board."

"You bet I will! Just the same, I wish we were goin' back to-night," added Billy, with a worried note in his voice. "The Carsons are down on you because you helped me, Chip, and they never overlook an injury."

"I don't think Bully will overlook anything for a day or two," said Frank. "I landed on his right eye twice, anyhow. Nonsense, Billy! He's tried for a cowardly revenge and he's failed, and that closes up the incident. We'll get back to Fardale to-morrow night if your mother doesn't kill us with that chicken dinner she promised for to-morrow."

"Yum!" and Clancy smacked his lips. "Billy, don't say anything more about our going back to-night, or I'll assassinate you! Wow! Your mother's chicken dinners certainly do hit me in the right spot!"

"All right," retorted Billy Mac. "But I'd bet you fifteen thousand dollars and a half that we hear from that crowd again!"

Merry flung the initialed hat into the street, and they went on their way. None of the three observed a shadowy form that followed them at a little distance, as if spying on their movements.

CHAPTER XIX.

FATHER AND SON.

Bully Carson, long after midnight, was still sitting over a washbowl in his room at home, bathing a startlingly black eye. It was a painful operation.

He was growling savagely to himself as he worked. There was a strong smell of arnica in the air, while his room was decorated with cigarette stubs and hastily discarded garments. These latter were calculated to be striking in appearance, and they were. When attired in all his glory, Bully Carson, as Billy Mac said, could be heard coming a full mile away.

Just at present he was attired only in his underwear, however, and in several bruises. He had been adorning these with arnica, but not with arnica alone, for ranged beside him were all manner of bottles.

At intervals of five minutes, Bully would anxiously pick up a hand mirror and examine his injured eye. It was something of a job, since he could only see out of the other one, and he gained little joy from it.

"He must 'a' hit me with a brick!" he muttered vengefully. His mutter mingled with a groan of despair as he took another look at his eye.

"Wow! I guess I'll get my auto and get out o' town fer a while—this is only gettin' worse every minute! Yes, sir, that's what I'll do, as soon's Ironton shows up. He's watchin' them fellers, and if they get the constable I reckon I'll have passengers in that car o' mine."

Bully Carson was disheartened, there was no doubt of that. He was also discolored, and realized the fact thoroughly. He had counted on flashing a particularly flamboyant necktie on the girls the next day, but the colors would not harmonize very well with his eye. And his eye was immense, and growing more so. Bathing only seemed to help it along.

He began to dress. Late as the hour was, he was determined to get his car and slink out of town, rather than display his facial adornments to Carsonville's admiring gaze. He realized just how admiring that gaze would be.

Suddenly he paused, at the sound of some one entering the house. He started, then recognized his father's step ascending the stairs. This was strange, for when Colonel Carson had left for Fardale he had expected to remain over Monday. A moment later the colonel opened the door of his son's room and stepped in.

"Still up, eh?" he said. Then his eyes took in the array of bottles, and he sniffed. "Arnica?"

"Arnica," repeated Bully sullenly, keeping his back to the light.

"What have you been doing?"

"I been sittin' on the roof eating scrambled eggs—what'd you suppose?"

Being used to Bully's disrespectful manner, Colonel Carson took no notice.

"When I left, you agreed that you would get Merriwell laid out," he said. "Did you succeed?"

"If I had, I wouldn't be packin' up," returned Bully. He moved around until the light struck his face. "See that peeper? Well, I'm goin' to take that car o' mine and beat it. I'll be back in a few days."

"Hold on, son, hold on," but Colonel Carson could not help smiling, angry though he was. "Do you mean to say that kid licked you?"

"Don't look that way, does it? He had about a dozen fellers hid in a doorway, and they jumped us with clubs. We couldn't do nothin'."

Bully reeled off this astonishing lie with assurance. His father examined the black eye with commiseration and rage.

"My poor boy! We'll make that fellow rue the day he ever came to Carsonville, son! So you were going away, eh?"

"Yes. I reckon I'll lay over in Orton fer a few days."

Orton was a small town fifteen miles from Carsonville, a mere country village, where it would be easy to remain and pass over the injury with any excuse. Colonel Carson nodded thoughtfully.

"That's not so bad, son. I dunno's it won't fit in pretty well, too."

Bully looked up suddenly.

"Thought you was goin' to stay over in Fardale? You must 'a' done some tall hustling to get back on that late train! Did you see Randall?"

"Yes," and Colonel Carson's hard face darkened suddenly. "He's no good the way we thought, Bully. He won't throw the game."

"Huh? Why not?"

"I didn't get down to reasons—didn't have to. He's one o' these here goody-goody fellows who believe in sport for sport's sake, prob'ly. Anyway, he shied when I mentioned it, so I changed my plans around a bit."

"You're a wonder!" and Bully chuckled suddenly, in unholy admiration. "You got the slickest brain I ever did see! What's the idea now?"

"Well," and Colonel Carson sank wearily into a chair, "you know that I want to get down some bets on this Fardale-Franklin game, Bully. The only thing is how to know which team will win, d'you see?"

"Sure—even with this eye," said Bully, with a grin. "Go on."

"The Franklin pitcher is a wonder, but they don't know it at Fardale. Randall thinks he can win easily, if he pitches. And he'll pitch if Merriwell doesn't show up, that's certain. So if Randall pitches, it's a dead sure thing that Franklin wins the game."

"And if Merriwell pitches——"

"Then it's not so sure. But listen here, Bully! Randall put me wise to something, something that made me alter my plans. We want to get back at Merriwell, at both of 'em, father and son. The father will get hit if Fardale loses, and the kid gets hit if he don't pitch."

"How so?"

"'Cause whoever pitches that game gets 'lected captain o' the Fardale team. I don't understand it all, but that's how she lays. If Randall pitches, Merriwell loses out all around, d'you see?"

"And if he pitched, then he'd get the 'lection?"

"That's it, Bully."

The son grimaced, as he knotted a yellow-purple necktie about his neck.

"Then he can pitch, fer all o' me. By thunder, I know when I got enough, pop. If you can figger out any way——"

"Hold on, son, hold on!" and Colonel Carson tugged at his goatee, smiling craftily. "You ain't never seen the old man lose out very long, have you? He ain't a-goin' to this time, either. Merriwell ain't goin' to pitch that game, see?"

"How you goin' to keep him out?"

"That depends. Where is he now?"

"Gettin' the constable to arrest me, mebbe," returned Bully easily. "I lost my hat, and he slung it away after seein' whose it was. Ironton is watchin' to see where he goes fer the night."

"Well, we can take care of him easily enough," announced Colonel Carson, with great complacence. "Your goin' to Orton will come in jest right, too."

"Me? Not on your life!" exclaimed Bully fervently. "You don't get me mixed in no more doings with that kid, Merriwell, pop. Not much! I'm done."

"Oh, no you're not!" said the other easily. "I'll get over to Fardale for that game, and I'll get a good bunch o' money down on Franklin. That cussed fool Merriwell done me out o' the Mc-Quade mortgage, and I'm goin' to make him and his kid sweat for it, you bet!"

"I guess he wasn't so much of a fool if he did you out o' anything," muttered Bully, under his breath.

"Yep, it's a good scheme, a mighty good scheme," mused his father reflectively. "I'll give you a rake-off on them bets, Bully. Ain't the kid got an uncle named Dick Merriwell?"

"Sure. What's the idea?"

Bully began to take a keener interest in the subject. He knew that the wily Colonel Carson was rarely bested at such an encounter as this, and hope sprang anew that his father could succeed where he himself had failed.

"You wait, son. I ain't got the precise details figgered out, but they're a-comin'. Yes, they're on the way, all right."

Colonel Carson fell to tugging thoughtfully at his goatee. An instant later there came a soft whistle below the windows.

"There's Ironton now," exclaimed Bully.

He crossed to the nearest window, and flung up the sash.

"That you, Bully?" came the voice of Ironton.

"Sure, it's me. What'd you find out?"

There was a trace of anxiety in his tones. He still half feared that Merriwell would arrest him for that night's work.

"It's all right, Bully. I heard 'em talking. They ain't goin' to do nothin' about it, but figure on goin' home to-morrow."

"Ask where Merriwell is," spoke up Colonel Carson hastily. Bully repeated the question.

"He and the red-headed guy went up to the Morton House," answered Ironton. "How's the eye?"

"Black," said Bully, with a curse. "I'm goin' to skip out o' town fer a few days. Much obliged, Ironton. See you later."

He closed the window. Colonel Carson had risen, and was reflectively fingering a telegraph blank he had extracted from his pocket.

"I'm glad to get that information, Bully. I guess I can fix Mr. Chip Merriwell without much trouble!"

"I'd like to know how," growled Bully.

"You will, as soon as you get your car out. I want you to do an errand over at Orton, and I guess there won't be any chance to go wrong this time. Get ready, and when the car's out come to my room."

And Colonel Carson made his exit, whistling softly to himself.

CHAPTER XX.

LURED AWAY.

No use—I can't sleep a morning like this!"

Chip Merriwell jumped out of bed and went to the window. It was early Sunday morning, and from the room at the hotel which he and Clancy occupied he had a clear view of the village green, the streets leading on down toward the river, and the green opposite slope of the valley beyond.

The air was heavy with apple blossoms, warm with spring richness, and Frank drank it in eagerly. From somewhere about the place he heard the pur of a motor car, but could see nothing of the machine.

"I don't believe I can stay indoors," he sighed softly, and turned to where his clothes lay on a chair.

Indeed, the morning was a perfect one. The little town lay still, deserted, apparently empty of all life. Yet its streets were clothed with freshness, and its feathery-leaved trees were green with new spring life. From the fruit orchards that hedged Carsonville there drifted renewed sweetness on every breeze.

Chip glanced at his chum, but Clancy was sleeping the sleep of the just. The red-haired chap put in his daytime most energetically, and when he slept he did it with just as much vigor.

"I'll let him pound his ear," smiled Chip, as he flung on his clothes, impatient to be outdoors. "Anyway, I'd just as soon have a walk all by myself for a change. I've a good notion to go down and take a dip in the mill pond, by gracious!"

At thought of the cool, inviting waters of the river, which he had explored with the aid of Billy Mac, he finished his dressing hurriedly. The hotel was still dead to the world, and Frank quietly let himself out into the silent corridor.

Downstairs, however, he found the clerk sweeping out the office. The clerk looked up with a cheery greeting and a wide grin, for Chip was already a popular hero in Carsonville, after the game of the day before.

"Up early, ain't you?"

"Too fine a morning to sleep," said Chip. "What's that machine I heard buzzing around?"

"The garage is down the street a ways," explained the clerk, leaning on his broom. "They've got one machine there for hire. Want to get it?"

"No, thanks," and Frank laughed. "I was only mildly curious. Clancy's car is all right?"

"Sure, I seen it out in the back yard only just now."

Merry nodded and passed on to the veranda. At sight of the upturned chairs he was attacked by sudden laziness, and with a yawn turned over one of the chairs and seated himself, drinking in the clear air greedily.

"Mornings like this make life worth living," he reflected contentedly. "I'll wager that if folks knew how good these early spring mornings were, they'd go to bed earlier and get up earlier. It's worth all the rest of the day!"

He sprawled out comfortably. He was still weary with his stiff game of the previous afternoon, and his long evening following, and soon realized that if he sat here very long he would be fast asleep once more. So, after five minutes, he forced himself to rise.

"I never thought I'd be getting lazy!" he murmured. "Well, down to the river and have a quick dip, then a rest on the long grass, and back to rout Clan out in time for breakfast."

He paused as he reached the steps, for he caught sight of a solitary figure that seemed to be approaching the Morton House.

The figure was that of a farmer, but this signified nothing in Carsonville, where every one owned farms or orchards, or else worked in them. The man was tall, round-shouldered, and his face was decorated with a yellowish wisp of beard. He seemed to be a powerful fellow, Chip thought.

As he approached the hotel, Merry caught sight of the man's face. It was not exactly a pleasant one, for the eyes were very close set, and there was a general look of shrewd cunning about the man which was not reassuring.

Frank would not have noticed him, had the man not been inspecting him rather closely as he drew near. It occurred to Merry that the fellow might be looking for him.

"Good morning!" he exclaimed. "This is certainly great spring weather, eh?"

"Purty good," and the man looked him over curiously. "Say, mister, mebbe you kin tell me if there's a feller at the hotel by the name o' Merriwell? Frank Merriwell, I guess the front part of it is."

Merry wondered. Without any undue self-glorification, he thought it odd that the man did not know him, for every soul in town had witnessed the game of the previous day. He himself had come in for a good deal of attention.

"I believe he's stopping here," he said. "In fact, you happen to be talking to him at this moment. Why?"

"Well, now!" The man stared up. "Are you him?"

"I'm it," laughed Frank. "Anything I can do for you?"

"Why, I was down to the railroad dee-po jest now, when a tellygram come in fer a feller o' that name. The agent, he couldn't come up very well, so I said I'd fetch it along and see if you was here."

While he spoke, the man began fishing in the pocket of his overalls, and at last pulled out a yellow envelope. Merry took it with a nod. He knew that there was no regular telegraph office in the little town, messages being handled from the railroad station, so he thought little of the matter.

"Well, I'm much obliged to you for your trouble," he said, taking out a quarter as the man handed him the message. "If you'll take——"

"No, thanks, mister," and the man turned away without taking the money. "I couldn't take nothin', thanks. So long."

"So long," said Frank.

He tore open the message, as the man slouched away down the street. It was a typewritten message, and had evidently been received at Carsonville some ten minutes previously.

"By gracious!" he said. "What the deuce has struck Uncle Dick, anyhow? And where or what is Orton?"

This was the message that caused him so much wonder:

Frank Merriwell, Junior, Carsonville: Have your father meet me not later than nine, Sunday morning, Orton. Very important. Keep destination secret.

Uncle Dick.

Merry stared down at it, frowning. There must be a place named Orton, though he knew of none in the vicinity. But what was Dick Merriwell doing there?

He turned at a step, to find the clerk sweeping out the refuse through the doorway of the hotel. Chip knew that he would be able to get information at once, and spoke.

"Where is Orton? Is that any place near here?"

"Orton? Sure, Mr. Merriwell!" The clerk jerked his thumb over across the valley. "It ain't what you might call a metropolis, no-how, but it's got a smithy and a couple o' stores and a school-house. Thinkin' o' goin' over there?"

Frank started. Going over there! Why, of course!

"How far is it from here?" he queried.

"About fifteen mile by road, I take it. 'Bout ten, as the crow flies."

While the clerk paused to stare at him curiously, Merry considered. If his uncle was at Orton, he must be expecting his father to meet him there. But Frank Merriwell, senior, had returned home on the late train! And Dick had stated that it was very important, so there was but one thing to do.

"Clan hasn't waked up yet," thought Chip, "so I guess I won't disturb him. I'll go down and see if I can get that garage machine, and if it's taken then I can rouse up Clancy and get the Hornet buzzing."

He turned to the clerk, with quick decision, shoving the tele-gram into his pocket.

"Yes, I just received a telegram——" he stopped, remembering the admonition in that telegram. "But, by the way, I'd rather you wouldn't say anything to any one about my going to Orton, will you?"

"Sure not," assented the clerk at once.

"Tell Clancy that I'll be back before noon," went on Merry, turning. "I'll get a car if I can, and be back by then, easily. Much obliged to you!"

"You got a good morning for the trip," called the clerk after him. "Good luck!"

Chip waved his hand in return, and walked down the street to-ward the garage. He glanced about for the messenger, but doubt-less the man had returned to the station, and he sighed.

"I see where I don't get that early swim this morning! Well, that's what comes of a fellow having a family!"

And with a whimsical grimace he saw the garage ahead of him. In front was an old-fashioned but comfortable-looking car, with a young fellow busily engaged in washing it off.

"Must be expecting Sunday traffic," thought Frank. "That looks a whole lot better than Clan's bumpy old scrap heap, just the same. Six-cylinder, too, so probably she can go some."

Approaching the washer, he inquired if the car was for rent. The young fellow hailed the proprietor of the garage, inside, and the latter came out and nodded to Chip at once.

"You're young Merriwell, ain't you? I seen that game yesterday, by thunder! Is it you who wants to get a car?"

"I want to go over to Orton and back," said Merry, "if your car's for rent."

"For rent? To you?" A wide grin came over the man's face. "Say, Merriwell, you couldn't rent no car off'n me, not if you was to offer me a cold million dollars!"

"Eh!" Merry looked at him in astonishment. "What do you mean?"

"Anybody that lays over Colonel Carson like you did yesterday, son, can have my car when he wants it, see? No, don't do any hollering. I won't take no pay, except for gas and the chauffeur. Just expenses. You'll have to get back by noon, though. I only got the one car, and it's engaged for the afternoon."

Finding that the man was absolutely earnest in his refusal to take money, Chip assented.

"We'll be back as soon as we can reach Orton and turn around," he said, getting into the car. "And I'm much obliged to you, sir!"

"Pleasure's all mine, son," returned the other, with a grand air.

CHAPTER XXI.

WHERE IS MERRY?

reat morning, Chip!"

Clancy was drowsily looking out of the window. His eyes had just opened, and he had not yet observed the absence of his chum.

"Wake up and take a look at things, you lazy——"

Clan turned over to give Merry a punch, then suddenly sat up.

"Well, by Jupiter!" he gasped.

He noticed for the first time that his chum's clothes had disappeared, as well as Chip himself. Then he turned toward the window, hearing a church bell ringing sweetly across the valley, and noticed the maturity of the morning.

"Jumping whippoorwills! I must have overslept a whole lot——"

At that moment there came a sudden, furious knocking on the door. Clancy paused, half out of bed, and poised a pillow to fling as the door opened.

"Come in!" he yelled. "I'm not deaf. Come in, you imitation of a real man! You don't fool me, Chip Merriwell——Wow! Get out o' here!"

Clancy had thought that it was his chum, but as the door opened wide his voice shot up to a shrill yell. For there, looking in with rolling eyes, was one of the two negresses who acted as waitresses and bell boys at the hotel.

"Get out o' here!" shrilled Clan, pulling the bedclothes around him. "Can't you hear? Shut that door! What d'you think I am, a moving-picture show?"

The door shut. From the outside came the voice of the startled negress:

"Ah thought yo' said to come in, suh. Ah suttinly did!"

"I was wrong," retorted Clancy, grinning in spite of himself. "I meant to say go climb up the flagpole and kill flies. What do you want?"

"Why, suh, dar's a gem'man downsta'rs askin' foh yo' an Mistuh Merriwell."

"What's his name, and what time is it?"

"It's dat ar McQuade boy. It's ten o'clock, suh."

"Send him up," and Clancy leaped for his clothes. "Great Scott! Ten o'clock! Say, there must be something in this Carsonville air! I haven't slept as late as this for a month of Sundays."

He tore open his suit case, and went into dressing with such furious energy that the room was filled with baseball uniforms and sections of underwear and clean shirts when Billy flung open the door.

"What's goin' on here?" demanded the astonished Billy Mac.

"Me, mostly," said Clancy. "Where's Chip?"

"How do I know? Say, are you just getting up?"

"No!" roared Clancy, half into a clean shirt. "I'm sitting on Brooklyn Bridge making mince pie, you bonehead!"

"Oh, don't let me disturb you," said Billy sarcastically. "If you haven't got your beauty sleep, old sorrel top, go right back to bed. It's only ten o'clock, and I thought maybe you'd like to take a sunrise swim down in the mill pond."

Clancy cut these remarks short by seizing a pillow and letting fly. Billy was sent back into the corner, and came up grinning.

"Where's Chip?"

"Look under the bed," retorted Clancy. "I just woke up. I suppose he's dug out for the river himself. There's no sign of a bathroom around this jay hotel."

"What d'you expect for three dollars a week? There, leave off that white shirt, Clan! We'll go down to the crick and meet Chip, then come back here and dress."

This program suited Clancy to perfection. On their way down to the street, however, he stopped and asked the clerk whether Chip had left any message for him.

"Sure, Mr. Clancy. Said he'd be back before noon."

"Huh? And when was that?"

"A little before seven this morning."

"Holy smoke!" cried Clancy. "Before seven! Then Merry's been gone for three hours, Billy! He isn't down at the river, you boob!"

"Quit calling names," retorted Billy, a trace of anxiety in his clear eyes. "It didn't improve your manners to go West, I reckon. Sure, we'll go down and see, anyhow. He might be asleep in the sun down there."

Clancy asked the clerk if he knew where Merry had gone. The

clerk, mindful of Chip's injunction, said that he "couldn't say," and the two friends went off toward the river in helpless wonderment.

Billy said nothing, but he was not a little worried. Clancy suspected nothing wrong, though he knew that it was not Chip's usual custom to disappear without leaving any word of where he had gone.

Upon reaching the mill pond they found no sign of Merry. Clancy scoffed at the fears of his friend, so they stripped and took a hasty dip, then dressed and made their way back to the hotel.

"If he don't show up pretty soon," said Billy, "mother will be all balled up with her chicken dinner, Clan."

"Well, we aren't going to wait for him," said Clancy firmly. "I want that chicken dinner, believe me! We'll give him half an hour, then we'll load into the Hornet and go up to your house. Maybe he's there now."

Mrs. McQuade had been requested to prepare an early dinner, as the three friends intended returning to Fardale in the Hornet that afternoon. So promptly at eleven-thirty Clancy got out his car and ordered the reluctant Billy to climb in. Since there was a strong possibility that Merriwell was at the McQuade house, Billy finally obeyed.

"Nothing could happen to him," scoffed Clancy, as they climbed the hill. "He's off on a walk, that's all, and probably has gone to sleep on the shady side of a tree."

Mrs. McQuade had seen nothing of Merry, and since her dinner was all ready and waiting, she put aside a generous portion to keep warm for Chip and insisted on Clancy and Billy pitching in at once.

They did so, but as the meal progressed Clancy began to feel the same anxiety that was worrying his friend. Finally he asked Mrs. McQuade to hold her pies in the oven for a little.

"Billy and I will run back to the hotel. He might be there, or on the way."

The two jumped into the Hornet, and Clancy hit only the high spots until they drew up before the hotel. A man came down the steps, and Clancy recognized him as the garage proprietor.

"Say, Mr. Clancy, where's Mr. Merriwell?"

"Isn't he here?"

"No," returned the man, in a worried voice. "I got that auto rented this afternoon, and——"

"Auto!" yelled Billy. "Did he rent your auto?"

"Why, sure! Didn't you know that?"

"Not yet, I didn't!" snapped Clancy. He wakened abruptly to the fact that there must be something seriously wrong. "When was this?"

"About seven o'clock."

"Where did he go to?"

The garage proprietor hesitated.

"Well, last thing he says was not to say anything. But mebbe you boys could go and see if anything's wrong. Anyhow, you're his pals, so I reckon he wouldn't mind me tellin' you so much. He went over to Orton, or said he was goin' there."

"What the deuce was he going to Orton for?" queried Billy, in astonishment. "Why, there's nothing there but a schoolhouse and a smithy!"

Clancy frowned. He looked to see the clerk coming down toward them in a hesitant way, having heard the conversation.

"There ain't nothin' wrong, is there?" inquired the clerk.

"Seems to be," and Clancy gave him a sharp look. "Didn't Merry say he was going to Orton?"

"Oh, you know about it, then?" said the clerk, looking relieved. "Why, yes, the telegram come from Orton, I think he said——"

"What's the matter with you?" sang out Billy. "There's no telegraph station at Orton, and you know it! Did he tell you that?"

"Well, he got a telegram, then he started askin' me about Orton," returned the clerk. "I didn't ask no questions, so I don't know where it come from. He seemed rather fussed, though."

"There's something wrong, Clancy," murmured Billy, leaning over and speaking in a low voice. "It isn't like Chip to go off like that."

"No," agreed Clancy, "that's not his regular trail at all."

He turned to the garage proprietor.

"Don't worry about the car, sir. We'll do a little inquiring around here, and then start out after it. But whatever loss you incur will be made good."

"I wouldn't give a whoop," explained the man, "only I'd promised the car for this afternoon to another party. Far's I'm concerned, Merriwell could have the car out all day without payin' a cent. But I hate to disappoint folks."

"Well, we'll see what can be done," said Clancy. "How far to this place?"

"Fifteen miles or less. The roads ain't none too good, but it ain't a long ride at all. The car was in good shape, too."

"H'm!" grunted Clan. "Mighty funny if it'd take a car five hours for that! But he might have had a breakdown somewhere. It'd be a good play to run out and take a look at Orton, Billy."

"Better look at that telegram first, Clan."

"Huh? Why?"

"Because we might learn something."

"Where's the office here?"

"At the depot. But I'd bet you thirteen thousand dollars and fifty cents that we'll find there hasn't been any message for Chip received."

"Say, what's got into you?" queried Clancy. "Too much chicken pie?"

"Oh, you know same's I do, only you won't say it," sniffed Billy forebodingly. "It's foul play, Clan. Merry has helped me, and those Carsons are getting even with him, that's what it is!"

"Well, I'm beginning to think so myself, all right," said Clan soberly. "Only I didn't want to scare you out."

CHAPTER XXII.

INVESTIGATING.

Once more assuring the garage proprietor that any losses he might incur would be made good, Clancy opened up the Hornet and started for the railroad station.

"Colonel Carson owns a lot of land over toward Orton," stated Billy gloomily. "He's mixed up in this somewhere, you can believe me!"

Clancy grunted, but made no reply. When they reached the railroad station they had no difficulty in finding the combination agent and telegraph operator.

"Morning, Mr. Martin!" sang out Billy. "Did you get a wire for Mr. Merriwell about seven this morning?"

"Not me, Billy," returned the agent. "Was he expecting one?"

"Not that we know of, but he got one," exclaimed Clancy. "Are you sure that none came in this morning or last night?"

"Nobody here last night, and nothing has come this morning."

The operator regarded them with curiosity.

"Did you say Merriwell got a telegram, Billy?" he asked.

"No, I said so," snapped Clancy. "He certainly got a telegram this morning, and if it didn't come through you, it's a mighty queer thing!"

"Yes, I reckon it is," returned the agent calmly. This merely exasperated the red-headed chap.

"Well it's a darned funny thing," he exclaimed, "that telegrams can be received here without the telegraph operator knowing it!"

"Ain't no message come this morning," declared the agent again, and with a nod to Billy, he turned and went back into his place of business.

For a moment the two friends were at a loss what to do. It was quite evident that Chip Merriwell had been called away to Orton by some important affair, yet this agent declared that no message had arrived for him!

"I guess we'll go back and grill those fellows over again," said Clancy, starting the Hornet. "We want to make sure about this telegram business."

"It's easy enough to send a fake message," suggested Billy Mac.

"We'll soon see, then."

Returning to the hotel, they questioned the clerk anew. By this time he was in enough anxiety to speak out fully, and stated emphatically that he had seen the telegram, and that Merriwell had mentioned it.

"I guess that settles it, Clan," exclaimed Billy, with a gloomy countenance. "He got a message, all right, but it didn't come through the station agent."

"Do you suppose that Colonel Carson or his son had a hand in it?"

"Sure I do! Only, what's their reason? Do you think they tried to get Merry where they could beat him up?"

"From what I saw of the colonel," said Clancy thoughtfully, "he wouldn't go into anything so raw as that, old man. Bully tried it and got all that was coming to him last night. Granted that Chip was lured away, there are some folks who would have a decidedly good reason to keep him out of sight for a day or two."

"Who?"

"Some of the Franklin Academy crowd. I may be doing him an injustice, but I'd be more apt to blame Bob Randall than the Carsons, Billy."

Billy Mac stared in open disbelief.

"Randall? But why should he try to keep Chip away from Fardale?"

"Because he wants to pitch in Monday's game against Franklin. It looks to me as if Randall was trying for the place Ted Crockett will leave vacant. If he won the Franklin game he'd be a popular hero——"

"Cut out this foolishness, Clan!"

Billy Mac leaned forward earnestly. He was a staunch friend of Merriwell's, but he had seen Bob Randall at his best, and both liked and admired the fiery, handsome Southerner.

"You're away off. Bob Randall isn't that sort, not by a good deal. He doesn't like Chip particularly, but it's an honorable, openfaced dislike, and it won't last. If he knew anything like this was going on, he would be the first one to warn Chip. No, if there's any one to blame, Clancy, it's the Carsons."

The red-haired chap nodded. He was quick to recognize that his words might have been an injustice to Randall, whom he did not know at all well. Moreover, if anything was wrong it was no doubt inspired by Bully Carson or his father.

"Yes, Billy, I got a bit out of perspective there, I reckon. Randall or the Franklin crowd wouldn't be down here. Well, our best plan will be to hit for Orton and see if Merry's car got disabled."

By dint of inquiries they soon found that there was but one road to Orton, and that if they took it there was no chance that they could miss Merry. Clancy was for going to call on Colonel Carson and putting it up to him straight, but Billy Mac persuaded him to adopt the more sensible course of taking the road to Orton and tracing up Merriwell.

"Let's go up to your house, then," said Clancy, "and load up with some rations. Chip may be pretty hungry when we find him, and there's no knowing how long we'll be gone. Besides, we'd better tell your mother nothing of what we suspect. No use worrying her, Billy."

This was sound argument, and when they arrived at the Mc-Quade home they said nothing of their uneasiness. Clancy stated that Chip had been called over to Orton very unexpectedly, and that they were going over to meet him, and might possibly proceed on to Fardale without returning.

So, loading the Hornet with their belongings and a generous amount of Mrs. McQuade's toothsome edibles, the two started out on the trail of Frank Merriwell, junior. Once outside of town, Clancy opened up the Hornet and showed what she could do.

"I took her off the scrap heap," he declared proudly, "and while she doesn't look up to much, she can certainly go some!"

Billy's interest was only perfunctory, however. He was still thinking about Chip and the Carson family.

"Funny we didn't see Bully around town, Clan. He usually sports around in his gay duds on Sunday, and runs an old car he bought second-hand. The colonel sticks to horses, but Bully likes to make an impression with his car."

"I guess Merry gave him a black eye last night," said Clancy. "That may account for his failure to sport around. I guess the whole crowd is laying low and keeping quiet for the present."

Billy grunted, but relapsed into silence.

The Orton road was a rough one, and after the first mile Clancy had to slow down a bit. They were going directly away from the railroad, and as they proceeded without seeing any trace of the garage car, they found that the country lost its prosperous aspect, and became a good deal rougher and wilder.

More than once they passed rocky farms that had been abandoned years before, although the flowering orchards around Carsonville had proved that, with industry and skill, the country could be made productive.

Mile after mile reeled off without any token of their quarry, other than tracks of auto tires in the road, which might have been left by any one of a dozen machines. At length they topped a rise and saw Orton itself, two miles farther on. It was a miserably small place, and Clancy's heart sank.

"There'd be an elegant place to hold Merry prisoner," said Billy, pointing to a deserted farmhouse that stood back from the road to one side. It was the fifth place he had pointed out with the same idea, and Clancy grunted.

"You're off, Billy. I don't believe Merry was ever in this jay town. There's nothing to it but a blacksmith shop and a couple of stores."

"But don't you think that's what's happened?" persisted Billy Mac.

"No, I don't. Chip may have been lured away, all right, but Colonel Carson has too much gumption to work that kind of a racket, according to my notion. No hotel here, is there?"

"No," said Billy anxiously. "We can find out if Merry was here by going to the smithy. The blacksmith lives just behind it."

Orton was not even large enough to be possessed of a church, it appeared. The little place seemed absolutely desolate in the Sunday afternoon quiet, but as the Hornet drew up in front of the smithy, Clancy saw that the blacksmith was standing under an apple tree, watching them.

Leaping out, the two hastened into the orchard behind the smithy, and proceeded to question the burly smith.

"I couldn't say," he responded to their inquiries. "I've seen two or three machines go past, but didn't pay much attention. Mebbe my wife did. Hold on a minute."

He turned and lifted a shout at the house in the rear. A tired-looking woman came forth, and made response that she had seen Bully Carson's machine early that morning, but had not noticed the others.

"Bully Carson!" exclaimed Billy, in a low voice. "We're on the trail, Clancy!"

Clancy considered. If they were to make inquiries through the place, it might be best to leave the Hornet here. Turning to the smith, he found that the latter sold gasoline to the few cars coming through the place, and arranged to leave the Hornet in his care.

Returning to the car, he brought it around behind the smithy, and with Billy made his way to the tree-bordered street. An instant later, Billy clutched his arm.

"I hear a car, Clan! It's coming this way!"

The two friends stopped, the slow exhaust of a motor car coming clearly from ahead of them. The car came into sight, running slowly toward them. There was a single figure at the wheel.

"By gracious, it's Bully!" cried McQuade excitedly.

The car rolled toward them at a slow pace.

"Get ready to jump her," ordered Clancy, in a tense voice.

"What you going to do?"

"We'll do a little kidnaping on our own hook, Billy. Watch out, now!"

CHAPTER XXIII.

THE THIRD DEGREE.

arson was evidently quite unsuspecting. Possibly he did not see the two figures that waited at the roadside. At all events his car rolled slowly past the smithy, and, as it came opposite to their waiting place, Clancy nudged Billy and leaped forth.

He believed in doing a thing thoroughly, when he was doing it. Consequently, as he saw Bully twist around in his seat with a start of alarm, Clancy gave him no chance to increase his speed, but put all his energies into a flying leap.

A cry broke from Carson, but he was too late. Clancy rose in the air like a bird and struck full against him, driving him down at once. The two fell in a confused tangle under the steering wheel, while the car went slowly along the road.

Meantime, Billy Mac jumped to the running board and piled into the tonneau. He leaned over the back of the front seat. Before he could lend assistance, the two figures came erect, and Clancy shoved Carson bodily over into the tonneau.

"Keep him there, Mac," he ordered.

"What you going to do?" gasped Billy.

"No time to talk," said Clancy, jumping to the steering wheel. "Throw a robe over that fellow's head! Sit on him, you chump!"

Carson, indeed, was rising to the occasion. He had landed in the tonneau on his head and shoulders, and was squirming upright, letting out wild yells as he did so. The peace of the Sabbath was being terribly shattered.

Billy Mac saved the day by adopting Clan's suggestion. Seizing the heavy blanket that did duty for an auto robe, he threw it over Carson's head, managed to evade the waving fists, and plumped himself on top of the big fellow.

Carson was forced to the floor of the car, which had leaped into speed under Clancy's touch. Billy McQuade being a chunky fellow for his age, made no light weight, and Carson's bellows for help were stifled.

So quickly had it all occurred, that, while Bully Carson must have recognized his assailants, he had been too startled to propound any questions. In fact, he had been hustled about so rapidly that when Billy came down on him he had no more breath left with which to shout.

After a moment Clancy stopped the car on a lonely stretch of road, and told Billy to shove their prisoner out. Billy did not stand on ceremony, but opened one of the side doors and sent Carson tumbling out like a bag of flour.

The big fellow landed in the dust, came to his feet, flung off the robe, and emerged, spluttering with rage.

"What's this mean!" he exclaimed hotly. "I'll have you dubs pinched fer this!"

Clancy grinned.

"No, you won't, Bully. You're liable to get pinched yourself for what took place last night. Where's Chip Merriwell?"

"How do I know?" demanded Carson, working himself up into a rage. "You'd better clear out, and do it quick, or I'll smash your carrot head in about——"

"No more of that talk," said Clancy. "You're a coward, my friend. If you try fighting, you'll get the worst of it by a good deal. Where's Chip Merriwell?"

Clancy gave no sign of his inward perturbation. He had conducted this assault absolutely without evidence, and on a momentary impulse. If he failed to extract any information, he was apt to find himself up against the law.

"I don't know anythin' about him," said Carson sullenly.

"Don't lie," said Clancy angrily. "You sent him a fake telegram that got him over to Orton this morning. Where is he?"

Carson went white.

"How'd you know that——" he began, then checked himself and tried to bluster it off. "You're crazy, you boobs! I ain't seen the feller——"

"You make me sick," said Clancy, with renewed self-confidence. "You gave yourself away right there, Bully. Now come across, or take the consequences."

Carson glared at him out of his one good optic.

"I'll show you!" he bellowed. "You ain't a-goin' to get clear with this kind o' doin's around here——"

And turning swiftly, he shoved Billy Mac aside and made a break down the road. Clancy grinned inwardly. Carson was not only scared, but he was extremely anxious to get away.

Clancy caught the big fellow within fifty feet. Carson showed fight, but the red-haired chap decided to waste no further time. Catching the arm of Carson, he twisted it behind the other's back, and had him at his mercy.

"Take his arm, Billy," he commanded. "Put him into the machine and keep him quiet. If he yells for help, twist his arm and it'll break just below the elbow."

Carson went green.

"Hey, what you fellers tryin' to do?" he whimpered. "Ouch! I'll go along—don't twist that arm, Billy! We allus been friends, ain't we?"

"Not much," retorted Billy Mac, with unconcealed contempt. "I always knew you were a coward, Bully, but I thought you'd show a little fight! Get along with you."

Clancy climbed into the driver's seat, feeling highly satisfied with himself. He had forced a practical admission from Carson that his suspicions were correct, and he grimly made up his mind to force a good deal more from the fellow.

"Where you goin', Clan?" inquired Billy, with some anxiety.

He had shoved Carson into the tonneau and followed him, still grasping his arm.

"Well," said Clancy, with a wink that Bully did not catch, "I think we'd better take him to that deserted house you pointed out, as we came into town. Then we can torture him until he confesses."

"Fine!" grinned Billy. "We'll do some fancy branding on him, and if that don't work, we can hang him up by the thumbs and roast his feet, eh?"

Unfortunately, perhaps, he overdid the matter. Carson's evil conscience had turned him into an arrant coward, but it had not destroyed his judgment by any means. He perceived that the two were trying to frighten him, and he relapsed into a sullen silence.

"You'd better tell us where Merry is," stated Clancy, turning to look into the heavy, surly features. "I'll warn you, Bully, that we're not inclined to show you any mercy."

"Go to thunder!" growled the captive, and followed it with a string of curses. Clancy flushed angrily and threw in the clutch.

"All right, my friend," he grated. "You'll get yours!"

Ten minutes later they drew up at the deserted house outside town. Clancy drove around to the side, installed the machine in the half-ruined barn, and reconnoitered the house. A door was swinging on its hinges, but the place in general was in tolerable condition. He returned to the barn and took out his handkerchief.

"Put his wrists together," he ordered.

"Give him a chance to talk," pleaded Billy. Clancy nodded.

Carson, however, merely poured out a string of curses and began to plunge in a furious attempt to escape. His twisted arm soon made him quiet.

"Take him up to the house," said Clancy, when he had been bound. "I'll get some stuff to make a fire with."

Billy obeyed. He deposited Carson in an empty room, tied his ankles securely, then returned to Clancy with an anxious face.

"See here, Clan, how far are you goin'? You don't mean to torture him?"

"I should hope not," said Clancy, with a grin. "I feel like it, but I don't believe I'd go that far. I'm goin' to walk back and get the Hornet. We'll have something to eat, and maybe you can scare him into talking before I get back."

Clancy's hope was vain. When he returned with the Hornet and their provisions, he found that Carson had absolutely refused to say a word on the subject. Billy was not a little anxious, but Clancy stood firm.

"Billy, I'm goin' to make that fellow talk if I have to bust every law on earth. Just stop to think—he's done something to Chip, and knows where he is. He seems to have a notion that we're throwing a bluff into him about torture and——"

"So we are," interjected Billy. "You know it blamed well."

"Sure," admitted Clancy, with a grimace. "But I'm goin' to make him think he's wrong, if I can."

There ensued a series of bluffs at torture on Clancy's part, but they had not the slightest effect on Carson.

But Bully Carson stood pat. The first shock of alarm over, he resisted all of Clancy's efforts with a grim silence that could not be broken. He knew that he was helpless, but he also knew that despite Clancy's talk the red-haired chap would not dare to proceed to extremities. And as long as he could hold silence, he intended to do so. Merriwell must be kept out of that Franklin game. He knew that his father had gone to Fardale and would doubtless plunge heavily on the result of the game. Since money meant more than anything else to the Carson family, Bully intended making a hard fight of it.

He did so. Clancy and Billy built a roaring fire in the old fireplace when darkness came on. This took the damp from the main room of the farmhouse, and rendered it habitable. They ate some of their provisions, refusing to give Carson anything to eat or drink. Finally Clancy gave up in disgust.

"All right," he said grimly to the prisoner. "You'll stay here a month if you don't loosen up, old scout. Billy, we'll take turns keeping him awake to-night. He must have been on the go most of last night and to-day, and that'll bring him to terms."

When morning dawned, Bully Carson was haggard and drawn, but still refused to open his lips. Clancy was desperate. Thirsty and hungry though their captive was, nothing seemed to have any effect. Yet their only hope of rescuing Chip Merriwell lay in making him talk.

"I've had enough of this," said Clancy, when the morning was half gone. "Billy, we're up against it. Right or wrong, that fellow's going to talk."

"You're not going to really torture him?" asked the white-lipped Billy.

"I am."

CHAPTER XXIV.

QUICK WORK.

Carson was worn out with lack of sleep and exhaustion. When Clancy dragged him to the fireplace, took a burning brand from the fire, and approached him, he let out one frightened yell.

The red-haired chap knew that he could not carry out his bluff, but he held so desperate a countenance that Carson was overborne. Even Billy himself half thought that Clancy meant to put his bluff into effect.

"I give in!" yelled Carson wildly.

Clancy drew a long breath of relief, but did not let Carson see it. "Where's Chip Merriwell?" he demanded grimly.

"Don't burn me!" yelled Carson frantically. "Give me a drink!"

"You'll drink when I get ready, and not before," roared Clancy. "Where's Chip Merriwell? Hurry up, you galoot!"

"He's at the Brundage Farm, on the other side of Orton," gasped Bully. "For Heaven's sake, give me a drink!"

The bully had given in completely and absolutely. None the less, he knew that since it was getting on toward noon, all hope of getting to Fardale for the game must now be over.

"Get up," and Clancy kicked him to his feet. "Billy, take him out to the car and you take the wheel. I'll come along in the Hornet. Make him guide us to this Brundage place, and do it quick!"

"Give me a drink first," pleaded Carson.

"You'll drink when you get there, not before. Jump lively!"

With a groan, Carson followed Billy. The fellow was in a pitiable plight, but at thought of Chip, Clancy lost all pity.

He soon ascertained from Billy Mac that Brundage was a farmer living on one of the Carson farms, just outside Orton, but on the opposite side of the town from where they were at present. Also, Carson loosened up with the story.

He confessed to having lured Chip away, and stated that both he and the driver of his machine were being held at the farm in question, in order that Chip should be detained from the Franklin game. At this Clancy climbed into the Hornet with a groan of despair.

"The harm's done, now!" he reflected bitterly. "Billy, Chip, and I will be out of the game for certain. That means that Franklin will have a walk-away, unless old Fardale comes up to the scratch, or a miracle happens."

Billy, driving Carson's car with the owner huddled in the tonneau, shot out on the road, while Clancy followed in the Hornet. Poor Carson was almost in a state of collapse, but Billy allowed him no sleep.

The two cars shot through Orton like a streak, giving Carson no chance to call for assistance. On the other side of town they came in sight of their goal—a large white farmhouse, set back from the road.

Billy turned in at the drive and whizzed up to the side of the house. As Clancy followed him, two men appeared, one carrying a shotgun. Clancy instantly perceived that their troubles had just begun, and took charge of the situation.

"Get a drink of water for Mr. Carson," he cried, and the man with the shotgun leaned the weapon against the side of the house and hurried toward the well. The other came forward.

"This Mr. Brundage?" inquired Clancy.

"It is. What ye want? What's the matter with Bully?"

Clancy turned and drew a breath of relief at sight of Bully, who had fallen sound asleep from utter weariness.

"We came after Merriwell," he stated, turning to the farmer. "Get him out here in a hurry. Bully is tired out, that's all."

This statement was perfectly true. At Clancy's air of haste, Brundage clawed his whiskers for an instant, then turned and hurriedly stamped into the house. Before the other man returned, Clancy caught up the shotgun and thrust it into Billy's hands.

"Climb into the Hornet and be ready to light out," he exclaimed. "Keep that fellow covered."

As the man approached, Billy ordered him to put up his hands. Clancy was already examining the barnyard. In one corner appeared an automobile, which beyond a doubt was that of the Carsonville garage.

The astonished farm hand obeyed Billy's abrupt order. Bully Carson was in no danger of awakening for the present, and Clancy made ready to depart as soon as Chip was produced.

"We've got to hit her up for Fardale, Billy. When Chip comes, you give him that seat and climb out to the running board——"

"Take Carson's car," suggested Billy.

"No. We'll do it in the Hornet. That old bone wagon of Bully's couldn't keep up with us for a mile."

At this moment Brundage appeared at the door.

"Shall I let the other feller out——" he began, then stopped abruptly at sight of Billy covering the farm hand with the shotgun. "Hey! What you fellers up to?"

"You send Merriwell out here and do it in a hurry," said Clancy, striding toward the door.

He started for Billy on the jump. Brundage slammed the door and vanished.

At the man's shout, Billy hastily examined the shotgun. He found that it was unloaded, and flung it to the ground. Clancy, flaming with anger and despair, returned hastily to the machine just as the farm hand leaped at Billy.

The red-haired chap was in no mood for argument. His fist shot out and caught the farm hand underneath the ear. The fellow gave a grunt, then slumped weakly to the dust, and lay quiet.

"We're up against it, Clancy," exclaimed Billy, looking at the house. "He would have fallen for it if he hadn't seen me holding that chap up, or trying to."

"It's all my fault," said Clancy, with a groan. "But we know that he's got Merry in there, and that's some comfort. We'll have to get him out."

"I don't see how——" began Billy, but at that instant he was interrupted.

A shrill yell arose from inside the house. Then there followed a wild commotion.

Without warning, there was a crash of glass, as a china plate came through one of the lower windows. Another followed, and another, then a chair burst through the window.

"Wow! Lemme out o' here!" came a shrill yell. "I want to go home!"

Through the window protruded a frightened countenance.

"It's the garage driver from Carsonville!" yelled Billy. "Come on, old scout!"

"Wow! Lemme out o' here!"

It was evident that the young fellow was scared almost out of his head. He took a flying leap through the window and landed in a rose-bush. In his hand he held two more plates, and as he scrambled to his feet he hurled them against the house.

Then, paying no attention to Clancy and Billy, he rushed across the barnyard and cranked up his machine. It was evident that he had broken loose, and was too frightened to do anything but hit it up for home.

"Let him go," said Clancy. "We'll get in that window, Billy!"

He started for the house. The chauffeur, wild-eyed and reckless, got his machine slewed around and went shooting down the drive like a crazy man.

"Wow!" he yelled, as he passed. "Git the constable! Wow!"

Renewed sounds of commotion came from within the house. Clancy dashed at the window. Billy gave him a boost to the sill, and the red-haired chap shot over the edge headfirst and tumbled to the floor inside.

He found himself in a darkened room, evidently the dining room of the farmhouse. It was in wild confusion. Chairs were flung around, the floor was littered with smashed crockery, and over in the corner Clancy made out two figures in furious combat.

As he rushed up, he saw that Chip Merriwell was being gripped by the enraged Brundage, and that the young athlete was fighting furiously for his freedom, despite the handicap of handcuffs on his wrists.

"Whoop-ee!" yelled Clancy, charging across the room. "Here we are, pard!"

Merry managed to break loose, and, raising his handcuffed wrists, he brought them down across the brow of the farmer, who toppled forward. Clancy caught his chum in his arms as the man fell senseless.

"Come along, Chip——" he cried, but Merry broke in.

"Get the key for these irons, Clancy! He's got it in his vest pocket."

Clancy leaned over, and, after a short search, found the key of the handcuffs in the farmer's pocket. Straightening up, he inserted it in the lock, and Merry's hands fell free.

"Bully for you, Clan! I thought you were never coming!"

"We'll put these fellows over the road," cried Billy, who had also entered. "This will land the Carsons in jail, all right."

"I guess they're all right," said Merry. "They got me over here on the pretext that Uncle Dick was here. This man Brundage slipped the irons on me, and they imprisoned me and the chauffeur. Where'd he go?"

"Went home on the jump," said Clancy. "What happened?"

"Brundage came in and released him. Then he went to the door a moment. The chauffeur was almost wild with rage and fright, and he started to smash his way out. I guess he did it, all right!"

"Looks that way, Chip! Say, do you know it's 'most noon Monday? Let's get out of this!"

The three hastily left by the window and ran to the Hornet.

"We're off for Fardale and the big game," cried Clancy exuberantly.

"You can't get us there in time, can you?" asked Merry anxiously.

"By thunder, I can try!" returned Clancy. "Hang on, Billy! We're off!"

And the Hornet darted away.

CHAPTER XXV.

WON IN THE NINTH.

Fardale field was clothed in gloom. The only bright spot was the stand occupied by the Franklin rooters, and they were certainly making things lively in that quarter.

The great game was on, but as far as Fardale's chances were concerned, it seemed to be all off. Inning after inning had run along, and time after time Fardale had been saved from disgrace only by mere good luck.

As it was, the eighth inning had started with the score four to one in favor of Franklin. And Peters, the Franklin pitcher, had tightened up after the first inning, and was invincible.

Randall, pitching for Fardale, had started out strong. In the fifth he had let in a run, and in the sixth his poor support had sent him up in the air. For Fardale had certainly put a poor team in the field, with substitutes behind the bat, on first, and in the pitcher's box.

Even so, Randall might have held Franklin had his own men been able to hit the swift curves of Peters. Once he loosened up, however, Franklin romped away with the game, and the slaughter was on. All Fardale could now hope for was to hold down the score, and she was fighting desperately to that end.

Coach Trayne and Captain Ted Crockett were talking anxiously together while the Fardale batters were being mowed down in the final half of the eighth.

"We're gone completely now," announced Crockett gloomily. "We'll get another chance next inning, but the game's over."

"I can't understand it," said the coach, in perplexity. "I've had no answers to any of my telegrams from Chip or Billy or Clancy. At noon I wired the hotel there, and they said that all three had left yesterday. Nobody knows where they are."

"Something's happened to 'em, all right," said Ted, as a storm of cheers swept out from the Franklin bleachers, announcing that Peters had fanned a second man. "Maybe that car of Clancy's has blown up. Did you wire Mr. Merriwell?"

"I've wired everybody in the country!" cried the coach desperately. "Nobody knows anything about it. Merry left Carsonville yesterday morning, with Clan and Billy. That's all. They've dropped completely out of sight."

"It's a rotten shame," muttered Crockett. "We had to put Randall in, and they have simply murdered him. The boys are all up in the air, too."

"Well, hold the score down," said Coach Trayne, in desperation. "That's all we can hope for now."

Another roar went up from Franklin as Peters fanned the third man. Villum Kess trotted out to right field in gloomy fashion.

"Ve vos complexicated now," he said, as Crockett joined him. "Ve make a losings ven Chip vos gone, yah! Ve vos our feet viped off der earth of, Ted!"

"We'll have to hold 'em," said the captain glumly. "We get one more chance."

Randall went into the pitcher's box amid a storm of cheers from the Fardale bleachers. The Southerner realized that he had been outclassed, but he was resolutely trying to hold his self-control.

"All right, Randall!" cried Crockett. "We're all with you, old man!"

"Yah, ve vos all mit you," piped up Villum. "But I vish dot Merry vos mit us, like plazes!"

As the first Franklin man came up, Fardale redoubled its cheers. It was the first of the ninth. If Franklin could be held to its four runs, there was still a slim chance that Peters might be pounded in the next half. But every one admitted that the chance was too slim to be hoped for. Peters had everything.

The batter fell on Randall's first ball, and cracked out a neat single. The next batter tried for a sacrifice, but he was unable even to put himself out. The ball rolled down to third, and the third baseman made a wild throw to first. Both men were safe, and the Franklin cheers redoubled.

It was too much for Randall. In his anger he sent a fast one at the plate, and Peters himself landed on it. The ball streaked down toward first, but the unhappy substitute, playing Clancy's position, muffed it. By the time he got through booting it around, the bases were filled, not a man was out, and Franklin seemed fated to run up a tremendous score.

The next man advanced to the plate with a wide grin at Randall.

The heavy end of Franklin's batting order was up. At this instant, however, a shrill yell ascended from the gate.

"Merriwell! Merriwell! Stop the game!"

The yell rose to a roar. Men rose in the bleachers, stamping and waving their hats. Every one knew of Merriwell's unexplained absence. Randall went white, and would have delivered the ball had not the umpire stopped him.

Across the field careered a dust-white Hornet, with three uniformed figures clinging to it. Ted Crockett turned with a wild yell as Clancy drew up behind third.

"Get in the game!" he shouted. "Merry, pitch! Take first, Clan! Catch, Billy!"

A renewed storm of yells swept the field as the sudden shift of players was comprehended. Randall, white-faced, tried to protest, but Crockett waved him off the field. The three friends had made shift to don their uniforms as they rode into town, not without difficulty. Coming through the village they had heard how the game was going, and had hastened on to the field.

While they took their positions, and Merry was given a moment to warm up, the crowd fell silent. Even the Franklin rooters had cheered, for they were clean sportsmen, but the Fardale fans began to realize that Merry had arrived too late.

"They can't do anything now except hold 'em down," declared Coach Trayne.

New life had been infused into the team, however. Villum Kess was capering around in right field trying to stand on his head, and almost succeeding. The ball was being snapped around the bases in wonderful fashion. One and all, the team were leaping into action as if the coming of Merry and his friends had turned the tide.

Yet the score stood four to one, and the bases were filled, there were none out.

"Play ball!" called the umpire.

The Franklin batter stepped into his box. Merry poised himself on the mound and nodded at Billy's eager signal.

Then Merry did a strange thing:

He knew that the men behind him had regained confidence, and he proceeded to show his confidence in them by lobbing over a slow, straight ball. The batter almost gasped with astonishment, but swung and took it on the nose.

"Wow!"

The crowd came up on its toes. The ball drove across the field like a bullet, so quickly that it could hardly be seen what had happened. The shortstop put out his glove, and the ball struck. Instantly he leaped to second.

The runners had leaped at the crack of the bat. Touching second, the shortstop whipped the ball to Clancy. It came straight and true, and the man on first tried to get back, but too late. Three men had been retired, in less than twenty seconds from the time the ball was hit!

"Great Scott!" gasped Trayne, watching with bulging eyes. "It's incredible!"

The crowd went mad with excitement. Such playing had rarely been seen on Fardale field since the time of Frank Merriwell, senior. The Fardale players had moved like clockwork, with such absolute precision that they had accomplished a triple play before they themselves realized the fact!

Small wonder that the fans went crazy as the team trotted in. The grand stand was in bedlam, screaming and shouting and stamping. The bleachers shrieked that the game was not lost yet, and implored Crockett to send Merry to bat.

Crockett did not lose his head in the excitement, however. He himself was up, and he was fairly confident of a hit. As he strode out to the plate, the uproar died away. After all, Franklin was three runs to the good, and the case for Fardale looked hopeless.

As it happened, Clancy, Billy Mac, and Chip would come to bat in the order named.

Crockett fell on the first ball for a clean safety, Clancy walked out and the Fardale followers greeted him with a storm of yells.

These died into a groan, as Clancy swung twice without result. Peters was a cool pitcher, and he tried to tease Clancy into a third strike, but in vain. With three balls, Clancy settled himself for a good one.

It came over—a sharp drop. Clancy chopped at it, and the ball went sizzling toward third. Instantly Crockett was speeding toward second, and managed to beat out the ball by an inch. Once more the crowd went wild with excitement.

"A hit, Billy Mac!"

"Billy Mac to bat!"

"Win the game, Billy!"

Yell after yell pealed across the field, as Billy Mac went forth. Peters conferred with his catcher, and steadied down his rather demoralized team, then went back to the box.

Billy looked like easy money. He swung widely at two teasers, and Franklin began to grin. With the next ball down, however, Billy suddenly changed his tactics and met it on the nose. The ball sailed up over second, continued its course beyond reach of the center fielder, and, before it was retrieved, two men had come in and Billy was grinning happily from third.

"Four to three! Hurray!"

The band struck into "Fair Fardale" and hundreds of voices picked up the song and thundered it forth as Merry was seen to step toward the plate, bat in hand. The chorus rose and shrilled up into a wild scream, drowning out the Franklin cries. Peters waited, then shot the ball down.

Frank struck—and missed.

Again Peters poised himself. Again he uncurled his slim length and sent the white sphere sizzling down. Again Merry swung wickedly at it, and missed.

The song died away and settled into silence. Peters grinned easily, glanced at Billy at third, and sent another hot one over the plate.

Merry struck. A sharp crack, and the ball began to rise. But the Franklin outfielders took one look at it, then flung up their gloves and ran in. It was a home run, and Fardale had won by one run!

CHAPTER XXVI.

CAPTAIN OF THE NINE.

Hey, Chip! We got him!"

The players grouped about Coach Trayne in the clubhouse turned. They had been waiting for the arrival of Clancy and Billy Mac, who was still to vote on the new captain, as the coach had demanded a written ballot.

"By gracious!"

The exclamation burst from Merry. Between Clancy and Billy was a drooping figure which he recognized as that of Colonel Carson. The man's clothes were torn, and by the fierce glances he cast around it was clear that he had not been captured without a struggle.

"We knew he was somewhere," explained the panting Clancy. "So we went to the gate and grabbed him. Let's tar and feather him, fellows!"

"Stop!"

Merry stepped out as the yell went up. He flung Billy and Clancy aside, and faced the frightened Colonel Carson.

"Colonel," he said quietly, "I think you'd better get out of town at once. You tried dirty work, and I fancy that you've paid up for it, since you intended betting on Franklin. Fade away, and do it lively."

Colonel Carson faded.

"He plunged pretty heavily, I hear," said Trayne, holding back the indignant Fardale men. "Let him go, boys. Merry's right. Get in here with your ballots, you fellows, and quit delaying things!"

"Hold on a minute, please," said Chip. "I only want to say that the fellow to be elected is Owen Clancy——"

"Pho! Shut up, you rube!"

"Yah! Listen to der peesness! Go vay und talk mit yourselluf, Frankie!"

"Clan didn't knock the home run!"

Coach Trayne quieted down the yelling mob, and roared for ballots. When he had written out his, Merry turned to the silent and unhappy figure of Bob Randall and held out his hand.

"Bob," he said, smiling, "I want to congratulate you on your game to-day! That Franklin chap, Peters, seems to have been a general surprise, and with a smashed-up infield behind you, I think you did remarkably well to keep them down!"

Randall hesitated, then accepted Frank's hand. There was a quick glitter in his dark eyes as he searched Merry's face.

"Do you mean it?" he faltered. "You—you're not sarcastic?"

"Well, I should say not!" cried Merry warmly. "Old man, if you'd had Clan and Billy in their regular positions to steady things down, you'd have won in a hand down!"

"Thanks," said Randall, and turned away. "It's—it's mighty good of you, Chip."

There were fifteen men present, counting the substitutes, who, of course, each had a vote. When the last ballot had been handed in, Coach Trayne read them one by one. Then he held up his hand.

"Men," he said, "I received fifteen ballots in the vote for a captain of the regular team to succeed Captain Ted Crockett, who leaves Fardale to-night. The results are as follows: One vote for Randall, the other fourteen votes are all for Merriwell, so I guess we can claim that the new captain has been unanimously elected."

A shouting mob surrounded Chip, who had, in truth, been surprised. His thoughts had all been with Colonel Carson, and he had failed utterly to consider the captaincy. Through the crowd pushed Randall, his eyes shining.

"And I want to congratulate you, Merry," he said simply, holding out his hand to Frank. "You're the man for the job!"

"Thank you, old man," said Merry, as he met Randall's eyes. "I'm proud to have you behind me!"

And their hands met, amid a renewed storm of cheers.

CHAPTER XXVII.

A CHALLENGE.

"Where's Bob Randall?"

"Search me, Chip. He didn't turn up for practice. Bet a dollar he's still sore over not getting elected captain."

"Nonsense, Clan! He came around finely, congratulated me——"

"Oh, I know all about that. But the galoot got hot all over again, when he got to thinking it over! I know his kind. He goes on impulse."

Merry turned away. Despite his efforts to convince himself to the contrary, he knew that Clancy was right. Randall "went on impulse."

"Well, I'll do the best I can," thought Merry anxiously. "Bob is too fine a fellow to do this. If I leave Fardale he ought to be captain, I think."

The first and second teams were at practice on the Fardale ball field. There was an hour left before the drums would sound assembly for supper formation, and Merry was putting his men through their paces.

"I hear there's no game for Saturday," said Billy McQuade, joining Merry.

"Right. Had to be canceled. I'm sorry, because I may have to leave next week, and I'd like to play one more game——"

Frank broke off abruptly as the cadet orderly from Colonel Gunn's office came up and saluted.

"Telegram, just arrived."

"Thank you."

Merry took the message and tore it open. A cry of amazement broke from him, followed by an incredulous laugh. Then he turned.

"Mr. Trayne! Clan! Come over here!"

Coach Trayne and Clancy joined him, and Merry proceeded to read the message aloud:

"Frank Merriwell, Junior, Captain Fardale Baseball Team: The Carsonville Clippers challenge you to a game next Saturday, at Fardale. Anxious to meet regular Fardale team. Wire my expense.

"Colonel Carson, Owner."

Frank looked up, his eyes twinkling.

"Say, fellows, talk about nerve!"

"Nerve!" cried Clancy. "After you went over to Carsonville, picked up a team, and beat them! After Colonel Carson and his son tried to keep you out of the Franklin game last Saturday by kidnaping you! Nerve's no name for it, Chip. Tell 'em to go to thunder."

"That fellow's a pirate!" cried Billy Mac excitedly. "Wire him a hundred words collect with a kick at the end, Chip!"

"There's something crooked behind this," declared Clancy hotly. "The Clippers are crooked clear through, Chip, and we'd better not mix up with them."

"They're an amateur team, though," said Coach Trayne doubtfully. "It'd be a good game, boys."

"Sure it would," added Billy Mac scornfully. "Colonel Carson wants to recoup for his losses, Mr. Trayne. He has the reputation of being a dirty gambler, and there's something behind the challenge, you can be sure of that!"

Frank smiled.

"His crooked work doesn't seem to have won for him, just the same! Look here, fellows, there's no game Saturday, so we might accept this. It will be lots of fun to pound Bully Carson out of the lot."

"I guess Bully won't pitch," declared Clancy, with a grin. "It'd take him more than a week to get over what I did to him, Chip.

"That's one thing that looks queer to me," continued the red-haired chap. "You can bet a fistful that Colonel Carson isn't out for sport, Chip. He's out for revenge and boodle, and he doesn't care how he gets either, so long as he gets it."

"Let him come after it," said Coach Trayne. "There's no prospect of getting another game for Saturday, and the athletic association can use the money. That game would draw a big crowd, Clancy."

"We don't want to let him yell that we had cold feet," said Frank.

Billy Mac grunted.

"But what's the sense in playing him, Chip? We ought to have that shyster put in jail for kidnaping you, and we could do it, and his son, too. Everybody knows his crowd is crooked and——"

"So much the more glory in beating them squarely," said Frank. "What do you think about it, Mr. Trayne?"

"It looks all right to me," returned the coach. "I'd say to take the game, and then lick the stuffing out of those fellows. We're playing the Clippers, you know, not Colonel Carson himself. They could certainty raise a holler if we refused, for they're the crack team of the Amateur League. We've no good reason for turning them down, except on the score of crookedness, which we can't raise against the team as a whole. Carson's private dirty work doesn't blanket his whole team, remember."

"That's true," said Clancy, "but the team is a bad lot, too. They tried to beat up Chip, Billy, and me down at Carsonville, after our pick-ups licked them. But you suit yourself, Merry. I'll stand back of you."

"Same here, Chip," said Billy. "I'd just as soon help to do the bunch up brown, anyhow."

"All right, then," said Frank. "I see the practice game is over, so I'll trot across to the office and phone down a telegram of acceptance."

"Oh, by the way, Merriwell," said Coach Trayne, stopping him, "who are you working out to fill Crockett's place?"

"Well, Mr. Trayne, my choice happens to be holding down second right now," and Frank looked across the diamond with a twinkle. "What do you think of him?"

The party turned. Standing awkwardly on second and waiting for a grounder from the batter was Villum Kess. He stood full on the sack itself, as though firmly determined not to let it get away from him. A burst of laughter went up, though Trayne kept silent.

"Him!" cried Clancy derisively. "He's done nothing but right field up to now, Chip! Why, he'll fall all over the infield!"

"He's a joke," said Billy Mac. "Oh, my eye! Look at that!"

Clancy gasped. As the batter sent a twisting grounder at the place Kess should have been standing, the German youth appeared to lose his balance and topple from the bag. He stumbled over his own foot, tried to recover in vain, and went headlong to the ground in front of the ball. By some weird chance it seemed to hit his glove, and as he sat up he grinned and tossed it to first.

"Dot vos der pusiness!" he squawked, as every one roared with laughter. "Yaw! Didn't you toldt me so? You pet!"

"Talk about luck!" gasped Clancy. "Surely you're not in earnest, Chip?"

"I am," said Merry. "Maybe it's luck, but I've noticed that Villum always makes the luck break his way, Clan. Get out to first and see if you can make him miss your pegs. If you can, I'll reverse my decision."

Clancy trotted off with a whoop, and Coach Trayne smiled.

"I wish you were going to stay at Fardale as captain, Chip! You'd either smash up the team or else it would be a wonder to behold!"

"Thanks for them kind words," said Frank, with a chuckle, moving away. "You can announce that game for Saturday, Mr. Trayne!"

And he departed for Colonel Gunn's office, in order to telephone his wire to the village.

CHAPTER XXVIII.

LAYING THE WIRES.

It was commonly reported around Carsonville that the estimable Colonel Carson could tug more Satanic inspiration out of his yellow-gray goatee than Satan himself. At the present moment he seemed to be highly satisfied with himself.

He was sitting in his study at Carsonville, and with him was his son. Bully Carson's face was decorated with a large black eye, over which he wore an eye patch.

He was clad in a loud checked suit, flaming-red necktie, and green waistcoat. From one corner of his mouth drooped a negligent cigarette. His face looked pasty and unwholesome, and reflected the same hard, unscrupulous look that shone in his father's eyes.

"Son, here's where we even up with them Merriwells for good and all."

Colonel Carson tugged at his goatee again, and glanced down at Merry's telegram of acceptance. He used the Clippers as a means to win money by gambling. And when he did gamble, it was usually a sure thing. This he proceeded to prove in his next words.

"Bully, I'm going to clean up a lot on this here Fardale game," he stated reflectively. "I got word to-night that Southpaw Diggs will come."

"Whew!" Bully peered at his father in admiration. "Pop, you're a slick one! Ain't you afraid they'll recognize him?"

"Not at Fardale. He'll take a fictitious name and shave off his mustache. I'm going to pay him well for it. Also, I've got a semi-pro catcher to take the place of Squint Fletcher, whom some of the town boys trounced. Squint was always insolent, anyhow."

"Yes," said Bully, with a scowl. "He didn't have no respect for me at all. Then you've got two other fellers from that outlaw league, ain't you?"

"For first and third," replied his father. "Our own second baseman is excellent, and with Southpaw Diggs we'll have a walk-away, son."

Bully nodded. Diggs was a famous professional pitcher. In his good days he was one of the best in the country, but he had been let out by the last team he had been with for drunkenness.

"Sure Diggs won't get boozed up, pop?"

"Quite sure. He has agreed to let me bet half the amount I am to pay him on our team. He's also agreed not to touch a drop meantime, and, as he needs the money, we can depend on him fully."

Carson, junior, looked down at the floor, then lifted his one good eye suddenly.

"Pop, I want some money," he blurted out. "I want to get down some bets on this game for myself, and I'm busted."

"Nothing doing," and his father's eyes narrowed. "I'll make a clean-up for the family, son."

"Aw, loosen up!" exclaimed Bully disgustedly. "You durned old tightwad, you got more dollars in the bank than I have cents! Why, you own the bank, yet you won't come over with a hundred!"

"I should say not!" cried Colonel Carson, horrified at the mere idea. "Ain't I brought you up all your life? Ain't I paid for them clothes you got on?"

"Well, you needn't holler so about it," retorted his son. "I want some coin, hear that? I'm tired o' lollin' around without any money to go on, and I'm goin' to have some."

"Get out and rustle for it, then, like I did," retorted his father grimly.

Bully grunted with contempt. He had the same keen love for dollars that his father had, but he did not possess the elder Carson's aptitude to pick up cents. However, he fully intended to get hold of some money to bet on the Fardale game.

There was no doubt that the Clippers would win, none at all. With Diggs on the mound the academy team would be helpless, to say nothing of the other professionals who would masquerade as amateurs for the occasion. It was a "raw deal," but Colonel Carson was famed in sporting circles for his ability to put raw deals over successfully.

"This is the surest kind of a good thing," he mused reflectively. "If Diggs shows up in good shape, Bully, I'll get down about a thousand that we shut them out without a run."

"You'd better go easy on them fancy bets," growled Bully. "That Merriwell kid is liable to connect with a streak of luck and jab out a homer, like he done against Franklin. You thought that was a sure thing, too."

Colonel Carson winced. Merriwell's homer on that occasion had cost him more money than he liked to think about.

"You may be right, Bully," he said slowly. "But he would be helpless before Southpaw Diggs."

"He's got the durndest luck you ever seen," insisted Bully doggedly.

Colonel Carson began to pull at his goatee once more, frowning at the floor. He knew that Merriwell's success was not so much due to good luck as it was to pluck, skill, and honesty. He could not blind himself to this, but the knowledge only swerved his mind toward vindictiveness.

"No," he replied slowly, "it isn't all luck, son. Just the same, I've no fears that he'll be able to buck Diggs. There's no harm in making sure against all chance, however. If we could get him out of the way, Randall would pitch. That'd cinch the whole thing."

"Huh!" sniffed Bully. "You said that once before——"

"Shut up!" snapped his father violently. "I've had enough of your insolence! We'll fix that kid this time, and no mistake."

"You will, you mean. Count me out right here, pop! I've had all I want o' that kid, and if there's any 'fixing' to do, I ain't goin' to mix in it. No, I'm cured, I am, and I reckon I'll stay cured quite a spell."

He felt his injured eye tenderly. His father continued to pull at his goatee, and suddenly he nodded in decision and rose.

Going to a cabinet that stood against the wall, he opened a small drawer and extracted a tiny folded paper. With this in his hand, he returned to Bully.

"All right, son, we'll let your goody-goody Cousin Bob Randall handle this for us. You go over to Fardale to-morrow and see him. Give him this"—and he held up the folded paper—"and tell him to get Merriwell to drink it any time in the forenoon next Saturday. It's a powder, and all Randall will have to do is to shake it into a glass of water. It'll fix him."

Colonel Carson's eyes were malevolent as he spoke. Bully hung back, however.

"No, you don't, pop," he cried, with something like fear, "I ain't goin' to mix up in no poisoning——"

"Shut up, you fool!" snarled his father, glancing around. "This ain't poison, but a powder that'll send him off into a sound sleep for a while. It won't hurt him in any fashion, but it'll put him out o' the game for sure."

"But what about Randall?" Bully queried weakly. "You tried to get him to throw the game with Franklin, and he got sore. He ain't the kind to do this, pop."

"Oh, I sized him up pretty well," chuckled the elder Carson wickedly. "Now listen, Bully: You work this right, and I'll give you ten per cent of all I win on the game, see? This part of it depends on you, and you can do it fine.

"Go to Fardale and get hold of Randall. Talk to him slow and easy, and get him madder and madder. He'll be sore about not getting elected captain, anyhow. Work on that string. Play him good and strong, and get him to promise that he'll give the stuff to Merriwell. Then we've got him. He's one o' them fellers who'll stick to a promise, no matter what comes. But you'll have to handle it right."

"You can trust me for that," said Bully, with a growl, as he took the paper.

His eyes shone with vindictive cunning. He had tried to injure Merriwell, but vainly. Therefore, it was quite natural that he should bear bitter hatred toward the fellow he had tried to injure.

He saw that by working through Randall he would be freed of all personal responsibility, and this thought cheered on his little soul. He was willing enough to do anything for which another could be made to suffer, and this sort of chicanery was precisely what he could do well.

None the less, he did not forget that he wanted money. He saw that his father's scheme depended upon him, and grinned evilly.

"Now, come across, pop!"

"Hey?" Colonel Carson glared. "What do you mean?"

"Come across, I said!" Bully lolled back negligently in his chair, and eyed his father coolly. "I ain't workin' for my health."

"Confound your insolence!" sputtered the other angrily. "You're working for me! I'll give you no money to squander, you reprobate!"

"Nothin' doing, then, old tightwad," and Bully made as if to hand back the folded paper. He carelessly took his cigarette from his mouth and exhaled a cloud of vile-smelling smoke.

"Why—do you mean—do you refuse to go to Fardale?" Colonel Carson was almost speechless with rage.

"Surest thing you know!"

Colonel Carson reached into his pocket and drew out two five-dollar bills.

"Here's ten dollars—take it or leave it. Go to Fardale and stay over Saturday. Use this as expense money."

Bully sniffed, and his father exploded:

"You'll do what I say! Take this expense money and work this business, and you get ten per cent of the winnings. Refuse, and you can go to the dickens for all o' me! I'll not have a worthless thing like you loafin' around here any longer, understand?"

It was the first time Bully had ever seen his father aroused against him, and he was cowed. Reaching out, he took the money and put it in his pocket with the paper.

"All right," he said, "I'll do it." But to himself he muttered sullenly: "And I'll have a wad to bet on that game—somehow!"

"Ah, I thought you'd come around, son!"

And once more Colonel Carson complacently tugged at his goatee.

CHAPTER XXIX.

A THOUSAND DOLLARS IN CASH.

With eight dollars in his pocket, after purchasing his railroad ticket, Bully Carson climbed aboard the express.

He did not go into a Pullman, for that would cost more money. Instead, he sauntered up to the smoking car, rolling a cigarette as he went. For this occasion he had abandoned his "swellest" clothes, being simply clad in a black-and-white, shiny-buttoned suit that shrieked aloud, a plain orange-and-white necktie, and a pair of patent-leather shoes with green uppers. Bully desired to avoid all prominence during his stay in Fardale, and so had picked out his meekest raiment for the trip.

He found the smoking car fairly well filled, and with his mind still occupied with the subject of raising some money with which to bet for himself, he dropped into a seat beside a small, dried-up little man.

Now, there are many people who gauge other people's importance by their clothes, and who do so without any regard for taste. Ezra Hostetter had run a laundry all his life, and he was the simplest-hearted person that ever ironed a collar. Being of extremely dull taste as regarded his own attire, he entertained an unlimited admiration for those fortunate men who could afford and carry off gorgeous apparel with perfect ease.

Consequently, he directed one startled glance at Bully's glorious harmony of colors, and was lost. With honest longing stamped on his face, he directed sly but highly admiring side looks that feasted on everything from the green-topped shoes to the scarlet-and-blue hatband incasing Bully's purple felt hat.

To be sure, the eye patch slightly detracted from Bully's appearance. Ezra Hostetter began to swell with importance at sitting next this ornate personage. Possibly it was a prize fighter, or, at the very least, a follower of sports!

Not being a judge of character, the little man stole further worshiping glances as Bully grandly lighted his cigarette and snapped the match away. Being an excellent judge of character and delighting in posing, Bully was not slow to detect the point-blank admiration of his seatmate, and to delight in it.

"Fine weather, ain't it?" he remarked condescendingly. "Goin' to Fardale?"

Ezra Hostetter jumped, then stammered out an overjoyed assent:

"Yes, I'm going to buy a laundry there, Mr.—— Mr.——"

"Carson," prompted Bully, settling his thumbs in his vest and leaning back. "Ed Carson, of Carsonville. I'm glad to meet you, Mr.——"

"Hostetter, Ezra Hostetter," said the dried-up little laundryman.

Bully positively basked during the next few moments. He had had little opportunity to do any basking around home, of late, and the chance was too good to be missed. And since he could also be very genial when he chose, he soon fell into a conversation with Hostetter which was extremely pleasant on both sides.

He did not uncase his splendor all at once, however. Having seen the simplicity of his companion's heart, he began to take a keen delight in letting him discover his grandeur by degrees.

It seemed that Hostetter had heard of Colonel Carson, and, upon discovering that he was talking with that famous man's son, his admiration eclipsed all bounds. After a little he ventured a timid query as to Bully's profession.

"I'm a ball player," announced Bully, with quiet dignity. "Not a professional, y' understand, though I may consider an offer from the Giants this summer."

This was the final straw. Poor Hostetter, blinded by the limitations of his own experience, carried away by the glamour of Bully's wondrous raiment, positively groveled. And Bully continued to bask in open-mouthed admiration of the other, until it occurred to him that he had better account for his black eye.

"I got this in my last game," and he lightly touched the patch. "I was pitching, and the batter hit out a liner at me. I tried to stop it, but the ball broke through my hands and struck my eye. Even so, I caught it before it reached the ground, and so won the game."

He reeled off this fabrication with amazing ease. Across the aisle was seated a man who had got on at Carsonville, and who knew nothing of how Bully had really obtained that injured optic. He grinned, and nudged the man beside him. Bully did not notice it, however.

Presently the conversation became even more personal. Bully discovered that his companion was proceeding to Fardale to invest in a laundry there, which was for sale. After a cautious glance around, Hostetter pulled forth a long black wallet and opened it out.

"Look at this!" he exclaimed proudly, anxious to prove to the great man that he, too, had symptoms of nobility. "There's a thousand dollars in cash—in cash, mind you! I'm going to buy that laundry with it."

Bully leaned over. At sight of the ten hundred-dollar bills his senses reeled, and sparks danced before his eyes. A thousand dollars in cash!

"By glory!" he gasped inwardly. "If I only had that much, what a clean-up I'd make on this Fardale game!"

He was more cautious in expressing his thoughts aloud, however.

"Why didn't you get a draft? You could 'a' cashed it at Fardale in the morning. Ain't you afraid some one will hold you up?"

"It's kind o' risky," admitted the little man, replacing the wallet. "But I don't like to trust to banks, Carson. I had a bank bust on me once, in Chicago, and I ain't never going to trust 'em again. I guess no one's going to hold me up, though."

Bully pulled down his hat over his eyes. He knew that they were glittering covetously, and he desired to hide the glitter from his companion.

A thousand dollars in cash! The words drove through his brain over and over, and fitted themselves into a refrain that chimed with the click and clatter of the wheels underneath him.

He had visions of himself nonchalantly sauntering through the grand stand, waving those hundred-dollar bills and petrifying the Fardale fans with his grandeur. The more he thought it over, the more the idea appealed to him, and the more he mentally condemned his father for a tightwad.

"He's just rolling in money," he thought sullenly, "and here I am almost without a cent! I'll have to run close to the wind to make this eight dollars last me, at that. If I only had that thousand in cash, I guess I'd cut a swath in Fardale!"

Bitter and black thoughts filled his mind during the remainder of the journey. Little by little his mind edged to the conviction that he was a badly injured person, and that he was quite justified in resenting the injury in any manner possible. After all, he had warned his father quite fairly that he intended to raise some money, and if his father refused to take the warning—so much

the worse for him!

"What hotel do you patronize here, Mr. Carson?" asked Hostetter, as the train was pulling into Fardale.

"Me?" responded Bully, with careless magnificence. "Oh, I usually frequent the Dobbs Hotel. Are you going there?"

"Well—well, to tell the truth, I—I think I will," said Hostetter. "It ain't expensive?"

Bully grinned to himself, fingering his eight dollars.

"Not 'specially so. I'd be glad to have your company, old man."

"Thank you!" and the other glanced about nervously. "You see, Carson, I'd feel a little bit safer if I had a friend in the vicinity. Of course there's no danger, only I can't transact my business till the morning, and——"

"Give your money to the hotel proprietor," suggested Bully.

"Not me! I'll keep it right on me all the time, and if I lose it, it's my own fault. I wouldn't trust any hotel man that ever lived!"

"Well, I dunno's you're wrong," said Bully, nodding sagely. "Come along—we'll get supper at a restaurant, if you like, then go up to the hotel."

At this proposal the little man fluttered with conscious pride. They left the train and entered a restaurant together. Here, Bully found that his raiment created a sensation, that was highly soothing to his spirits. After supper they went to the Dobbs Hotel and registered, being given rooms directly across the hall from each other.

Bully Carson had already sent a message to Randall, informing him of his arrival and stating that he wanted to see him that evening at the hotel. He knew that his cousin would have little difficulty in evading the academy regulations about being out of the grounds after taps.

However, Bully's thoughts were still running on that thousand dollars in cash. Reaching his room before Hostetter arrived, for the latter had paused to telephone the men with whom he was to do business, Bully covertly took the key from his own door and tried it in that across the hall.

The key worked both locks!

A few moments later the little man arrived at the room which had been assigned to him. He soon came over and knocked on Carson's door, entering with a worried expression on his face.

"The bolt on my door is broken," he exclaimed. "Do you think it'll be quite safe there, or had I better get another room?"

"Oh, you're all right," Bully said carelessly. "Lock the door and put the key in your pocket—don't leave it in the door, or it can be turned from outside. Then shove that wallet under your pillow, and you're safer'n if you was locked up in a vault. It's a cinch, old man!"

"Well, I'll take your advice," said Hostetter, with a relieved air. "Much obliged to you, I'm sure!"

Saying good night, he vanished. Bully could hear him lock his door and withdraw the key.

Carson sat smoking until the room was so full of smoke that he was forced to open the window, much against his will. A thousand dollars in cash! The words seemed to burn into his brain. He walked up and down, trying to fling off the black thoughts that filled him, but finally he paused and brought down one fist on the table.

"I'll do it!"

At that instant there came a soft knock at the door. Bully started, and swung around. The door opened.

"Oh, it's you!" he cried, and laughed a little. "Come in, Bob. I was waiting for you."

CHAPTER XXX.

CRIMINAL WORK.

Bob Randall slipped quickly inside, shut the door swiftly behind him, and stood as if listening.

On his high, dark, and undeniably handsome face there was a look of mingled worry and anger. His eyes seemed haggard, and Bully Carson chuckled to himself as he recalled what his father had said about Randall brooding over a fancied injury. It was quite plain that Randall was in good shape to be worked on.

"What's the matter?" inquired Bully. "What you listenin' for?"

Randall dropped into a chair, wiping his brow.

"I thought old man Dobbs had seen me come in," he explained nervously. "You see, I got held up at school, couldn't get away earlier, and had to sneak past the guards. I came in the hotel by the back entrance."

"How'll you get back to your room?"

"Easy," said the Southerner. "Rope to the window. I won't want to be seen around here, though, or I might get reported. Old Dobbs knows me by sight."

Carson nodded, and flung himself into a chair.

"I hear you got beaten to the captaincy of the nine," he observed. "That kid Merriwell seems to cop out everything."

Randall's face flushed.

"What did you want to see me about?" he said, with a scowl.

"About Merriwell," Bully stated calmly. "Of course, he's got you slated to pitch against the Clippers Saturday?"

"Yes he has—not!" Randall lost his temper, and slipped into his Southern dialect as usual when he became excited.

"I wouldn't pitch if he did! I've had enough of these heah Yankee ways! I'm goin' to leave Fahdale, Cahson, for wheah a man doesn't hog it all because his fatheh is a big athlete! I cain't swallow it and I won't!"

"Good for you!" said Bully approvingly. "He has certainly treated you mis'ably, old hoss. You ought to be captain of the Fardale team right now! It ain't fair treatment, I say."

"I reckon not! These low-down Yankees truckle to him abjectly, Cahson. You-all haven't any idea of what goes on heah! When we played Franklin last Satuhday, that fellow held out the best men on the team until I was beaten. Then he showed up, put 'em in, and managed to win with luck."

Randall leaned back, trying to collect himself. Bully chuckled quietly. It was evident that his cousin had worked himself up into a riotous state of mind.

Randall was honestly convinced that his version of the Franklin game was the true one. Had he pitched and won, he would have been elected captain. He pitched, and was being knocked out of the box when Merry arrived in the ninth inning and saved the game.

All Fardale knew that Merriwell had been held prisoner, and that Clancy and Billy Mac had rescued him, all three appearing in the nick of time. Yet Randall only accepted that as a story put forth by Merry.

He had brooded by himself, had pointedly avoided Chip on the baseball field, and gradually managed to get himself into a badly overwrought condition. Twisting every little incident, seeing everything in the light of his jealousy and bitterness, it was not hard for him to convince himself that he was the victim of a cleverly executed plot.

His state of mind was a bad one, and would require some severe and sharp correction before his angle of vision could be straightened. Fortunately for himself, he had not attempted to convince any one else on the subject.

"That's right," Bully encouraged him, playing his cards cunningly. "He's done you dirt, Bob, for a fact. You ought to get even with him."

"What chance have I?" Randall asked bitterly. "I'm all alone here."

"Oh, I dunno about that. Pop and me, we figure to stand by our kin, Bob. Didn't he try to help you by keepin' Merriwell out o' that Franklin game?"

Randall nodded, forcing himself into a strained calmness.

"Yes, and I want you to thank him for me, old man. It was no use, though."

"Virtue is its own reward," quoted Bully. "We done our best. Now, pop would like to see you pitch against the Clippers on

Saturday, Bob. O' course, we mean to beat you, but I ain't goin' to be in the game, and pop would like to——"

"No chance," broke in Randall, with renewed bitterness. Then he glanced up, half suspiciously. "Why is your father so interested?"

"Because he likes you, Bob."

Bully was too wise to persuade Randall along crooked lines. He sneered at his cousin, in his own mind, for being a "goody-goody" fellow.

"I'd like to even up with Merriwell, Bob," he went on cautiously. "We'd like to have you pitch Saturday 'cause you're a better pitcher than Merriwell. We've got a new pitcher for the Clippers, and if we beat Fardale at its best, there'll be all the more glory in it."

"I suppose Colonel Carson intends to do some betting?" Bob queried keenly.

"Oh, a little, mebbe. Not much. Now see here, Bob: This guy Merriwell ain't used you right, to my notion. He's played dirty against you, and he's got all Fardale persuaded that he's a little tin god on wheels, with a bell to his neck. There ain't no use tryin' to hit back at him fair and square. We got to use his own methods."

Bully worked himself into a virtuous glow. He almost believed his own words.

"You tried 'em last Sunday," retorted Bob gloomily. "They didn't work."

"We didn't know just how slick he was, Bob. He could 'a' got away from us sooner, only he wanted to come in at the last minute for a grand-stand play. He thinks that if he pitches against the Clippers he's sure to win. But we'd sooner have you pitch, 'cause you ain't crooked. We want to play a clean game; get me?"

Randall nodded. Wrapped up in his own thoughts, he did not even attempt to penetrate Bully's sudden show of conscious virtue.

"That's right, Carson. And I'd sure like to hand him one hot one before I leave school!"

"You'd hand it to him if you pitched against the Clippers, Bob. I'll pass it to you on the quiet that we don't know much about our new pitcher, and he might pan out wrong. If he does, you stand a chance o' winning the game. Of course, I want to see the Clippers win, but if you could beat us square, I'd be satisfied. It'd make this Merriwell kid squirm ten ways from election."

Randall could readily understand that, according to his notions of Merry's character.

"Yes," he assented, growing excited as the golden vision arose before him. "Yes, I reckon yo' ce'tainly have it doped out. If that could come about, he'd sho' learn a bitteh lesson, the low-down scoundrel!"

Bully grinned to himself. He could read his cousin like a book, and was playing on the other with beautiful precision.

"Well, Bob, pop and I figgered up a plan. It ain't a nice plan, but this is our last chance to slip one over on Merriwell. He ain't played the gentleman in his dealings with you, and we don't mind fightin' fire with fire for once."

This amazing display of innocence did not astonish Randall. He knew little of his precious relatives, and Bully's assumed hesitation seemed quite natural to him.

"Neither do I!" he growled, in return. "Where he is concerned, Carson, I'd feel justified in doing anything!"

"Then do this, Cousin Bob."

While he spoke, Bully took from his pocket the carefully folded paper that had been given him by his father. Randall looked at it.

"Here's the plan we figgered out, Bob: To get Merriwell out o' this here game, we got to keep him out by force. It ain't no use appealing to his fairness. He ain't got any such thing!"

"Force won't work, here at Fardale," muttered Bob.

"But this powder will," said Bully, leaning forward and dropping his voice. "Hold on!" he cried, as Randall gave a quick start. "It ain't only a sleepin' potion, Bob. If you could get Merriwell to drink it any time Saturday mornin', which is to-morrow, he'd sleep clear through till supper time. They couldn't wake him up, and if they did he wouldn't be no good."

Randall flushed, drawing back.

"It's a bad business," he faltered.

"So's your losing out for captain, Bob. Go in and win this game. What if Merriwell does know you doped him? He can't prove it. If you win the game, you'll show him up for fair. If you get beat, they'll say he got cold feet. You win comin' and goin', and we'll even things up with him once and for all. What say?"

Randall still hesitated. Looking at the folded paper which his cousin held out to him, the criminality of the thing appalled him. His chivalrous nature rebelled at the very thought.

But Bully's cunning words worked on his mind. His fancied wrongs loomed up large on his mental horizon. Once more a flood of bitterness swept over him, and he felt himself justified in doing anything.

"I'll do it," he said thickly, and took the paper.

"Promise?"

"My word is my promise," cried Randall, half angrily. Then he glanced around with sudden alarm. "Say, I've been here too long. See if any one's in the hall, so I can get out the back way to the side street."

Bully opened the door and announced that the coast was clear. On this Randall silently shook hands with him, then stole off down the corridor on tiptoe.

For a moment Bully watched, then his eyes went to the opposite door. In the silence he could plainly hear a gentle, regular snore. Still watching that door, he drew the key from his own lock.

Then he snapped off his own light, and in two quick steps was across the hall. For an instant he fumbled at the door, with deft fingers that turned back the lock in perfect silence. Slowly and cautiously he pressed the knob and opened the door.

Half a moment later he reappeared and locked the door as silently as he had unlocked it. Darting swiftly into his room, he switched on the light and drew something from his pocket, examining it swiftly. His eyes glittered, and he again snapped off his light and undressed in the darkness, carefully stowing away the object in his coat pocket.

"A thousand dollars in cash!" he murmured, as he crept into bed. "Pop, if you could only see me now!"

CHAPTER XXXI.

BEFORE THE GAME.

Dow's everything, Chip?"

"Great, Mr. Trayne! We're going to do some topside playing this afternoon!"

"Glad to hear it," said the coach, with a smile. "Have you decided to keep Kess at second?"

"If you approve, sir. Lowe at third, Harker at short, and O'Day in Villum's place in right. It's a new line-up, but I think it's tremendously strengthened."

Coach Trayne nodded quick assent.

"You've done wonders with those chaps already, Chip! Crockett was a dandy captain, but he seemed content to keep the men in their old positions. This change of yours is going to give the fans a big surprise."

"And a pleasant one, I hope." Merry's smile suddenly died away. "Only I'm not quite certain about the pitching end."

"What!" Coach Trayne's face expressed sudden concern. "Aren't you going in?"

"I hope so. But I was thinking what would happen if anything went wrong with me, or if I got pounded badly. You see, Randall is our best substitute man, and he's been acting badly lately. He refused to come out to practice the last two days, and virtually announced that he was through with baseball."

"I know," and the coach looked worried. "Personally, I'd like to kick him around the block, Chip! But for the school's sake we ought to try to placate him."

It was late Saturday morning, the day of the game with the Carsonville Clippers. Everything looked bright for Fardale. The Clippers were due to arrive on the noon train, and, as their reputation was great, a record crowd was expected. Word had spread around that this might be Chip Merriwell's last game for the season, and excitement was intense.

"I wouldn't worry, though," advised the coach. "You're all right, old man, and those Clippers will never get to you. We won't need Randall."

"I don't know, Mr. Trayne. The Clippers are amateurs, but they're crack players. Still, I wasn't thinking of the game alone. I may go away next week, and if Randall can only be brought into a right frame of mind, he'd make a great captain."

Trayne flung him a keen look.

"Do you mean it? After the way he's acted toward you——"

"Yes," said Chip soberly, "I think that he's merely viewed things wrongly, and I feel now that he'd make the best captain of any one on the team. I think I'll run up to his room right now, Mr. Trayne. I'll have a frank talk with him, and it may be that I can win him around."

"That's not a bad idea, Merriwell. If you can do so, it'll surely be a great good thing for Fardale. We can't afford to have a man of his caliber brooding over his imagined wrongs. Good luck to you, and let me know how he shows up."

"I will," said Chip, and he turned away toward the barracks.

As regarded his leaving Fardale, Chip himself knew very little. He had heard from his father that they were going West, together with Dick Merriwell, and that he must hold himself in readiness to leave when his father sent for him at a moment's notice. Therefore, it was possible that this was his last diamond work for Fardale.

The cause of this summons was a mystery to him, but he knew that he would find out in due course. In fact, he was looking forward to the trip with no little anticipation. Frank Merriwell, junior, was a chip of the old block in nickname and in fact, and he knew that with his father and his Uncle Dick he was apt to experience a lively time.

He quickly made his way to the room in barracks occupied by Bob Randall. At his knock, the Southerner's voice called "Come in!" and Frank entered.

"You!"

Randall came to his feet, fists clenched and eyes flashing. He had been sitting beside a table, on which lay a pitcher of water and some books. Evidently he had been trying to get through some study.

"I'd like a talk with you, Bob," said Merry quietly. He took no heed of the other's constrained attitude.

"Sit down," said Randall, his innate hospitality showing through his anger. "I'm rather surprised to find you coming here, Merriwell."

"I thought you would be," and Frank coolly plunged into the discussion, without any false premises. "I've observed that you're worked up over something, Randall. More than one fellow has told me that you're sore at me over my getting elected captain, and I wanted to straighten things out with you if I could."

Randall trembled with anger, and seemed on the point of a violent outburst. Then he made an effort and curbed himself. Forcing his voice down, he spoke slowly and with apparent calmness, which did not deceive Frank.

"That's quite right, Merriwell. You fooled me at the time, but I've been thinking it over since then, and I've seen how you jockeyed me out of that election. Naturally, it looked like anything but gentleman's work."

Chip flushed a little.

"I think you've made a big mistake, old man," he returned. "I thought you understood me better than that, and I can't see how you imagine that I didn't play fair."

"Perhaps you did, from your viewpoint. You kept Clancy and Billy Mac out of the game and smashed up the team. Then, when I was beaten, you sailed on the field, slapped the team together, and won out. That's why you got elected. I'd have won with the whole team behind me, and you know it!"

"Keep your temper," Chip said crisply. "You're away off, Bob. I was kidnaped, and those two fellows pulled me out. If you'd won the game I'd have been the first to congratulate you. As it was, I had already proposed you for captain, if you'll believe it."

"You had?"

"Yes. Ask Coach Trayne or any of the fellows. I don't think you've given me a square deal in this, Bob, and yet I can see how you look at it. I'm sorry that I didn't come to you before and have it out frankly, but I've been pretty busy, and didn't understand just what was behind it all."

Randall was not at all convinced. He stared down at the table, and his eye fell on a tiny folded paper inserted in his Cicero. His cheeks flushed a trifle, and he gave an imperceptible start.

"In that case," he said slowly, his clenched hands at his sides in self-repression, "I—I may have been wrong. But it seemed to me that you hadn't been the one to hand out a square deal, Merry. I was helpless in trying to fight you for an elective office. Everybody around here seems to toady to the Merriwells——"

"Hold on, right there, Bob," Chip interrupted quickly, his eyes flashing with a hint of anger.

"You know that's not the case. If there's any one who hates to be truckled to and toadied to, I'm the one. I didn't go after the captaincy, in this particular instance, and it was handed to me before I knew it. As to toadying, you ought to know the fellows too well to lay that charge, Bob."

"Haven't you everything your own way?" demanded Randall. His eyes still held to that folded scrap of paper, and his face looked troubled. "You run everything around here, and nobody else gets a look-in——"

"Old man, for Heaven's sake get your brain untangled!" Chip leaned forward earnestly, setting aside his own irritation. "I don't want to run anything. Whatever I have done has been done for Fardale, and I've had nothing further in view than the best good of the school. Let me prove this by something which I ought not to tell you."

He found Randall staring at him with a peculiar look, and fancied that his words were bearing fruit.

"I was just talking to Coach Trayne about who will be elected captain if I have to leave school—which may be at any minute now. I urged you for the place, since I honestly believe that you're the man for it. He could not understand why I overlooked the way you have acted lately, until I explained that I hoped to talk it over with you and straighten things out for the good of Fardale. I don't care a whoop about myself, Randall. I'm only thinking of the school, and I want you to do the same. Now, slip into your things and come over to the gym with me. The fellows will know that the hatchet's been buried, and you will leap up at a bound in their estimation, and everybody will be happy. Will you do it, old fellow?"

Randall had turned, and was gazing out of the window. Merriwell could not see the dark flush of anger that flitted across his face, but after a moment he heard the low and tense voice of Randall.

"I'll do it, Chip. I'm sorry."

Randall turned quickly to the closet and pulled out his shoes, for he had been at work in bath robe and slippers.

"Good!" Frank cried, in delight. "Get on your duds, and we'll forget it all!"

He walked over to the window, looking out on the campus, and stood watching the flitting crowd below. Randall had come around all right, he thought, and, with a little careful handling, would soon be his old self.

Meantime, however, Randall had given a quick glance at his

back. A crafty smile leaped to his face, and, while still watching Merriwell's motionless figure, he reached out and seized the folded paper.

Tearing off one end with a quick motion, he emptied a flickering white powder into the glass that stood beside the pitcher. Still covertly eying Chip, he deftly obtained a second glass from the closet shelf and placed it on the opposite side of the pitcher. Then he poured water into both glasses.

The white powder dissolved instantly. At the sound of the pouring water, Merry turned, and Randall straightened up with a smile that set queerly on his features.

"I say, Merry," he called, with seeming candor, "let's drink a toast to the success of the team to-day, and the continuance of our friendship—a toast in aqua pura!"

"Bully!"

Merriwell stepped forward, with a smile. At this instant there was a sudden interruption, however.

The door was flung open, and a panting cadet orderly appeared as the startled Randall swung round.

"Mr. Randall! Colonel Gunn wants to see you at once in his office."

This summons could mean only one thing—trouble. Randall had already slipped into his clothes, and he seized his hat, instantly forgetting everything else. Was it possible that his visit to the village of the previous night had been discovered?

"Wait for me, Merry," he said hastily. "I'll probably be right back!"

"I'll be here, old man," Chip assured him, and Randall left hurriedly with the orderly.

CHAPTER XXXII.

WHO GOT IT?

oo bad we didn't drink that toast!" murmured Merriwell, as the echoing steps of the orderly and Randall died away down the corridor. "Still, I'm mighty glad that Bob saw fit to come around. It'll clear things up wonderfully."

He crossed the room and sank into a chair. Picking up a magazine, he began to turn over its pages. As he did so, his hand went out to the nearer of the two glasses, and he brought it to his lips, sipping slowly.

With a sigh, he emptied the glass and replaced it on the table. Five minutes passed, and Merry flung the magazine back to its place, rising.

"Wonder what kind of a row Randall has got himself into now?" he mused, going to the window and looking down on the campus, with a frown.

Colonel Gunn was the principal of Fardale, and if Randall had been in some kind of a scrape, it might injure his chances on the diamond. However, there was a chance that the Southerner had been guilty of some infraction of the military routine of the school which would merely get him a "call-down" and a few black marks.

Suddenly Chip turned, as a sharp knock sounded at the door.

"Come in!"

The door opened. Merry gave a gasp of astonishment, for framed in the doorway, stood Bully Carson. The latter turned and shut the door, not observing him.

"You came over to see the game?" Merry asked pleasantly.

Bully whirled with a swift cry, his face black.

"You! Why—why—where's Bob Randall? Isn't this his room?"

The startled surprise of Colonel Carson's son was quite evident. In fact, he was wildly disconcerted. He had expected to see his cousin, and instead he found Merriwell.

"Don't get scared out, Bully," said Chip. "Bob will be right back. I was waiting for him myself, so I hope you won't mind my company."

Merry thoroughly enjoyed the confusion of the other. He bore Carson no malice, for he knew that the other had been thoroughly punished for his wrongdoings. He fancied that Bully's confusion sprang from fear at being found in Fardale—fear of new retribution for the past.

"Sit down," he urged pleasantly. "Sit down and rest your eye, Bully. One of 'em looks pretty tired. Hot day, isn't it?"

Bully growled out something inarticulate and sank into a chair with a scowl at Merry. Since he had blundered into it, he was determined to stick.

As Chip remarked, it was a warm day for that time of year, and no mistake. Bully Carson was heated by his walk from the village, and he was perspiring profusely. He pulled out a handkerchief of purple silk with red bars, and mopped at his face, eying Merry furtively. Seeming to conclude that he was safe for the present, he regained his composure slowly.

Chip knew that Carson was a thorough bully and coward. In fact, he had himself presented Bully with that black eye, when the other had attempted to "beat him up" in Carsonville the previous Saturday. He scanned Bully's attire with a humorous twinkle in his eyes.

"You ought to be more careful, Bully," he remarked, with mock solicitude. "If you were seen on the Fardale streets in those duds, you'd be in danger of arrest."

"Huh? What for?" Bully growled suspiciously. He looked down at himself.

"For disturbing the peace," said Chip, with a laugh, dropping on the window seat.

"Think you're cussed smart, don't you?"

"Not a bit of it," Chip gravely assured him. He found Bully capital amusement. "I only wonder at your nerve in coming here!"

"You should worry," retorted Bully, with a scowl. "Ain't I got a right to visit my cousin?"

"Sure. Only, if you had another cousin in jail, you'd have a better right to visit him, seems to me."

"Huh?" Carson turned pale and mopped at his face again. "What you goin' to do about it?"

Chip knew that he could have both Bully and his father arrested for what had taken place at Carsonville. This, however, was far from his thoughts.

"Nothing. Make yourself right at home, old man. Only I wouldn't advise you to light up that cigarette in here."

Bully had started to roll a cigarette. He paused, looking up quickly.

"Why not?"

"It's not allowed. Go ahead and suck it all you want to, but don't light it. We don't approve of coffin nails at Fardale, and if the guards smelled smoke they'd throw you out of here in a hurry."

Carson grunted. Nevertheless, he apparently decided to take Chip's warning in good part. There was an undernote to Merry's voice that told him the other was not joking this time.

He finished rolling the cigarette, licked it, and carefully inserted it into one corner of his mouth. Then he lolled back in his chair, glanced around, and favored Chip with a black look.

"You fellers are goin' to get the hide licked off you to-day," he announced. His confidence was returning, as Merry made no hostile move.

"Thanks for the news," said Chip easily. "Are you going to pitch?"

"No. We got a new feller named Green. He'll show you dubs what real pitchin' is, and I'm goin' to back him to the limit."

"I hope he'll show us more than you did," and Frank settled himself among the pillows in the window seat. "We're always willing to be shown, Bully."

Bully grunted.

"You get yours to-day, all right."

"Who's Green?" asked Chip curiously. "Is he an amateur?"

"Sure!"

"And I suppose your father is going to bet on him, as usual?"

Bully grinned, and patted his pocket knowingly.

"Pop's goin' to do a little betting, I reckon. So'm I."

"Why don't you bet on Fardale, for a change?" Merry queried pleasantly. "It might get you something, old man!"

"I suppose you think I'm a piker, hey?" scowled Bully. "I suppose you think I ain't got money myself?"

"You always were good at supposing," said Chip. "This time you hit it dead right."

"That shows how much you know! I got a thousand dollars in cash, right here in my pocket, and I'm goin' to meet a feller now and bet on the Clippers, see?"

Chip was somewhat amazed at this intelligence, though he gave no sign of it. He knew that Colonel Carson himself was a heavy plunger, but from what he had seen of Bully he had not thought that the latter was exactly flush with money.

"You must have bet on Fardale during that Franklin game," he murmured gently. "Or has your respected father become generous?"

"None o' your business," said Bully, with a growl, finding the subject abruptly distasteful. "Whew! I'm certainly het up. I guess I'll run along and place that bet, then come back here and find Bob."

"Suit yourself," chirped Merry. "If you're warm, take a glass of water. When you get outside, light that cigarette. Then you'll get nice and warm again, and it'll fur up your tongue."

Bully merely grunted at this sarcasm. He seemed to decide that part of the advice was good, however, for he caught up the other glass that Randall had filled and carried it across the table to his lips.

"I suppose you'll pitch to-day?" he inquired, pausing.

"Once more your suppositions are correct," returned Chip ironically.

Bully grunted and gulped down the water, replacing the glass on the table with a deep sigh, then threw his sleeve across his lips.

"That certainly tastes good! Well, I hope you'll get pounded out of the box, Merriwell. Green will shut you fellers out without a hit."

With this pleasant wish Bully came to his feet and moved toward the door, inspecting a few pictures and pennants as he went.

"Don't hurry," pleaded Chip, with mock anxiety. "You're not going to tear yourself away so soon, I trust?"

"Tell Bob I'll be back later," said Bully, with a grunt.

"With pleasure. Maybe you'd like to have me throw the game for you to-day?"

Carson merely scowled and passed outside, slamming the door viciously after him. From the window Frank could see him start across the campus in the direction of the riding hall, stopping to light his cigarette.

"Big brute!" he thought, disgusted. "I wonder how Randall ever got a cousin like that? But—what on earth is he doing here? If he and Bob are getting thick, I feel sorry for Bob."

This thought was disquieting to Merry. Could it be possible that Carson was back of Randall's queer actions?

It seemed improbable, for Randall had been keeping to himself, and Carson had not been seen at Fardale previous to this. Yet Frank knew that Bully possessed a crafty and cunning mind. He felt disturbed over Carson's impudence in daring to show himself about the place.

"Oh, well, I guess Randall can take care of himself," he mused, and dismissed the subject lightly, and settled himself among the pillows again.

He had been up early that morning, and it was a warm spring day. Consequently, it was only natural that he should feel drowsy. Taking advantage of the moment to relax utterly, Merry put back his head and closed his eyes. Almost before he knew it, he had dropped off into a light doze.

He was roused by a sharp knock at the door, and sprang up instantly with a shout to enter. The door swung back and disclosed Colonel Gunn's orderly.

"You're wanted at the office, Mr. Merriwell," said the cadet, with symptoms of flurried haste. "Colonel Gunn sent me after you on the run."

"What's up?" queried Frank, in surprise. "Is Randall in trouble?"

"In up to his neck," said the cadet. "But I'd better not say anything about it, I guess."

"All right," and Merry seized his hat. "Come along!"

CHAPTER XXXIII.

ACCUSED OF THEFT.

olonel Gunn was fat, ponderous, and highly digni-
fied. He owned his military title by virtue of having
been an aid on the governor's staff, but none the less
he was an extremely capable man.

Merry had no inkling of what trouble Randall was mixed up in,
for the orderly had wisely refrained from discussing it. Upon entering the office of the principal, Chip found Colonel Gunn seated
at his desk. Before him was Randall, white-faced and evidently
badly frightened, while at one side stood the constable from Fardale village.

To judge by the general air of things, the situation was anything
but pleasant for Bob Randall. Merry came to attention.

"Ah, Mr. Merriwell," exclaimed the colonel, in his ponderous
style, "I sent for you at—ah—Mr. Randall's request. There is a
considerable—ah—difficulty, and Mr. Randall seems to think that
you can—ah—help matters out. I'm sure I hope so."

"Yes, sir," returned Frank, quite in the dark as yet. "I didn't
know that Randall was in any trouble, sir."

"I did not intend to convey that—ah—intelligence, Merriwell. I
merely ventured the—ah—statement that there was a difficulty.
You will please note that there is not only a technical, but a moral,
difference—I might say a tremendous difference—between leve-
ling an accusation of—ah—guilt, or presupposing such a conclu-
sion, and making a statement of bare and unvarnished fact."

Merry was tempted to smile, but knew better.

"Yes, sir," he gravely answered. "I beg your pardon, Colonel
Gunn, for having unintentionally miscomprehended your prior
remark. If I may be allowed a word with Randall, sir, it might
serve to——"

"Ah—certainly, certainly!" wheezed the colonel.

Merry turned. Until then, Randall had not dared to break silence, knowing that the principal was a stickler for discipline. Now he leaned over the table toward Frank, his face white and tense.

"Chip, I swear that I didn't do it!" he cried passionately. "I never dreamed of such a thing!"

"I hope not," returned Frank, his eyes twinkling. Then, noting the terrible strain that Randall labored under, he became serious. "What is it, old man? What kind of trouble are you in?"

"This heah officeh says that I stole a thousand dollahs last night!" cried out Randall, indicating the constable.

Merry smiled. To any one who knew Bob Randall, the preposterous absurdity of such a charge was evident. Randall might be a murderer, but never a thief.

"Why, old man," said Frank, "surely there's no evidence for such a charge? You have plenty of money, for one thing. For another, any one who knows you must believe you incapable of such a thing."

"Yo' sho' ahe true blue, Chip!" Randall cried eagerly. "Of co'se, no one would accuse a Randall of theft, except a low-down Yankee——"

Colonel Gunn cleared his throat heavily. His face looked troubled, and Chip saw that he also found it hard to reconcile the charge with Randall's character.

"You—ah—are presupposing a good deal, gentlemen," he declared ponderously. "In the first place, allow me to make the assertion that—ah—no one has accused Mr. Randall of the theft. Is that not right, constable?"

"Yes, sir," said the perplexed officer. "I didn't accuse him, exactly. I only wanted to know how much he knew."

"A distinction with a difference," said the colonel.

Frank made a grimace of despair. If he was going to get to the bottom of this before time for mess, he would have to wade in.

"Excuse me, sir," he exclaimed, "but I know nothing of the circumstances referred to. I don't see how I can help Randall, but if you'll be good enough to explain the nature of the difficulty I'll be only too glad to tell anything I know, or to do anything I can to help out matters."

"Ah—quite so, quite so, Merriwell!"

Colonel Gunn swung around in his chair, taking a paper from the desk before him, and proceeded to elucidate.

"Putting up at the Dobbs Hotel in the village, Merriwell, is a gentleman named—ah—Hostetter, Ezra Hostetter. It is his assertion that at some time last night, some person or persons unknown did feloniously gain admittance to his room at the hotel, and

did—ah—remove from beneath his pillow a black leather wallet, containing—ah—certain papers. The wallet also contained a
thousand dollars in hundred-dollar bills."

"He must have been pining for adventure, sir, to carry that
much around with him in currency," observed Frank. The colonel's mouth twitched slightly. "But if the thieves are unknown,
where does Randall come in? He was in barracks last night, as
would be easy to prove."

"That is just the—ah—difficulty," observed the colonel heavily,
fixing his eye on Randall. "According to the inspector's report,
Mr. Randall and his roommate were asleep at the proper time. But
when I asked Mr. Randall whether he had been to the village last
night, he admitted it. Is not that correct, sir?"

"Of course, Colonel Gunn," said the Southerner proudly. "There
was a dummy in my bed to fool the inspector. But when you
asked, of course, I would not lie about it, sir."

"A highly proper—ah—sentiment, Mr. Randall," said the colonel. He stopped Merry with uplifted hand. "One moment, sir! Mr.
Randall was seen to enter the hotel in question, and to leave, each
time by the back door, and in a stealthy manner. When I asked
him for an explanation, he—ah—asked that you be sent for."

Merry looked at the Southerner in astonishment. Randall stood
erect, a dark flush in his cheeks, his eyes desperate. But he had
regained his self-control.

"I was frightened, Chip," he said quietly. "Of course, you know
nothing about it, only the evidence seemed so terribly circumstantial that you were the first person I thought of."

"I'm glad you did think of me, old man," said Chip, smiling.
"But let's get this business straightened out. May I ask who observed Randall's entry and departure, Colonel Gunn?"

"Mr. Dobbs himself," stated the colonel, referring to his paper.
"But allow me to—ah—mention that Mr. Randall makes no deni-
al, and no explanation."

Frank glanced again at Randall, in perplexity.

"What's the answer, old man?"

"I received a letter from my cousin, Edward Carson, the son of
Colonel Carson, of Carsonville," said Randall. "He asked me to
meet him at the hotel on important business. I was unable to get
away before taps, so I left my room by means of a rope, and entered the hotel quietly, hoping to avoid observation."

"Ah, Mr. Randall," wheezed the colonel, "and what, may I in-
quire, was the nature of the—ah—important business to which
your cousin referred?"

"I must refuse to answer, sir," and Randall suddenly went white. "I give you my word, sir, that it was entirely personal and private. More than that, I cannot say."

A little silence ensued. Frank studied Randall, but could find no trace of guilt in the dark, handsome features. Nor did he believe the Southerner guilty.

"You know nothing of the theft, of course?"

"Nothing, Chip."

"I must say, colonel," exclaimed Frank, turning to the principal, "that I do not think Randall at all guilty. He could have easily lied out of the whole thing, and the inspector's report would have borne him out. The fact that he refused to do so must surely count in his favor?"

"Most certainly, Merriwell. It has just—ah—occurred to me that if we could locate this Carson, we might thus exonerate Mr. Randall completely. Such a consummation would be—ah—highly pleasing to me."

"He ain't at the village," spoke up the constable. "Mr. Hostetter was lookin' fer him, sir."

"Hostetter knew him, then?" inquired Chip quickly.

"They was friends," replied the constable. Frank turned.

"Carson was at Randall's room just before I left, Colonel Gunn. He departed across the campus, and he might be easily located, I think."

"Ah—by all means!"

The principal hastily summoned his orderly and ordered a dozen cadets dispatched in search of Carson, who could be easily recognized by means of his black eye and patch. Randall was looking at the floor, a tumult of emotions in his face.

How much Merry knew of the attempt to drug him, he could not guess. Yet Frank was doing his best to help him out of his scrape. The Southerner was smitten with remorse and self-condemnation, but dared say nothing.

"We'll clear you, old man," said Merry warmly. "This might be a plot to ruin your character—and knowing Carson, as I do, I would not put it past him."

He briefly recounted to Colonel Gunn his late experiences at Carsonville. The principal, however, did not agree that there could be any plot against Randall, and Frank himself had only suggested it as a forlorn hope.

"Your anxiety for your friend—ah—does you honor, Merriwell. Yet I would point out that until Mr. Dobbs volunteered his—ah—information, Mr. Randall was not thought of in connection with the unfortunate matter."

Poor Randall was miserable enough, and looked it. He could not doubt Frank's sincerity in helping him, and his conscience smote him. He wondered whether Merry had drank that glass of water, but Frank gave no signs of being drugged.

Going over the facts once more, Merriwell was forced to admit that things looked black for Randall. If he should be arrested and brought before a jury, there was little doubt but that he would be convicted on circumstantial evidence. And yet it was incredible that he should have stolen the money!

One by one the searchers brought back word that there was no sign of Carson anywhere about the grounds, and on telephoning the hotel, Colonel Gunn found that he had not returned. Randall's entire hopes of vindication rested upon his cousin.

"I'm sure the constable will be willing that Randall should remain here in your care, colonel," suggested Merry. "Carson is sure to turn up at the game, and he can be brought over at once to clear Randall."

"Good!" cried the colonel, the constable nodding assent. "And to express my—ah—belief and confidence in Mr. Randall, he shall sit in my box during the game!"

Randall tried to thank Merry with his eyes, as the bugles rang out for mess, but Frank departed with an uneasy feeling that something was certainly weighing on the Southerner's mind. Could he be guilty by any chance?

CHAPTER XXXIV.

A MYSTERY.

There was no doubt that the Clippers were a drawing card.

Although their team was one of the best in the Amateur League, the rumor had spread abroad that it had been largely reconstructed by Colonel Carson for this game, and the near-by towns had sent their contingents of fans, in no little expectation.

Fardale field was crowded long before the time for the game. Before two o'clock the grand stand was sold out. There was no overflow crowd, since the long bleachers were full able to handle every one, but automobiles were parked by the score at all available points, and it looked as if ground rules would have to go into effect.

There had been a big shift in the Fardale team, also. News of this had leaked out, and consequently both cadets and baseball fans were eager to see what Captain Merriwell had done in the way of a shake-up.

Man after man purchased a score card, and then gazed at it in blank amazement. If he happened to be a Fardale rooter, the amazement was tinctured with dismay. If he was a Clipper fan, he stared at his card in perplexity, and began to ask questions of the men around him.

This was the line-up that caused the crowd so much confusion:
FARDALE.
Lowe, 3d b.
O'Day, r. f.
Kess, 2d b.
Clancy, 1st b.
Merriwell, p.
Harker, ss.
McQuade, c.

Chester, l. f.
Lang, c. f.

CLIPPERS.
Ironton, ss.
Murray, 2d b.
Green, p.
Smith, 1st b.
Olcott, c.
Johnson, r. f.
Craven, 3d b.
Runge, l. f.
Merrell, c. f.

"That's a queer proposition," said a Clipper fan, turning to the man behind him. "Who's this fellow Green? And Smith?"

"Search me. All we got left o' the old Clippers is short and second."

Over in the Fardale bleachers there was little short of a sensation, for Chip's line-up had not been made public before the game.

"We're gone!" groaned one man despairingly. "With Kess on second and O'Day out in the field, it's 'good night' for us!"

"Merriwell must be crazy," exclaimed another. "That blundering Dutchman can't hit beans! And Lowe and Harker switched around, and a substitute in left field! I wish Ted Crockett had remained captain, by thunder!"

"Oh, pickles!" scoffed a plebe derisively. "Who left the door open for you to get in? You wait and see what happens to those Clippers!"

None the less, Fardale was anxious. So were the Clipper sympathizers. When the time for practice drew near, the crowd was literally on its toes, watching for the first sight of the players. Both teams were an unknown quantity, in their present shape, and the only comfort remaining to Fardale was that Merriwell was slated to pitch. The umpires were two Yale men, specially obtained for the occasion.

Frank was forced to dismiss his worry over Bob Randall, as the time for work drew near. Nothing had been seen of Bully Carson, and Randall was due to witness the game from the principal's box—partly as a guest, partly under surveillance. The village constable was somewhere about the field, hunting for Carson.

Colonel Carson himself was in evidence in the grand stand, laying as many bets as he could find Fardale takers. Most of these latter were out-of-town men, for there were few among the ca-

BURT L. STANDISH

dets themselves who cared to do any gambling. The colonel knew
nothing of his son, it appeared, and had not seen him that day.

"I've heard a lot about this Merriwell guy," stated a Fardale fan
to the world at large. "Has he got anything?"

"Has he!" A fat man below him turned around, brandishing a
fan in one hand and a pop bottle in the other. "Say, ever see the
old Frank Merriwell pitch?"

"Uh-huh, once."

"Well, the kid is a chip of the old block, take it from me!"

"I guess I'll not let Colonel Carson slide past me, then," and the
Fardale rooter took out his pocketbook.

Finally a tremendous burst of cheering started in the bleachers
and gradually spread around the field. The two teams had arrived for practice work! Every head was craned to look, and a
howl of expectation rose as the Clippers took the field first.

The howl rose to a roar of applause as the ball began to whip
around. The new Clipper infield was a wonder! Their precision
was magnificent, and the way they put the sphere to the bases
made Fardale gasp.

With Coach Trayne, Merry stood watching them work. Off to
one side, Green was limbering up with his catcher, Olcott. He was
a tall, slender, wiry man with a very brown face and terrific speed
to his practice ball.

"Chip, that fellow is a tartar!" murmured the coach. "Watch
how easily he puts those sizzlers down, eh? He moves as if every
muscle was run by clockwork!"

"He certainly is a beautiful pitcher," Frank said admiringly.
"And look there—see that fellow Craven pick up that hot one!
Ironton and Murray are the only infielders left from their old
team, but I guess Colonel Carson knew his business!"

Wild cheers went up as Craven picked a sizzler from the ground,
darted to his base, and sent the ball across to third like a bullet.
Just then a bat boy touched Merry's arm.

"A man in one of the boxes wants to speak to you, Chip."

Frank followed his guide back to the grand stand. A keen-eyed
man with a long black cigar in his mouth was standing by the
netting, and beckoned.

"You wanted me?"

"Yes. Say, Merriwell, do you know that fellow Green—the Clippers' pitcher?"

"Why, no," returned Chip, smiling. "He looks mighty good,
though."

"Well, I'm a traveling man, but I'm rooting for Fardale. Did you ever hear of Southpaw Diggs?"

"Often. He's one of the best pitchers in the country, if he'd let booze alone. What's on your mind?"

"That fellow Green is a dead ringer for Diggs, Merriwell! He ain't got Diggs' big rainbow mustache, but I've seen Diggs work too often not to recognize that wind-up."

Frank looked up at the man, startled.

"Impossible, my friend! The Clippers are all amateurs——"

"Oh, rats! I know too much about the game to swallow that talk, Merriwell, especially when Colonel Carson talks it."

Merry looked troubled. He knew Carson was crooked as a corkscrew, but it was incredible that such a barefaced thing could be attempted.

"If you can swear that Diggs and Green are one and the same," suggested Frank, frowning, "we could protest him."

"No," returned the traveling man regretfully. "I never seen Diggs close up, but I could recognize that wind-up a mile away. I couldn't swear to it very well, though."

"Then the game has to go on," said Frank.

At this point the man next to his informant, who had been listening, chipped in the conversation.

"Old man Carson is betting all kinds of money, Merriwell. If that fellow is really Diggs, would it queer the bets?"

"Not exactly," said Merry. "If we could prove it, of course, the bets would be off, and so would the game. But I see no chance of proving it."

"Well, I'm backin' your crowd," went on the man anxiously. "I had a bet at even money with the colonel's son, but he must have got cold feet. He ain't showed up."

"Was it much of a bet?" asked Frank.

"A thousand even."

"You'd better keep your money in your pocket," advised Chip, turning away. "Betting is mighty poor business, especially where the Carson crowd is mixed up in it."

He stood looking across the field, suddenly thoughtful. A thousand dollars—and Bully Carson also had boasted that he had a thousand in cash to bet—and Hostetter had been robbed of exactly that amount!

"That's a mighty queer coincidence," reflected Merry, worried. "Hostetter and Bully were friends, according to Colonel Gunn. Could it be possible that Carson did steal that money? But where is he now?"

That was a mystery. Evidently Bully had failed to meet the man with whom he was to bet, yet he had left Randall's room for that express purpose.

"I believe he can explain that theft," muttered Frank. "And I'll make it my business to find him after the game."

Returning to Coach Trayne, he repeated the information given him by the traveling man, and Trayne watched Green closely.

"He does resemble Diggs in general outline," admitted the coach. "And his wind-up and delivery are exactly similar. Chip, I've a good notion to stop this game now!"

"You've no proof, Mr. Trayne. The Clippers are vouched for as amateurs by their owner, and even if he has put in a few ringers, that can't hurt our standing, if we play them. And it would be a bad business to start something we can't finish."

Trayne saw the justice of this argument, and Merry caught up his glove, as the bell rang, and ran out. While he was warming up with Billy Mac, the other Fardale men began to work, and Merry's judgment was soon vindicated by the fans, except in the case of Villum Kess.

The Dutch lad seemed awkward. He committed no glaring errors, but it seemed to the crowd that any one would have been better at second than he. However, Fardale was now committed, and every rooter hoped for the best as the Fardale yell began to ring out: "Ha, ha, ha! 'Rah, 'rah, 'rah! Rigger-boom! Zigger-boom! All hail—Fardale! Fardale! Fardale!"

The Clipper sympathizers had no regular yell, but they made good with a thunder of feet stamping, and a roar of shouts and yells. For an instant these fell silent while the two umpires announced the batteries, then they rose again into a wild storm as the Fardale nine trotted out and took the field.

"Play ball!" cried the strike umpire, adjusting his mask. Ironton stepped out.

The game was on.

CHAPTER XXXV.

THE FIGHT OF HIS LIFE.

"Ve vos all pehind you, Chip!" squawked Villum Kess, capering around second.

"Take your time, old man," advised Clancy.

"Let this boob hit it," grinned Billy Mac, as Ironton stepped into the box.

Frank paused. He had seen clearly that Green was a whirlwind, and decided to hold his best ball, the jump, in reserve. If Green was really Diggs, then he had his work cut out for him.

"Get on to that guy on second!" yelled a fan.

Villum Kess had come to rest plumb on his bag, and stood waiting.

"Play off there, you lobster!" shrieked another rooter frantically.

"Blay off yourselluf," returned Villum hotly. "Shud oop und say less. Make a glam of yourselluf if I vas a lopster yes, no! Yaw! You vait till you show me!"

Frank nodded to Billy, and put over a low, straight ball. Ironton waited.

"Strike—one!"

The Clipper shortstop was a wicked hitter, as Merry knew. Seeing that he stood up close to the plate, Chip put over a sharp inshoot, and again the umpire called a strike, as Ironton swung vainly.

He refused to bite at two teasers, however, and again Merry used his in. As if sensing the ball, Ironton pulled back and chopped.

Crack!

Merry reached after the hot liner in vain. It went straight toward the position that Kess should have been playing, while Ironton dug down toward first, amid wild whoops from the bleachers. Then Villum did a surprising thing.

Flinging himself out toward the ball, he lost his balance and slid forward, whirling around. He came down in a cloud of dust.

"By glory, he sat on it!" yelled the fans.

Villum reached beneath himself and pulled out the ball, staring at it in mild astonishment.

"Put it over, you boob!" shrieked Clancy.

Kess looked up, saw the runner nearing first, and scrambled to his feet. With astonishing precision, he sent the ball to Clancy, and the umpire motioned Ironton out.

"It was an accident!" cried Craven, on the coaching line. "He's an idiot!"

"Go avay mit yourselluf!" squawked Villum, brushing the dust from his shirt. "Vait till I vos shown you how you don'd blay, yes, no!"

Murray advanced to the plate, and with evident determination to hit. After trying to connect with three sharp curves, Murray slung away his bat and yielded up his place to Green.

Frank saw the wiry pitcher pull down his cap and dust his hands, and the quiet confidence of the man went far to show that he was no amateur. Grimly resolving to fan him, Chip wound up for the double shoot, and the ball hummed down.

Green did not attempt to strike. Then a swift look of astonishment overspread his lean brown face. Merry had changed from his right to his left hand!

"Great Scott!" gasped Green. "It's impossible!"

"Go on and knock it over the fence," chuckled Billy Mac.

Green tried to, but the double shoot fooled him completely. With a smile, Frank delivered a sharp out with his left hand, and Green reached for it in vain.

"We've got 'em!" whooped Clancy as he ran in. "One, two, three!"

"Easy money," cried Billy, and Chip touched his cap to the yelling grand stand as the Fardale cheer ripped out.

Fardale's hopes received an abrupt shock, however. Smiling a little, but saying nothing, Green put over nine pitched balls, and retired Lowe, O'Day, and Kess!

"He can't pitch anything but strikes!" gasped Clancy.

"Don'd you see dot sbeed!" muttered Villum. "Dot pall a pullet vos, so hellup me!"

"We're up against something pretty hard, fellows," said Chip, as they went out. "Everybody pull together, now, and we'll win."

His confidence had been sorely shaken, however. Smith strode out and landed on Frank's first ball for a foul that went up over the grand stand. Twice more he fouled, but the double shoot retired him finally.

"They're all bad actors," cried Lowe from third. "Let 'em hit it, Chip!"

Olcott, the new Clipper catcher, was a short man, with tremendously wide shoulders. Chip tried him with a low fadeaway, but Olcott chortled with glee and fell on it. The ball rose and began to travel for the right-field fence.

O'Day raced back, then stopped short. The crowd hooted, for the ball seemed certain to go far beyond him. The fans had forgotten the wind, however, and, when the sphere came down it nestled into O'Day's glove, and stuck there. Johnson fanned, and the Fardales went to bat.

That is, they went to bat technically. Clancy was the first up, and although usually a slugger, he was retired on three pitched balls. Merry took his place, with the bleachers screaming for a hit.

Green studied him a moment, then changed his position abruptly. He used something that he had hitherto held in reserve—a remarkable spit ball. Frank guessed it, but could not hit.

Again Green used the same thing, and again Merry missed it. He touched the third one for a high foul, however, that cleared the grand stand. With a new ball thrown out to him, Green deliberately put over three balls that were wide of the plate.

"Put it over!" snapped Chip. "You're scared to put it over, Green!"

Green looked at him, and grinned tantalizingly. Then he calmly sent over the ball, ten feet wide of the plate. Frank angrily flung his bat away, and walked.

The Fardale rooters went wild, but Chip was not fooled. He knew that this was a deliberate effort to rattle him, and that Green had meant to show his contempt. This was proved when Harker was sent down on three pitched balls, though Green again held his spit ball under cover.

His curves were wonderful, and would have fooled better men than Fardale owned. Seeing that he was marooned on first, Chip made a desperate attempt, and stole second, but only got there safely because Murray dropped a terrific ball, that Olcott placed perfectly. Billy Mac immediately struck out, and the inning was over.

"That man Green is beyond anything I ever saw!" cried Coach Trayne, as Chip came in to confer with Billy. "Watch out for Craven, Merry!"

Frank nodded toward the bench. Craven was a slender, lanky fellow with a large jaw. He was chewing tobacco, and carried his bat easily.

Using his right hand once more, Merry resorted to the double shoot, refusing Billy's agonized plea to use the jump ball. Craven fanned twice, seeming to be awkward at the plate, but on the third ball he struck too quickly, whirled, and the ball hit him between the shoulders.

He went down to first, apparently badly hurt. But Chip caught a quick grin from him, and realized angrily that the umpire had been "worked" very neatly. He fanned Merrell, then Runge, but Craven romped down to second without hindrance, exchanging compliments with the enraged Villum, as he did so.

Ironton again was at bat. Chip sent the ball sizzling over for two strikes, but Ironton had solved the double shoot. He connected with the next ball and dropped it over second for a neat single—the first hit of the game. Craven went to third, with the crowd frantic, and Murray was up.

Chip switched hands in desperation, and Murray fanned twice. Then Ironton tried for second, and Billy Mac made a wretched throw that Villum barely hung on to, a yard from the sack. When Frank put the ball down again, Murray cracked a liner at Lowe—and Lowe fumbled it, booting it across the infield to Harker.

The crowd came to its feet, as Craven raced over the rubber. Harker lost his head and made a throw ten feet wide of the plate. Billy went after it, but Ironton came in like a whirlwind. Frank ran in and put the ball on him as he slid, but the umpire called him safe, and the Clippers had secured two runs, with Murray on third and Green up.

"For Heaven's sake use the jump!" implored Billy desperately, conferring with Chip. But Merry, grim-lipped, refused.

"I've got to hold it, Billy. This game is only three innings old."

He walked back, determined to retrieve the errors that had overwhelmed his team. Green faced him with a wide grin, the Clipper fans howling for a hit to bring in Murray. And Green was confident of getting it. Murray's lone hit had started things.

Frank did the very last thing Green expected. With a lengthy preliminary, he sent in a fast straight ball over the heart of the plate. Green had watched his fingers, and expected a drop, striking a foot beneath the ball.

"That got him!" yelled Clancy.

"Another of the same," cried Billy.

"Sure, give me another," begged Green.

Chip smiled. He knew that Green would now be certain of a swift curve. So, making as if to throw an out, Chip sent down another straight ball.

"Strike—uh—two!"

"That's headwork, old man!" cried Harker.

"Led him dood it!" cried Villum. "Ve vos all behind you, Frankie!"

Merry stood quietly. He refused Billy's signals time after time, knowing that Green was watching him like a hawk, until the crowd yelled for action. In desperation Billy tried the signal for another straight ball, and Merry nodded.

Again he wound up carefully. This time he cut loose with every ounce of speed at his command, and the ball went down fairly scorching. Green hit, but hit too late, and Billy was taken off his feet by the speed of the ball. None the less, he held on to it; Chip had fanned his rival with three straight balls!

Not only those in the grand stand, but the bleachers had also noted the fact, and there was a deep roar of cheers as Fardale came in. Merry passed Green, and the latter gave him a quick smile.

"Merriwell," he said quietly, "I take off my hat to you! That was magnificent."

Chip looked at him, found sincerity in the wrinkled eyes, and warmed instinctively.

"Thanks," he said significantly. "Coming from you, that means a good deal, Mr. Diggs!"

Green started, gave him one keen glance, then passed on with a laugh. But in that moment Chip knew that he now knew his man.

"That man is Diggs, right enough," he said to Coach Trayne, as his next three men proceeded to fan. "But he's not beaten us yet."

"Yaw!" squawked Villum from behind. "Dot vos right, Chip! Two runs don'd a pasepall game make, you pet me! Vait till I dood it!"

For the second time, Green retired Fardale on nine pitched balls.

CHAPTER XXXVI.

THE JUMP BALL.

he fourth inning started off badly, Smith beating out a bunt to first, but he held on while Merry tightened and fanned the next two men with the double shoot. At this Smith went down to second, where Villum was standing on the sack as usual.

Billy Mac sent down a perfect throw from the plate, but Villum appeared not to see it, for he was staring at Smith.

"Jump, you chump!" yelled Smith, and flung himself down in a beautiful fall-away slide.

For the second time that day, Villum sat down suddenly. The ball plunged into the cloud of dust, and a groan from the bleachers. When the dust cleared off, Villum was seen to be smiling blandly at Smith, holding the ball against the latter's chest; Smith's leg was hooked about Villum's waist, and the Clipper was staring up with wild astonishment.

"You vas oudt," exclaimed Villum. "You vos hooked me aroundt vhere I down sit, und you thought it vos der pase, yes, no?"

"Well, I'm jiggered!" gasped Smith.

The crowd roared with laughter at this evidence of Villum's playing, but it fell into somber silence once more as Fardale came to bat and O'Day struck out.

Then Villum came up to the plate, and, in trying to hit the first ball over, he lost his balance and was hit himself. The umpire hesitated, then motioned him to first, and Olcott's protest went unheeded.

"Yaw!" triumphantly blatted the Dutch lad, as he trotted down. "I toldt you I'd dood it! Britty soon der ball vill hit Chip a home run vor, you pet me!"

"Sacrifice, Clan," ordered Merry quietly. "You can't hope for a hit."

"Why not?" said Clancy, pausing as he was going forth.

"Because we're up against Southpaw Diggs. Bunt it."

The red-haired chap tried hard to obey, but failed. Villum went to second, however. Murray stood square on the base line, trying to block him off, and Villum arrived at about the same time as the ball. He flung himself straight at the sack and Murray went down amid a cloud of dust, from which the ball was seen to roll. Instantly Villum jumped up and went tearing toward third, regardless of Lowe's orders to hold second. Murray pegged the ball down to Craven, but made a poor throw. It was a close decision, but Villum got the benefit of the doubt.

"Bring him in, Chip," said Clancy.

For the second time, Merry faced his rival, and for the second time Green resorted to his wonderful spit ball. Once Chip fouled, and once struck in vain, then at the last instant he choked his bat and met the third ball for a bunt.

The slippery ball twisted along toward first, and Merry sped after it like a deer. Green went for it, but Chip beat out the throw, and Villum was safe with the first run for Fardale. Harker fanned, and the inning was ended.

"Well, that showed that they aren't invulnerable, fellows," said Merry cheerfully. "We'll even up pretty soon!"

"You're the only one of us who has a hit so far," said Billy Mac.

"And that was a bad scratch," chuckled Merry. "Well, go to it!"

Craven, the dangerous third baseman, was again up. He could not solve the double shoot, however, and Merrell and Runge went down, also. Merry had repeated Green's feat of retiring the side with nine pitched balls.

As he walked in and met Billy, however, he shook his head doubtfully.

"I'm using that ball too much," he said, in a low voice. "I don't want to use the jump unless I have to, but I can't throw the double shoot all the time, Billy."

"Change arms, then."

"I have. Well, let's see what happens."

Billy, Chester, and Lange went down in regular order to the smiling Green, although Lange managed to send up a pop fly that was gathered in by Murray. The sixth started with the heavy end up, and Ironton came out confidently.

Frank tried to avoid using the double shoot, with the result that Ironton poled a hot liner toward third. Lowe made a beautiful stop that drew an admiring yell from the bleachers, but dropped the ball, and Ironton beat it out.

The next man up was Murray, and Chip handled him carefully,

forcing him to put up an infield fly, that Villum easily absorbed. Then Green strode out, smiling.

Chip gathered every energy. He put over the double shoot, reversing from an in to an out, and Green fanned. Then, using his left hand, he reversed the shoot, and once more Green struck in vain, Ironton going down to second. Knowing that it was useless to attempt luring Green, Frank once more threw every effort into a terrifically swift, straight ball—and again Green fanned.

The speed of that ball was too much for Billy, however. It went through him and rolled back to the grand stand, while Green tore to first and Ironton to third. Both were safe, and Smith advanced to the plate. Frank signaled to Billy to come up.

"It's no use, old man," he said quietly.

"I'm sorry, Chip," and Billy was almost in tears. "They can't touch you, and if you only had a decent catcher——"

"None of that," said Merry. "You're all right, Billy. But I daren't use the double shoot again. I've pitched nothing else, and I can't give away the jump ball just yet. I'm going to try the spit ball, so watch out for bad ones."

The almost constant use of the double shoot had been a tremendous strain on Frank's arm, and Billy was forced to assent. Merry did not half like using the spit ball, as he had not practiced it for some time, but the need was imperative.

In fact, his first two balls went wide of the plate, and nearly let in a run. Then he found himself, and Smith fanned twice, Billy vainly trying to catch Green at second. By sheer good luck, Smith connected and walloped out a beauty to the left garden, which Chester gathered. But Ironton beat the ball to the plate for the third tally.

"He's gone!" came a voice from the grand stand that Frank recognized for that of Colonel Carson. "Knock him out of the lot! He's gone!"

"I'll show you something, you old scoundrel!" muttered Chip angrily, as Olcott pounded the rubber and begged for a good one.

He seemed unable to fulfill his prediction, however, for Olcott bunted the first ball to Harker, the shortstop made a poor throw to first, and Olcott was safe. Johnson came up, but ended the inning by popping a foul, that Billy Mac neatly garnered.

"Four to one," said Lowe, with a groan, as they came in. "We're done!"

"We're not," said Clancy warmly. "Chip hasn't begun to pitch yet."

Merry smiled faintly, and stared aghast as Green again put over nine pitched balls and retired Fardale. The man seemed made of iron!

In the first half of the seventh it seemed that only luck saved Fardale. Chester dropped Craven's fly, and Merrell let the ball hit him. Runge fanned, and Ironton came up with second and third filled, and one out. He knocked a hot one to Villum, who promptly dropped it; while every one yelled at him, the Dutch lad stared at the runners in astonishment.

Then he picked up the ball and slammed it to third, catching Merrell, and Lowe snapped it to Billy for a double play that retired the Clippers.

"Get a hit, Clan," said Merry quietly. "Green's weakening."

Clancy brightened up perceptibly, and though Green showed no sign of weakening, Clancy was hit by the ball, and went to first. Merry came up, made a quick guess that Green would give him an in, and swung with all his strength. He hit the ball on the nose.

"Wow!"

A shrill yell went up from every fan as the ball sailed out, cleared the fence, and was no more seen. As Merry jogged in from third he grinned.

"All luck, Green," he cried.

Frank had netted two runs with that homer, but the eighth opened with the score four to three in favor of the Clippers, and Craven at bat. He grounded out to Clancy, Merrell fanned, and Runge flied to Lowe. Green again fanned three men, leaving Kess up, and the ninth inning was on.

"All right, Billy," said Chip quietly. "Every ball a jump."

"Hurray!" yelled Billy, in delight. "Nine balls, Merry!"

Ironton was up. Merry put the first ball down to him right in the groove, and he swung viciously at it. The ball seemed to leap over his bat into Billy's glove.

"Hey!" cried Ironton, amazed. "What's the matter with that ball?"

"Take another look," said Chip, with a grin.

Again he sent it squarely over the plate, and again Ironton failed utterly to find it. The third ball looked even better, and with wondering desperation Ironton brought around his bat.

"Out!"

"What kind of a ball is that?" demanded Ironton savagely.

"Plain straight ball," chuckled Billy. "Couldn't you see it?"

The grand stand began to appreciate a change in Merriwell's pitching as Johnson came into the box and proceeded to strike out also.

"He's using a new ball!" yelled the traveling man who had recognized Green-Diggs.

"Look at Johnson swing!" shrieked another fan excitedly. "Where'd he get that ball? What is it?"

Johnson watched the third one come, and tried helplessly to find it. He was motioned out, and flung his bat away heatedly.

"There's some crooked work here!" he cried.

"And it smells like Southpaw Diggs," chirped Clancy, as Green came out swinging two bats. He flung one away and stepped into the box.

The Fardale fans began to pluck up hope. They roared out hoarse entreaties to fight it out, and as he glanced at the grand stand Merry saw Colonel Gunn standing up and excitedly waving his hat, dignity utterly forgotten, while Randall clutched him around the neck and yelled like a crazy man.

"Here's a nice straight one for you, Green," said Chip.

Green evidently believed him, for he swung at the ball wickedly. But the sphere took a queer upward jump into Billy's mitt, and Green stepped back with a single gasp of amazement.

"What you got on that ball?" he queried wonderingly.

Smiling, Merry sent down another, square in the groove. This time Green stood back and watched it, then grinned.

"Let her come!" he cried, and Chip knew that he had solved the jump.

With that, he sent down a straight ball. Green grinned again, struck a foot above it—and was out!

But the Clippers were still one run to the good.

CHAPTER XXXVII.

A DESPERATE FINISH.

ardale field was a pandemonium.

Grand stand and bleachers alike were crazy with excitement. The band, unheard, blared forth amid the din. Men shouted and shrieked for the score to be tied, begged Merry to crack out another homer, hit each other over the head, and threatened to smash the stands with their frenzied stamping.

With suddenness that was almost appalling, the din died away as Villum Kess was seen walking out to the plate. The rooters held their breath.

"That settles it," groaned a man near Colonel Gunn's box. "That dunderhead will be the first out—it's all over."

"Confound your impertinence, sir!" roared the irate colonel, twisting about and threatening the fan with personal violence. "It's not—ah—all over till the last man has—ah—gone down!"

Then he turned and sent another roar at the field.

"Get a hit! Get a hit!"

The crowd took up the swinging words. "Get a hit! Get a hit!" rose the thunder of many voices, pierced by the shrill yells of the Clipper fans, who implored Green to "Hold 'em down!"

Then Kess stepped into the box, and instantly the silence fell anew.

"Yaw!" squawked the Dutch lad, his voice sounding distinctly all over the field. "Didn't I toldt you I vos goin' to dood it! You vos a skinch, so hellup me!"

"You'll get skinned, all right," yelled Olcott. "Let the Dutchman hit it, old man! He's easy!"

"Shut oop mit your mouth!" retorted Villum, turning angrily.

As he did so, Green unwound and the sphere came down like a bullet. Villum tried to strike, but overreached himself and fell forward, sitting on the plate.

"Vot der matter vos?" he inquired blankly. "Vhere vos der pall?"

"Get up or you'll have another strike called," said Olcott.

Villum scrambled to his feet. His actions disgusted the excited crowd, however, and a storm of objurgation began to rain upon him.

"Take him out! Send in a ball player!"

"Get the hook! Get the hook!"

"By Yimini, you shoot oop!" roared Villum, waving his bat at the grand stand. "How vos I to hear der pall coming vhen you vos making such a yelling?"

Green smiled and once more put the ball across while Villum was glaring at the crowd. He whirled around as the ball plunked home.

"Vot vos dot?"

"Strike—two!" called the umpire.

"Vell, by shinks!" gasped Villum angrily. "You vos der advantage oof me dake, yes, no?"

"Watch out," advised Olcott, with a wide grin. "Here it comes again."

Villum spat on his hands, pounded the plate, and settled down. Even the nonchalant Green was laughing, but his laugh ended suddenly.

For, as the ball came glinting down, Villum gathered together, swung mightily, and connected!

"He's done it!" shrieked the fans, coming to their feet with a howl.

The ball went sizzling along the ground to Craven, while Villum Kess labored toward first. The third baseman was so astonished at his hit that when he scooped up the ball he fumbled it. Then he picked it up again and whipped it to first.

"Look oudt!" yelled Villum. "I vos coming!"

He came, too, in an unheralded slide. Smith, the semipro, had probably never seen any one slide for first before in all his life. He was so startled at the action that he missed the ball, which went past him.

Instantly Villum gained his feet and plunged toward second, repeating his bull-head effort of the fourth inning. While Smith chased the ball the crowd began to yell encouragement at him, remembering that he had scored the first tally.

On reaching second, Villum took a look over his shoulder and started for third. Smith had gained the ball, and was sending it across the diamond to Craven, but none the less he pounded on, head down and elbows working.

He was only halfway from second when Craven picked up the

ball and started for him with a grin. Villum never slacked up, despite the frantic yells that were directed at him. Just as Craven reached out to tag him, however, he stumbled over his own foot and fell like a shot, headfirst.

He struck squarely against Craven's knees. The latter's hand was distinctly seen to fly out, while the ball dropped and rolled away. Out of the whirling arms and legs emerged Villum, bounced to third, and turned toward home.

"I toldt you I vos a home run got!" he bellowed.

This time, however, this amazing luck seemed to have deserted him. Craven rolled over and got the ball, and quickly snapped it home. Olcott stepped out to get it, flinging aside his mask, and a groan swelled out from the crowd.

"He's done for!"

"Nefer!" roared Villum, bouncing along desperately.

Once more he shot to earth, just as the ball came whizzing along over him. Olcott took the ball and fetched it down, but Villum had already come to a stop, hands outstretched before him.

"Shudgement!" he squawked at the umpire. "You pet me dot I vos safe!"

He had the tips of his fingers on the plate—and had effected a home run without making a hit!

"Yaw!" he shrieked, in delight. "Vot vos I toldt you! You pet me der score she vos died, yes, no?"

"Right you are, Villum," laughed Chip, escorting the Dutch lad to the bench in mingled wonder and joy. "Take off your hat!"

Villum did so, then looked at it curiously. His eyes went to Chip's face, then to the grand stand, and for the first time he seemed to realize that the crowds were yelling at him in frantic madness. He bowed, stumbled, stood on his head, and vanished under the players' shed.

As Clancy walked out, Green seemed to lose his composure for the first time.

"Wake up, you boneheads!" he shouted wrathfully at his amazed team, who were still trying to find out what had happened. "They've got four runs on us, with only two hits. And Merriwell got them both! Wake up and play the game!"

"Here's where we get another hit, Southpaw Diggs," said Clancy merrily, as he danced into the box. "Put her over, old sox!"

Green obeyed, and the ball had so much speed that Clancy merely leaped backward in actual terror.

"Hey!" he cried. "You don't need to kill a fellow!"

Green smiled, having regained his lost poise, and brought out his spit ball in this emergency. Clancy swung at it vainly.

"Strike—two."

Once more the ball sped down like a white streak. This time Clancy connected with a crack that fetched the crowds up standing. But the roar was followed by a groan, as the ball lifted into deep center field and Merrell went after it.

Merrell was more intent on the ball than on the ground, however. Clancy was running along to first and watching him when Merrell stumbled and fell. The ball came down a yard beyond him, and O'Day sent Clancy on to second, while once more the roar swelled out from the bleachers.

"Green's blown up! Merry to bat!"

"A hit, Merriwell! Get a hit! Get a hit!"

"One run wins the game! Get a hit!"

That fly, which fell well within Merrell's territory, and should have been fielded easily, went as an error instead of a hit. Therefore, in spite of the fact that Fardale had four runs, Merry was the only one who had so far been able to hit Green. One of his two hits was a scratch, and the other was a lucky jab by his own admission. Therefore, as he came up to the plate, he was anything but confident.

He had already given Clancy the hit-and-run signal, for he himself had little hope of making another decent hit. As he stepped in the box and faced Green, he saw the man's lean brown face smiling at him, and knew that the other was even cooler than he himself.

For the second time, Green read danger in Merry's eyes and resolved to take no chances. He sent down a wide one, and Chip lashed out at it in order to give Clancy a chance.

The red-haired chap went to third, safe by a narrow margin. After that, Green sent down no more wide ones, but instead he placed them so high that Olcott was forced to get on his toes to reach them. Yet they never went too high for him; Green was a perfect master, and his control was absolute.

Three of them sang past, while Merry waited desperately. He knew perfectly well that Green intended to pass him, in order to strike out the next three men.

"I'd sooner die fighting than be left at the post," he muttered grimly, taking a firm grip on his bat.

Again Green smiled, scarcely taking the trouble to wind up for the throw. He sent the ball down to Olcott, far too high for a good strike, but Chip was past caring whether it was good or not.

With an effort, he swung up and reached for it. There was a

crack, and the sphere shot out over second base—for his third hit off Green!

Merrell made a hard run in for the ball, secured it on the first bounce, and relayed in a beautiful throw to Olcott. Clancy was tearing for home, and he ran along as he had never run before. Glancing around, he saw the ball almost even with him, and as he neared home he went down in a desperate slide.

Olcott received the ball perfectly, and there was a moment of suspense as the dust rose and hid the play. Then the umpire's figure emerged, hands down.

Fardale had won on Merry's hit—the closest finish ever seen on Fardale field.

CHAPTER XXXVIII.

CAUGHT WITH THE GOODS.

"It's Merry's game, all right!"

"I'm not so sure of that, fellows," said Merry, as he entered the dressing room and heard Lowe's remark; "I'd say that it's Villum's game. Didn't he get the run that tied, and get it without assistance?"

A roar of laughter went up. As Merry went to his locker, however, he was approached by Colonel Gunn's orderly, who shoved hastily through the crowd.

"Come outside, Mr. Merriwell!" cried the cadet. "The constable wants you!"

"Tell him I'll be dressed in a minute," returned Chip.

"No, get a move on right now!" insisted the other excitedly. "Colonel Gunn is waiting, too."

"That's a horse of another color, then," said Chip, and made haste outside.

He found the constable, who greeted him eagerly.

"Say, Merriwell, come along over to the riding hall. Colonel Gunn's gone over, and said to bring you along."

"Me? What for?"

Merry had forgotten all about the affairs of Randall in the excitement.

"Why, they found that feller Carson, and he seems to be drunk, or hurt, or something," explained the constable hurriedly, as they started out. "One o' the boys phoned over to the grand stand just before the game ended."

"That's bad," commented Merry. "You don't know any more?"

The constable did not, except that he had seen Colonel Carson slinking away from the grounds in woeful plight. It was said that the colonel had lost a large sum of money on the game.

With the orderly, they hastened to the riding hall. Grouped in the rear, they found a small crowd of cadets, in the midst of whom stood Colonel Gunn and Randall, while a motionless figure could be made out on the ground.

"Ha—Merriwell!" cried the principal, who had recovered his momentarily lost ponderous manner. "Here is the—ah—individual of whom we were in search. He appears to have been in this posture for some little time."

Merry and the constable pushed through, to see Bully Carson lying on the ground. He was motionless, and was breathing stertorously. Although his one good eye did not open, he seemed dimly conscious that others were around him.

"Go 'way!" he muttered thickly. "Go 'way!"

"He don't look drunk, exactly," observed the constable, "and he ain't hurt."

"No, he does not—ah—appear to be under the influence of liquor. Perhaps he is merely—ah—reposing in the arms of Morpheus."

"No, Murphy was lookin' for him to-day," rejoined the constable, referring to his assistant. Colonel Gunn's lips twitched.

"See if you can resuscitate him, Merriwell. The sooner we could—ah—relieve Randall of the unfortunate difficulties surrounding him, the better."

Merry knelt over Bully and raised his head, shaking his shoulders in no very gentle fashion. Bully grunted and opened his eyes in a dazed manner. At the same instant a small, very much flustered man pushed through the group.

"Hello, here's Hostetter now," announced the constable. "Colonel Gunn, this is him."

"I heard that Carson had been found," exclaimed Hostetter. "Nothing has happened to him, I trust?"

Bully answered for himself. Sitting up suddenly and pushing Merry away, he glanced around with dull and yet frightened eyes.

"Who's that?" he muttered thickly. "Where's Hostetter?"

"Right here, old man," cried the little laundryman fervently. "Have you managed to locate my pocketbook? You know you said this morning that you might be able to get a clew."

"Nothin' doin'," said Bully thickly. "I must 'a' been asleep—it was that there glass o' water, I'll bet a dollar!"

He tried to get to his feet, Chip assisting him, but stumbled and fell back. As he did so, a long black object fell from his pocket. Hostetter pounced on it with a shrill yell.

"My wallet! How——"

As he examined it feverishly, Bully once more came to life. He clapped a hand to his pocket, then staggered up.

"Where's my wallet!" he growled, clutching for support.

"Your wallet!" cried Merry. "You mean Hostetter's wallet. Where'd you get it, eh? Are you the one that stole it?"

Bully seemed to shrink suddenly into himself, muttering and mumbling.

"Who says I stole it?" he grunted defiantly, only half conscious yet. He gave a lurch and caught at Merriwell for support. "Hostetter—durned little fool——"

"What do you mean?" exclaimed Merriwell sharply. Bully tried to rouse himself. "Here, one of you fellows get a bucket of water, will you?"

"Lemme go," grunted Bully, trying to reel away. "I got to place bet—thousand-dollar bet—little fool Hostetter handed me his money——"

"That's a lie!" snapped Hostetter suddenly. "I believe you stole that money, Carson!"

"I believe so, too," said Merry dryly. "Constable, you'd better get ready to take charge of him when—ah, here's the water now!"

One of the grinning cadets arrived with a pail of water. Bully had already relapsed into slumber, and Merry took the water and soused it over his head.

A second later Bully was on his feet, shaking his head and bellowing in fury.

"That's enough out o' you," said the constable, tapping him on the shoulder. "I guess you can come along to the lockup, my man."

Bully let out a yell of fear.

"What fur!" he wailed, as the constable gripped him firmly. "I ain't done nothin'! Take your hands off'n me!"

"For the theft of Mr. Hostetter's pocketbook," said Colonel Gunn, in his most military voice, facing the astounded Bully. "You, sir, have been—ah—apprehended with the stolen property on your person. While still in a condition of semi-coma, you made certain admissions which most undoubtedly will—ah—be put to service in the cause of justice."

"I'll give it back!" wailed Bully. "It was only a joke—I didn't mean——"

"Constable, remove the—ah—prisoner!"

The constable did so. The last that was seen of Bully Carson, he was trailing along and tearfully expostulating. Colonel Gunn turned to Randall.

"I congratulate you, Mr. Randall, on being thus—ah—exonerated of all the faint suspicion which—ah—clung to your footsteps, in a manner of speaking. You will kindly report at my office Monday morning to state why you should not be punished for leaving your room and the school grounds without permission last evening. Gentlemen, I bid you good day! Oh—one moment, Merriwell! That—ah—that was the most remarkable, I think I may say the most spectacular, game of baseball I ever witnessed. Sir, I heartily congratulate you on your playing!"

And with a stiff bow, Colonel Gunn beckoned his orderly and strode away.

Merry looked after him, then turned to Randall with a smile, his hand out.

"It's all right, old man!" he said. "Come along over to the gym while I get into my clothes, will you? I've got something I want to say."

Randall gave him a half-frightened look, but merely nodded assent. The two walked to the gym together, and more than one cadet looked after them significantly, with the remark that Randall had been fetched around, after all.

"What do you suppose was the trouble with Bully?" queried Chip, as they entered the gymnasium building. "It looked to me rather as if he had been drugged, Bob!"

Randall flushed.

"Maybe he had," he said bitterly. "I knew that he was pretty bad, but I never suspected that he could stoop to being a thief."

"I guess there are a whole lot of things about your cousin that you never suspected," returned Merry dryly.

They found the dressing room almost deserted, the members of the team having disappeared long since. Merry had his shower and rubdown, and returned to his locker where Randall was waiting.

"That was a great finish to-day, Chip," said the Southerner, rather awkwardly. "And your pitching showed me a whole lot I had never even guessed. If I had been in your place, they'd have pounded me off the mound in two innings, Chip."

"Not much," said Chip. "Luck broke with us, that was all. By the way, their pitcher was Southpaw Diggs, Bob. Some credit in beating him, eh? I was almost gone in the seventh, for a fact."

"Diggs!" Bob gasped. "I guess you had mighty little luck in that game, Chip, and a whole lot of good playing! I heard a fellow near us saying that he thought the first baseman was a semipro player from Buffalo."

"Likely enough," said Chip thoughtfully. "I wouldn't be surprised if Colonel Carson had got professionals all the way through, because he expected to clear up a big wad. It must have cost him a lot, even besides what he lost! Well, that only goes to show that a fellow gets exactly what he gives, Bob. Your attitude toward the world will be bound to be reflected back at you from the world."

"I suppose that's about right," and Randall's handsome face clouded.

"By the way," said Chip suddenly, "I may leave Fardale almost any time now, old man. I had a notion of having a team meeting to-night or Monday, and putting it up to them about electing you captain——"

"Hold on a minute, Chip," broke in Randall, his eyes fixing those of Merry in a peculiar fashion. "Did you and Carson drink those glasses of water I had poured out?"

"Eh?" Merry's thoughts went back swiftly to the scene in Bob's room. "Why, yes!"

"Then that's what's the matter with Bully," and Randall faced Merry, white-faced but firm. "I had doped one glass of water, hoping to put you out of the game for the afternoon. He got it by mistake. I pretended to be placated by your words this morning, Chip, and—well, I began to see differently later, that's all. Now go ahead and do anything you want to—I'm glad that I've made a clean breast of it."

"So am I," said Chip quietly. "As I was saying, I hope you'll be elected the captain, to succeed me when I leave, Bob."

CHAPTER XXXIX.

CONCLUSION.

ou what!" gasped Randall, staring. "You're joking with me!"

"Not a bit of it," said Merry. "I suppose Bully persuaded you to dope me?"

"Well, he had a little to do with it," admitted Randall, too proud to cast the blame where it rightly lay. "I can only apologize, Chip, and you——"

"Why, old man, forget all about it!" exclaimed Merry, catching the other about the shoulders and turning toward the door. "There was nobody damaged in any way except Bully."

He broke off suddenly, and laughed.

"Look here, Bob! He tried to make you the goat to put me out of the way, see? He probably figured that Southpaw Diggs could handle either one of us, but without the double shoot Fardale would get pounded. Then he got hold of that stuff by accident and it laid him out. Except for that, you might still be under suspicion of stealing Hostetter's money! It was only his being doped that really saved you!"

"That's right, Merry!" and Randall's eyes flashed. "I believe he'd have let me suffer for it, too, the cowardly cur! Look here, old man, will you take my hand and accept my apologies?"

"Great Scott, how often do you want me to tell you so?" returned Chip, with mock despair. He wrung the Southerner's hand heartily.

"Now let's get out into the open air. I'm about ready for something to eat, if you want to know it!"

They left the building behind and started across the campus for the barracks. It still being some time before assembly and mess. As they neared the barracks, they were approached by a tall figure neatly clad in a dark-blue suit. He gave them a keen glance, then stopped them quietly.

"This is Mr. Merriwell, isn't it?"

Merry flung him a look, and started.

"Hello! It's Green—or I should say Diggs!"

"Yes, Southpaw Diggs," and the other smiled as he held out his hand. "I just want to congratulate you on winning a remarkably fine game, Merriwell—one of the best I ever saw, in fact. If you'd only consider big-league work and——"

"No, thanks," said Merry. "I've had a sample of professional ethics this afternoon, when you and your friends masqueraded as amateurs. That's one reason, though I don't blame you as I do Colonel Carson."

"What can a fellow do when he needs the money?" and Diggs shrugged his shoulders good-naturedly.

"He can get busy and make it cleanly," retorted Chip, watching the other. With a quick impulse he added: "And if he'd cut out the booze, Diggs."

Diggs flushed and his eyes kindled. Then he smiled again and nodded.

"Right you are, Merriwell, and I know you mean me. Well, I'm only twenty-four, and if I brace up I'd have a few years ahead of me of baseball. I've been thinking it over, and, to tell you the truth, I've not had a drink for a good while. I was testing my nerves out on you fellows to-day, for one thing."

"I hope they suited you?" said Merry.

"Oh, mine were all right until you pulled that last bag of tricks. Well, so long, son, and good luck go with you!"

"And the same to you, Diggs," said Merry earnestly.

He walked on with Randall, neither speaking. At the door of the barracks they came upon Clancy and Billy Mac, who immediately met them with wide grins.

"Buried the hatchet, you two?" queried Clan.

"I think so," said Chip. "By the way, I'd like to ask a special favor of you fellows, sight unseen. Will you grant it?"

"Surest thing you know," returned Clancy.

"Anything you want, old man," said Billy Mac.

"Well, I'm thinking of proposing Bob for captain in my place, and I want you two fellows to second it. How does it strike you?"

Clancy looked at Randall, and grinned.

"Sure," he said. "Only I'll give you a run for your money, Bob, because I'm going after that job myself. I'll second you, just the same."

"Same here," said Billy. "But I guess I can see right now where

Carrot-top Clancy gets snowed under about two miles! Shake, Cap Randall!"

Merry smiled.

THE END.

Lightning Source UK Ltd.
Milton Keynes UK
UKHW041114130920
369836UK00002B/12